LANDFALL: ISLANDS IN THE AFTERMATH

LANDFALL: ISLANDS IN THE AFTERMATH

BOOK IV OF THE PULSE SERIES

SCOTT B. WILLIAMS

Lightning Struck Press

ISBN-13: 978-1537048970

Cover photograph: © Scott B. Williams

Cover design: Bayou Cover Designs

Editor: Michelle Cleveland

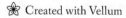 Created with Vellum

This one is for my friend, David Halladay, of Boatsmith

CHAPTER 1

AT FIRST, Russell thought he might be seeing a mirage, or that after all this time alone with the relentless tropical sun beating down upon his bare head, perhaps his mind was playing tricks on him. No boats had come to call at the tiny island since he'd arrived here, and he'd about decided that none probably would. He didn't know the name of the rocky, windswept and sun-scorched cay, only that it was supposed to be in the Exumas, that chain of unspoiled islands in the Bahamas he'd been so desperate to reach. For nearly a month he'd paced its perimeter and explored virtually every nook and cranny of its interior as well as the shallow, reef-strewn waters lapping its shores. There was no decent harbor here and his best guess was that the island was far enough off the normal sailing routes that the chances a boat would call were slim to none.

But as he stood there and stared, he finally accepted that the glossy white hull and shiny metal fittings of the pretty sailboat anchored near the west end of the island were real. And across the narrow rocky point separating the protected side of the island from the surf-pounded northern shore, two more masts, both attached to the same twin-hulled catamaran, protruded into the sky from an area where no vessel its size should ever venture. That the boat was in trouble, trapped there among the rocks and coral, Russell had no doubt. He'd explored those reefs on the calm days when there was little surf, and he knew it was not a place a sane captain would intentionally take his boat.

As soon as he realized that what he was seeing was indeed no illusion, Russell worked his way a bit closer to get a better look, keeping to the higher ground among the rocks and trees and well away from the open beach. With no way to leave and few places to hide on such a small island, it wouldn't do to be seen by the people in the two boats until he sized them up to determine whether or not they were a threat. No strangers could be trusted entirely at this point, but their presence here could be a game changer for him if they weren't set on killing him on sight. Whether he revealed himself or not, they were bound to discover him here if they spent any time on the little island. His tracks were all over the beaches, and on the east end, opposite from the two boats; he'd constructed a small lean-to from broken saplings and palm fronds woven into some semblance of a roof. That they'd not already found him told him that they'd been seriously occupied with their boat troubles. Russell had been laid up sick in his miserable hut since the day before yesterday. It was fever of some kind, and it had left him exhausted and unable to move until it broke. This morning was his first time to venture out since it had hit him, so he didn't know for sure how long the boats had been there.

Much of the shoreline in the area immediately adjacent the boats was rocky almost to the high tide line, and Russell usually walked the water's edge at low tide when he made his rounds, so the footprints from his last circuit would have been quickly erased. Anyone venturing to his end of the island would have seen his tracks everywhere though, and would have spotted him in his camp, so he was quite certain they had not been there. The makeshift shelter had no walls, and the roof did little to keep the rain off. But rain was far less of a problem here than the relentless rays of blistering sun, and even when he wasn't sick he spent the better part of each day sprawled in the shade of his pathetic abode, doing his beachcombing and foraging late in the evening and early in the morning.

Other than the two days he spent too sick to move, every day was pretty much the same for Russell. He would walk the beaches around the island with an eye on the tide-line, looking for anything of use that may have washed up since his last stroll. Most days that was very little, a plastic bottle or a useful piece of driftwood; sometimes a bit of rope or fishing net, but so far, nothing that would significantly improve his life here or help him get off the island. That was, until today. The arrival of two sailboats was the biggest event of his entire stay.

He had spotted them in the first few minutes after

sunrise, and at that hour there was no sign of the crew of either boat stirring on deck or ashore. Russell assumed they were all still asleep, and that was good, because it gave him an opportunity to study the scene. He pondered where they might have come from as he sat there staring at them, and wondered why they stopped here when no one else had, and why one boat was safely anchored while the other was aground on the wrong side of the island.

Whoever had made the mistake of sailing the catamaran into that situation had taken great pains to secure it afterwards. Russell counted no less than four separate anchor lines. Two of them were stout looking white nylon ropes leading from the front beam of the boat to the beach well above the high tideline. Russell couldn't see them, but he figured they led to anchors buried there. The other two lines extended out at roughly 45-degree angles to either side of the stern, where they disappeared under the surface of the water, no doubt leading to a couple more anchors. But the tide was out now and the big catamaran was beyond the reach of the waves, which was probably why whoever was aboard it was still asleep. It looked to Russell like they probably knew what they were doing, despite their navigational mistake. The more he thought about it, the more he figured they'd arrived there during the night, when the unlit island would be difficult to see even in good weather. But as he was well aware after being drenched again and again while he tossed with the fever, there had been lines of passing showers and squalls night after night that would have made it even more difficult.

The other boat that was not aground was a nice-looking, more traditional cruiser, maybe much older but nonetheless well equipped and maintained. It was typical of the size and type of boat one saw most often along the island cruising routes, and Russell figured like most of them, it was probably American or Canadian. No ensign flew from the stern though, nor the obligatory Bahamian courtesy flag at the spreaders that would have surely been present on any foreign boat in these waters before the collapse. That the two boats both arrived here since he'd last been to this side of the island was almost conclusive proof to Russell that they were sailing together in company. But none of that told him anything about the crew, and he knew that until he saw them, it was risky to make any assumptions. For all he knew, they had murdered the rightful owners of the two yachts and were here seeking a hideout until they decided who to rob and kill next.

Russell knew he had to be careful, or he would end up dead, like so many already had, but he was also getting desperate. He was weak from the fever, but even before that he was barely eking out an existence on the island and he doubted he could last much longer without help. If not for the mostly pristine reefs, easily accessible in the shallow waters that ringed the little cay, he would have already starved. He had nothing in the way of tools aside from a sturdy folding knife, dive mask and a pole spear, but the sea provided enough easily acquired food that he'd managed to stay alive thus far.

The wild goats that roamed the island had him salivating for a change in diet, even if it meant eating raw meat, but they were elusive and wary, defying all his attempts to either brain one with a rock, impale one with his fish spear or simply run one down and tackle it. And so he had been living on whelks, small clams, conch, and the occasion fish he managed to get with the spear. His raw seafood diet was supplemented with coconuts and a few other plant foods such as hearts of palm, prickly pear and the salty leaves of the seaside purslane. It was getting old, eating everything uncooked for more than a month, but he had no way to make fire and had failed at his attempts to emulate primitive methods he'd seen on TV and in the movies before the collapse. Fire by friction was hopeless with his lack of skill or knowledge of the necessary materials, and on the limestone island there were no rocks containing flint for striking a spark. He kept hoping to find a glass bottle with a bottom of the suitable shape to work as a magnifying glass that would focus the sun's rays, but so far he'd not even managed that.

But now none of that mattered. He was sure the people on these two boats had food—and probably lots of it. They would also have matches or a lighter they could give him, at the very least, and probably fish hooks and line or maybe a Hawaiian sling and other gear for underwater hunting. These would all help him survive here more comfortably, but of course that wasn't what he really wanted. What he *really* wanted from these strangers with boats was a *ride*. A ride to anywhere but here, where he could live like a human being again.

And so he watched and waited, growing impatient, but not daring to get any closer until at last he saw a hatch on one of the catamaran hulls slide open. A man's head emerged, and Russell judged him to be in his mid to late 30s. His face was deeply tanned and bearded; his hair a sandy blonde bleached even lighter by the sun. After slowly looking around in all directions, first out to sea and then back across the nearby island, the man climbed the rest of the way out of the hatch. He was shirtless and bare-foot, wearing nothing but a pair of khaki cargo shorts. Russell saw him step to the shrouds on the other side of the boat, where he held on with one hand and relieved himself over the side. Finished with that first task of the day, the man walked around the decks to each of the anchor lines securing the boat, first check their tension and the cleat knots that held them before studying the two off the stern as if trying to decide what to do next.

To Russell he looked like a long-time sailor, a man clearly at ease aboard a boat, though he appeared to favor one arm as if it were injured. He didn't look like the sort that would have murdered the real owner of the catamaran, but then, these days one could never know. Whoever he was, he was in quite a predicament with his boat in a real jam. If he were alone, Russell figured he would be marooned there just as surely as he was. But with the other yacht anchored across the way, he might have several people available to give him a hand. Russell would continue to watch and wait for now, to see what happened next.

CHAPTER 2

THE NIGHT HE MET SCULLY, Thomas Allen was certain the challenges he and Mindy had survived since the blackout were about to come to an end. Both of them would die there on an uninhabitable island that was little more than a clump of mangroves, their bodies left for the crabs and birds and their dreams of a life of adventure stolen from them forever. The bullet to the head would come, Thomas knew, but not before the two men made him watch what they were going to do to her. When they appeared out of the tangled, jungle-like vegetation, Mindy had tried to duck into the tiny cabin of their miniature cruiser and hide. But the men had already seen her and while one held Thomas at gunpoint, the other one waded out to where *Intrepida* was anchored to drag her back to the narrow strip of mud and sand that was the only dry place Thomas had found to build a cooking fire. The pistol aimed at his face left him helpless to intervene as Thomas waited for the inevitable.

Thomas knew he had failed Mindy; just completely and utterly *failed* her. He thought they were doing okay, after all these weeks of keeping to the backwaters of the Keys and anchoring in places bigger vessels couldn't go. They had talked often of the Bahamas, and Thomas had been trying to work up the nerve, but neither of them had ever sailed that far offshore, and as long as he'd been living in Key West he'd heard nothing but dire warnings about the hazards of the Gulf Stream. Now he knew he shouldn't have listened. They could be somewhere safe in those islands right now, instead of here, facing death, if only he'd had the *cajones* to set sail. But he had not. Thomas had failed to take Mindy to the islands and now he would fail to protect her from these men as well.

Thomas knew nothing of firearms, and he'd certainly never had the slightest interest in owning one. He didn't grow up around them and before the collapse; he could not have imagined why anyone but a criminal or a policeman would ever need one. No one in his family owned guns, and nor did any of his close friends, as far as he knew. He and Mindy had felt perfectly safe in the Keys and it was just something that never crossed his mind back then. Most people there were cool and laid back, and not prone to violence. Sure, there was petty crime like bicycle theft and the occasional break-in, but the bad stuff happened up in Miami and elsewhere on the mainland, not in Key West, at least not then.

But everything changed when the pulse from the solar flare cut off the Keys from the outside world. Food and other essentials in the local stores disappeared faster than Thomas and Mindy could have ever imagined. The only reason they weren't completely caught without was because like most people living there, they had long been in the habit of keeping extra supplies on hand for hurricane season. But this was so much worse than any hurricane. The relief everyone on the island expected never arrived, because unknown to them, there was nowhere for help to come from that wasn't equally affected by the same event. The idyllic island life the two of them had known became a living hell within a week. The little sailboat they'd christened *Intrepida* was the only reason they'd made it out and lasted even this long. They had bought the boat as a way to get a taste of the sailing life they dreamed of while they both worked hard to earn the money they would need for a real cruiser. But the Montgomery 17 had a good reputation as a seaworthy boat despite its small size. Designed by a renowned naval architect, it was a proper little ship with a good ballast to displacement ratio and of stout construction. Other people had sailed them across entire oceans—but not Thomas Allen. Before the collapse, he wouldn't have contemplated crossing even the Florida Straits in anything less than 35 feet, and preferably longer. But the 20-year-old Montgomery had turned up for sale at a price too good to pass up, and so they had bought her as a way to spend some time on the water, learning how to sail and navigate in their free time. After all, what would be the point of living in the Keys and not owning a boat?

Mindy got to spend most of her days on the water anyway, working as a deckhand on a tour boat that took tourists out to the reef for two-hour snorkeling trips. It wasn't sailing, but it kept her keen on the life they envisioned. Thomas did his part to contribute to the dream fund by working as a chef in a popular Duval Street eatery. Sailing *Intrepida* was what he looked forward to on his one day a week off. They'd kept her on a mooring just a short bike ride and dinghy trip from their over-priced, one-bedroom apartment, and when it became apparent that it was no longer safe to stay in town, Mindy had suggested they move aboard and leave.

"We can sail to Fort Jefferson," she said. "I've heard a lot of people with boats saying they were going to go out there until things were back under control. It's a good place because no one can get there without a boat. The other boat people won't bother us."

The old fort was part of a National Park in the Dry Tortugas, some 70 miles west of Key West. But unlike crossing to the Bahamas, there was no treacherous Gulf Stream current to worry about, and they could stop along the way at the Marquesas Keys to break up the passage. It had seemed like a good plan at the time, and much better than just sitting around in a dark apartment, running out of food and sweating in the heat with no idea when or if relief would ever come. And at least on the water they could find food. Both of them liked to fish and they had fishing gear already on board, as well as several day's worth of canned goods and snacks they kept in the lockers for their weekend getaways. It wasn't much, and the boat was small, but once they cast off they realized they were better off than those stuck on the island with no boat at all.

Until this terrible night when it was all about to come to an end, they had managed okay aboard *Intrepida*. Sure, it was cramped, especially when it rained while they were at anchor, confining them to the minimal cabin. There was little below but bunks for two and barely adequate room to sit. But they realized the discomfort was worth it as they began meeting other sailors, particularly those who had sailed there from the mainland. The stories they told sent a chill down Thomas' spine. As the days without power stretched into weeks, entire cities were swept up in rioting and violence. The police were overwhelmed and unable stop the looters from the beginning. And once store shelves were stripped, the gangs began targeting houses and even entire neighborhoods. They took what they wanted, killing anyone who stood in their way. From everything Thomas and Mindy heard, returning to any large population center would be a fatal mistake.

But the population at Fort Jefferson kept increasing and the anchorage had gotten crowded long before the U.S. Navy arrived and made them leave. Problems began to arise even among the boaters who had sailed there to avoid problems and violence. Disputes over anchoring spots and collisions and damage caused by the less experienced led to fistfights and brawls and even two fatal shootings. Thomas and Mindy had been frightened as the tensions grew worse, but aboard their little boat they were able to avoid most of it by anchoring in the shallows where larger vessels couldn't. With no idea where else they could go, they'd made the best of the situation until the day the ship arrived, dispatching a boatload of armed commandos who informed everyone there they would have to leave.

Some of the refugees aboard larger cruisers decided to set sail for horizons beyond U.S. waters, opting to cross the straits to Cuba or Mexico, or sail east directly to the Bahamas. Thomas and Mindy considered all those options, but the thought of Cuba or Mexico frightened them as much as Miami. How could it be any better in any densely populated nation if the conditions were as bad as they'd heard they were in south Florida? Because there were so many uninhabited islands there, the Bahamas seemed like the only safe alternative in the region. But instead of risking such a long direct passage from the Dry Tortugas, they decided to make their way east in that general direction by sailing back along the chain of the Keys as they worked up the nerve to cross the Stream from a closer jump-off point. They avoided all the islands connected to the Overseas Highway and anchored mostly in the remote wildlife refuges, the majority of which were clusters of mangrove islands with little or no dry land to be found. With their relatively short mast and shallow draft, they had been able to tuck into seldom-visited hideaways, and had so far managed to catch enough fish and collect enough rainwater to survive.

They had encountered a few others in small boats living out among the mangroves, but until this encounter, no one had threatened them directly. It just so happened that the hidden anchorage where they were now was midway between Key West and the mainland, and less than a mile north of one of the most developed islands in the Middle Keys. They had seen no other boats when they approached it though, the tall mangroves completely obscuring their view of the land to the south and they hoped, hiding their presence from anyone still living there. With *Intrepida* anchored in waist-deep water just a few feet off the one little pocket beach, Thomas and Mindy had felt as safe there as anywhere else they'd stopped. What they didn't know though, as they were settling in for the night and he was combing the nearby mangrove roots for pieces of driftwood to start a fire, was that their every move was being watched. Mindy had gone back to the boat to get a skillet out of the cabin when the two men stepped out of the dark mangroves. When she saw that they had guns, her first instinct was to hide, hoping they hadn't seen her. When they saw that Thomas had nothing of value, maybe they would leave him alone. But they *had* seen her, and as it turned out, *she* was the one thing he had that they wanted.

Thomas did nothing as he watched the other one pull her out of the cabin of their little boat by the hair. He knew that if he moved to help her, the one with the pistol pointed at his face would pull the trigger, so he didn't. Mindy struggled but the man who had her was much bigger, and he slapped her before pushing her over the side into the water and jumping in after her to grab her again. When she got to her feet in the shallows, he had her by the upper arm and was forcing her with him to the beach. Thomas saw her look his way, the fear in her eyes visible in the firelight. She knew as well as he did that the two of them were as good as dead once these men had their fun. Thomas considered his almost non-existent options. Would it be better to jump up and try and grab the other man's pistol, even if it resulted in getting shot dead immediately, or wait and be forced to watch what was coming and be shot anyway? The man who had Mindy had a gun too, not a pistol but a long one of some kind slung over his back. Thomas knew that even if he could grab the pistol from the nearer one, the other one would likely shoot him before he could figure out how to use it. He had about made up his mind to try anyway when out of nowhere a thunderous gunshot rang out, and the man standing over him suddenly collapsed into the sand.

Thomas stared for a moment in disbelief before turning his attention back to Mindy. Two more shots sounded before either could speak and the man holding her fell too, his hand slipping from Mindy's arm before he splashed face-first into the water. Mindy ran to the beach screaming, and Thomas jumped to his feet, his eyes straining into the dark for what new threat they now faced from somewhere unknown. He didn't know who did the shooting, but he was certain that the man sprawled in front of him would never harm anyone again. A quick glance at the corpse was all Thomas could stomach before he had to look away. The bullet that took him out blew the man's head apart, and something Thomas was sure could only be brain matter oozed from the opening and onto the bloody sand.

Mindy ran straight into his arms despite the uncertainty of what was going to happen next. But as he embraced her for what he feared might be the last time ever, Thomas heard a voice calling out to him. The two dead attackers where white, but this was the West Indian lilt of an islander, unmistakable from his years in the Keys, where he encountered Jamaicans and Bahamians on a daily basis.

"IT'S OKAY, MON! NOT GOING TO SHOOT! ONLY KILL DE BAD GUY TO HELP YOU OUT, MON!"

CHAPTER 3

WHEN LARRY DRAGER opened the companionway hatch and stuck his head out, he was not surprised to see that the sun was already well above the eastern horizon. He had gotten little sleep his second night on Green Cay after discovering the *Casey Nicole* aground on the surf-bound and reef strewn northern shore. The crews of both boats had worked for hours through the darkness doing the best they could to secure the 36-foot catamaran so that it wouldn't be swept to sea or bashed to pieces against the rocks. Thankfully, the tide was falling, so that made their job easier. It would not have been feasible to try and get her back out through the surf in the dark and the rain, and the next high tide cycle would be in full daylight. Once he'd been reasonably sure the boat would still be there in the morning, Larry had turned in below, his first night aboard the catamaran he'd built in nearly two weeks. His brother, Artie gladly relinquished his bunk and followed his daughter, Casey back to Tara's *Sarah J.,* anchored across the island on the sheltered side. Jessica and Grant stayed aboard with Larry, like everyone else, too exhausted to move and in need of at least a couple hours of sleep.

Larry knew Grant felt terrible, because he'd been the one at the helm when the *Casey Nicole* went aground. But Grant had never set foot on a sailboat before the voyage that brought them here, and Larry hadn't expected him to learn the intricacies of seamanship overnight. His brother didn't have much more experience than Grant, but Larry had trusted that the *Casey Nicole* was in good hands, because he'd left Scully, his first mate of many years in command. But Scully was missing. That thought hit Larry hard as he stepped on deck and had a look around. Scully had been left behind in Florida, and from what Artie and Grant and Jessica told him, it was not going be easy to go back and get him, even if they knew where to start looking.

Larry already knew about the presence of the navy at the Dry Tortugas, as they too had been turned away as they tried to approach what had been their destination for the first leg of the voyage. He'd sailed on because there was little else he could do, but he'd expected to reach the Jumentos Cays and find Scully and the others on the faster catamaran already waiting there. Instead, they'd made this unplanned rendezvous on a seldom-visited cay at the edge of the Tongue of the Ocean. Though it would seem an unlikely coincidence to those unfamiliar with the islands that both boats could end up in the same remote place, to Larry it wasn't surprising at all that it had happened that way. Sailing routes through the islands were determined by navigable channels through the banks and the prevailing winds. Both boats had left Florida to sail around the north end of Andros Island before turning south, and Green Cay just happened to lie near the logical route from there to the Jumentos. If not for the water pump failure on the *Sarah J.,* Larry would not have bothered to stop there, but because of that he did, and then his brother and the rest of the crew on the catamaran had chanced upon Green Cay simply because their navigation was off track enough that they literally ran into it!

As best he could tell in the dark when he'd first checked, the *Casey Nicole* hadn't suffered any major damage, but her hulls had been cracked in two or three places and she was taking on water into some of the lower compartments that were sealed by watertight bulkheads. It would take a lot more than a few minor breeches to completely flood her two hulls, but still, the cracks had to be taken care of before she could sail again. Larry knew they had their work cut out for them—probably days and possibly nearly a week of it. At least Green Cay was off the beaten path, and from what he'd seen of it since they'd been here, they had it all to themselves.

He went back below to light the stove for a pot of coffee —a luxury they would be running out of soon, but one that he needed to face a day like the one before him. When the others were awake, they would start working. The first job was to offload as much gear and other stuff from the cata-maran as possible to lighten the hulls, so they could winch her high and dry onto the beach. That alone would take half a day, and by then Larry knew the tide would be back and they would have to move fast to prepare for the next steps.

Artie Drager was so happy to see Casey again he wasn't about to let her out of his sight for long. After they were done setting anchors and mooring lines to secure the catamaran, Artie followed her back to the *Sarah J.* and fell asleep on one of the quarter berths. When he woke to daylight streaming in the portlights of the cozy teak cabin he knew he probably hadn't slept more than an hour or two. But he was well used to an erratic and often interrupted sleeping schedule after the long voyage from Cat Island. He couldn't have slept longer if he'd wanted to, restless and worried as he was about what would happen to the *Casey Nicole,* and wondering how they would get her repaired and safely back beyond the reefs guarding the beach.

Artie felt terrible about letting his brother's pride and joy go aground. The catamaran could have been a total wreck if it had not narrowly missed the worst of the reefs by a turn of luck. The keels had certainly kissed rock in a few places and sustained some damage, but the boat had come to rest in an area of mostly sand bottom inside the reef.

Grant had been at the helm simply because it was his turn to stand watch, but Artie knew it wouldn't have mattered who was steering. None of them could have seen the dark outline of such a low island on a night like last night. The first warning Grant had that something was wrong was the roar of breaking surf. None of them had thought they were anywhere near land, as their dead-reckoning navigation had put them sailing southeast down the middle of the Tongue of the Ocean: the deepest channel in the entire Bahamas Archipelago. But dead reckoning was prone to error, as his brother had pointed out to him time and time again. Scully could have pulled it off without making such a mistake, but Scully had not been aboard. That they'd managed to end up on the same island where the other boat stopped seemed almost miraculous to Artie, but made more sense when Larry told him they had sailed the same route around the north end of Andros before the engine issue forced them to stop. Both boats would have passed within a few miles of the isolated cay anyway, if all had gone as planned.

Before they'd hit it in the dark, Artie had never really noticed Green Cay on the chart. It was at the extreme end of a large area of shallow water extending west of the Exumas, which he'd intended to avoid, but his sights were set on the more distant Jumentos Cays and Ragged Islands. That was the only area in the Bahamas of interest to him, because that's where Larry had said they should eventually go when they set sail from the northern coast of the Gulf. Getting the two boats separated at sea wasn't in the plan, nor was the unexpected encounter with the U.S. Navy off the coast of Florida. But sticking to a plan in this new reality had proven difficult and once again, Artie found himself separated from his daughter after all he'd been through to sail to New Orleans to find her. He doubted that would have happened though if not for their chance meeting of Tara Hancock before they left. How could his single brother resist a good-looking, divorced woman who knew how to sail and had her own classic sailing yacht? He couldn't, and he hadn't, and because of her, their party had been split up, despite Larry's best intentions to keep the two boats within sight of each other on the crossing. The weather and the whims of Tara's depressed teenaged daughter derailed that plan, and no matter what Larry said now, Artie knew it was a bit of a miracle they were all back together again in such an improbable place. All of them, except for poor Scully, that is.

Artie felt far worse about leaving Scully behind in Florida than he did about the grounding of the *Casey Nicole*. How in the world would he ever get here, left as he was on the wilderness coast of the Everglades with nothing but Larry's sea kayak? With police or military gunboats like the one they'd encountered aggressively patrolling the coastline, had Scully already been arrested for remaining in the restricted zone? Or worse, had he been shot? If they found him and saw the AK-47 he was carrying, but no passport or any other form of I.D., they would likely assume he was just another looter or bandit out taking advantage of the lawless situation. Artie wondered if they would ever know, but he should have known that as soon as he told his brother what had happened, Larry would say he was going back for him. Of course he was. Scully was like another brother to him, and Artie agreed they needed to do everything they could to find him, but what Larry proposed didn't involve any of them. Artie didn't like the idea of splitting up again, but he agreed it didn't make sense for all of them to risk arrest or worse. It was just that his dream of a safe refuge with all the people he loved together in one place had fallen apart again. And now he wondered if it would ever come true or forever remain just out of reach.

CHAPTER 4

THOMAS ALLEN WAS SO startled by the shooting and then the voice calling out to him from the dark that he didn't even think to pick up the dead man's pistol, lying there in the sand within easy reach. All that registered was that the two men who had attacked them were dead, and that Mindy was in his arms, safe for the moment. He had no way to know if whoever did this would be any less a threat than the two he had just killed, but hearing the unseen shooter's voice assure him otherwise gave Thomas a bit of hope. Anything else would have been futile anyway. There was no escape other than to try and flee into the impenetrable mangroves. Whoever had done the shooting was approaching from the dark waters beyond their moored boat, leaving them no option to try and board it without making themselves easy targets if he wanted to stop them.

But more shots never came, and momentarily, Thomas saw a long, sleek sea kayak emerge from the gloom. The sound of the paddle was barely perceptible and now he understood why neither they nor the two dead men had heard anything until the sudden gunshots. When the bow of the kayak slid up onto the little beach and stopped, Thomas saw that it was paddled by a shirtless, muscular black man with dreadlocks that hung all the way down to the deck behind him. Just as he'd known when he heard the man's voice, Thomas could now see that the man was indeed a West Indian islander. His wild appearance might be frightening to many, but Thomas and Mindy saw guys like him every day in Key West, and his friendly smile and another greeting before he stepped out of the boat assured them he meant them no harm. After introducing himself as "Scully", he checked to make sure the two men he'd shot were indeed no longer a threat to anyone. Then, he bent and picked up the fallen pistol, making Thomas feel stupid for leaving it there when he had no idea if they were still in danger or not.

Pointing it away from them though, the stranger did something with it that Thomas correctly assumed involved removing the bullets to make it safe. Then he put the gun and the bullets in his pocket and dragged the man with the shattered skull into the foliage where the body would be out of sight. This done, he was ready to talk, and after finding out Thomas and Mindy had been to the Dry Tortugas, told them that was exactly where he was headed.

"You might as well forget about going there," Thomas said, "The entire area around the anchorage and the fort is completely off-limits. But even if it wasn't you couldn't get there in that kayak."

Scully listened patiently and seemed to accept what Thomas was telling him about the restrictions. He told them of his own encounter with a gunboat on the coast to the north, and how he'd paddled here after his friends were forced to leave him on the beach. He said they were supposed to rendezvous with more friends in another sailboat at the Dry Tortugas, and he seemed undaunted by the prospects of paddling all the way out there in the kayak. But of course this news of the blockade left him doubting the wisdom of that plan now. If his friends couldn't stop there, what would be the point?

"They didn't tell us much of anything, really. Except that the entire coast was under a naval blockade."

"Some of the other boat people out there were saying it was like they had essentially declared martial law," Mindy said.

"Whatever they are doing, all I know is that they made everyone leave. If your friends were already there, they won't be now, and if they were still trying to get there, they would not have allowed them to enter the anchorage. They were serious about it."

"An' de ship, dem U.S. Navy? Dat fo' true, mon?"

"Yes, they were U.S. Navy. At least they told us they were, and their small boats had Navy markings on them. But the men who came ashore looked liked soldiers."

"I think they were SEALs or Marines or something like that," Mindy said.

"Whoever they were, they were *serious*," Thomas said. "Some of the boat people tried to argue with them, but they said that anyone who wasn't out of there within 48 hours would be arrested, and their vessels confiscated. When some people asked them where they were supposed to go, they said they didn't care, but that they couldn't stay at Fort Jefferson. They said they were locking down the whole coast and that any boats coming in from offshore would be turned away. They said that applied to all of the Keys and the Florida mainland too, but we came back here by staying closer inshore to the mangroves and shoals, well away from their big ships. We haven't seen any sign of them in these waters, but we figured we're going to have to move on to the Bahamas to find someplace safe for the long term."

"We wanted to go there in the first place," Mindy said, "but we weren't sure we could make it in *Intrepida*. She's only 17-feet long and we haven't done any real offshore sailing. The trip to the Dry Tortugas was much farther than we've ever sailed before."

"She's only 17-feet long," Thomas said, "but she *is* a *Montgomery* 17. They are proven boats."

Thomas nervously watched for the islander's reaction to this, but he was pleasantly surprised when Scully agreed with him, saying that he could tell by her lines that the little boat could make it to the Bahamas. But what was even more surprising was that he said since his friends had likely sailed on to the Bahamas if they couldn't enter the anchorage at the Dry Tortugas, he might as well change his plans and go there too.

"In that kayak? Are you completely crazy?"

"Only little bit crazy mon, but de kayak she can go. Only problem is dat place in de Bahamas Larry sailing is very far from de first island. Hundreds more miles after crossing de Gulf Stream, an' against de wind too. Big problem to take enough watah in de kayak for de drinkin' all dem days."

"Well, I guess if he can cross the Gulf Stream in a kayak, we can do it in *Intrepida*," Thomas told Mindy.

But much to his surprise, after sitting there staring at the two boats, seemingly lost in thought, Scully turned back to Thomas with a proposal: he would sail with them, and take on the duties of captain, if they would agree to tow the kayak behind *Intrepida*. Thomas countered that the boat was very small for three people aboard, but Mindy liked the idea. After all, this man had just saved their lives and he clearly knew something about boats and offshore seamanship.

"Give us a minute to talk about it," Thomas told Scully.

The islander gladly complied, taking the opportunity to wade into the water beyond his beached kayak to retrieve the weapon from the body of the other dead man, still in the water nearby.

"He saved our lives, there's no doubt about that, Mindy. But we don't know anything about this man. How do we know he won't shoot us both or push us overboard once we're out at sea?"

"We don't know, but I'd rather take that chance than stay here in the Keys and run into more men like those two.

I think he's telling the truth. His story makes sense to me, and it makes sense that he would want to help us get to the islands in exchange for a ride. As small as our boat is, it's a lot bigger than his and it has sails. I think we should go, Thomas, and take him with us. What have we got to lose at this point?"

Thomas couldn't argue with that. They didn't have much of anything to lose but their boat and their lives, and if they stayed here much longer they were likely to lose both. At least they might have a chance if they could make it to the Bahamas.

"I know it's going to be crowded and uncomfortable Thomas, but we can make it work."

"Okay. I'll tell him. But if we agree to his help crossing the Gulf Stream, we're going to have to take him farther, to the part of the islands he's trying to reach. That's what he wants."

"That's fine with me," Mindy said. "It's probably a better place anyway. That's why that captain friend of his wants them to meet there. The farther off the beaten track the better, I say."

Thomas waved Scully back over to the fire and told him they would take him where he wanted to go in exchange for his navigation and sailing expertise. But when he asked Scully when they would leave, he wasn't expecting the answer he received, especially since there were still many hours of darkness before dawn.

"Now, mon. We sailin' now. Nevah know how many friend de dead mon dem got. Mehbe on de way already, comin' in de night outta de bush like dey friend. I seh we go tonight, leavin' dis place far behind. An' if de sea, she at peace, we be sailin' to de island come mornin'."

It took Thomas a minute to grasp the enormity of this. After all this time of dreaming and procrastinating, they were about to sail to the Bahamas, and they were leaving right away! It made him a bit nervous, but looking at the other body half-afloat at the tideline, Thomas knew the island man was right. They needed to get out of here and they needed to do it now. It would be foolhardy to remain here all night after their new friend had just killed two men. Thomas was almost certain someone else would come before morning, and Mindy nodded in agreement when he told Scully they could do it. The only thing she suggested was that since Thomas already had a fire going, they should cook the snapper they had caught earlier and eat before they left. Scully didn't argue with that. It only took an extra twenty minutes and then Thomas kicked sand onto the fire to put it out and they waded out to their boat. Scully pulled his kayak into the water as well and waded around to the stern of the sailboat, where he tied his bow painter to a cleat to serve as a towline.

Thomas wondered how they were going to manage, with the three of them living aboard the 17-foot micro-cruiser for several days or longer. There were only two bunks down below, but Scully assured him he wouldn't need one. He said he preferred to sleep on deck and stretching out in one of the cockpit seats to check it out, pronounced it plenty long enough for the purpose.

"All we need doin' is haul in de anchor mon."

"Are we going straight to the Bahamas tonight?" Mindy asked, still unsure of the plan.

Thomas wasn't clear on it either. Everything was happening so fast. And now he'd turned over the decision making to their new captain.

"We wait an' see in de mornin'" Scully said. "Sail outta dis place an' keep away from de land where people livin'. If de wind, she good, we goin' when de sun rise. But first we need to make de pass to south of dem Keys, under de bridge. You got de charts, to find de channel, mon?"

"Yes, we have all the charts for the Keys. There are several passes with enough bridge clearance for our mast. We've just been staying on the Gulf side because the chart showed a lot more mangrove islands and places to hide here." From what he could tell looking at the charts, the Atlantic side of the Keys looked a lot more open, with many of the inhabited islands built up on that side an few places to duck out of sight between them and the reefs farther offshore. It might have proven fatal tonight if not for Scully's arrival, but until then the strategy had worked. But now it was time to go to a better place.

With the anchor up and the rode stowed in its locker, Mindy and Thomas got the sails up without Scully's help and *Intrepida* began moving in the light nighttime breeze. The Montgomery did surprisingly well in light air and was reasonably close-winded. Thomas and Mindy had been sailing her long enough to know how to handle her well, it was just that they had not sailed offshore enough to build the confidence for longer crossings. But with a real offshore sailor on board, Thomas felt they absolutely could now.

Scully had little in the way of possessions other than the long, two-man kayak that he said belonged to his best friend, Larry, and his weapons. In addition to the military-style rifle he carried, he had a long, razor-sharp machete and the pistol and rifle taken from the two attackers he killed. Thomas found a safe place in a locker down below for the dangerous blade and the recovered firearms but Scully insisted on keeping his personal rifle close at hand as long as they were in sight of land. As they were tacking away from the anchorage at the mangrove island, Scully answered more of their questions about where he had been and what he had seen since the pulse.

"Lights out everywhere, mon. Dem out in St. Thomas, Puerto Rico, New Orlean. All de place I an' I see. Mehbe all de world, got de lights out. Only Jah knowin' mon."

Scully's report only confirmed what Thomas and Mindy suspected; the damage to the grid *was* widespread. Some of the other sailors they'd met at the Dry Tortugas said the same. Most of them had come from other parts of the Florida peninsula: Tampa, Ft. Myers, Miami, Ft. Lauderdale... Scully was the first person they'd talked to who could verify the same conditions as far away as New Orleans and St. Thomas. If the situation was truly global, then it was far worse than he'd imagined. The damage was the same anywhere they could conceivably go, so would things be any better in the Bahamas? When he asked Scully what he thought, their new captain replied with the

SCOTT B. WILLIAMS

story of the attack from another sailing vessel on the Cay Sal Bank. Even in such a remote place, they'd encountered violence, so maybe no place was truly safe, but Thomas already felt better with Scully in charge. And now there were three firearms aboard as well. Thomas would have never thought them necessary before the collapse, but after what just happened, he felt good knowing the guns were close at hand. And when they reached the Bahamas, he intended to ask Scully if they could keep one of them, maybe the pistol, and if he could teach them how to use it. Never again did he want to experience that helpless feeling of knowing he was about to be murdered, along with the woman he loved, and that there was not a thing he could do about it. From this point forward, Thomas realized they were going to have to adapt to a harsh new way of life. The rules were different now, and the only authorities they had encountered had simply ordered them to go away. Thomas wanted to survive this, and he knew Mindy did too. With Scully's help, the prospects of doing just that suddenly looked a whole lot better.

CHAPTER 5

THE LONGER RUSSELL WATCHED, the better he felt about his new neighbors with which he now shared this tiny Bahamian cay he didn't even know the name of. After seeing more of the crew from the two sailboats, he began to feel fairly certain that they were not cutthroat murderers out roaming the islands to take from the less fortunate. Instead, they appeared to be quite normal looking folks. That they were a mix of men and women, even *young, good-looking women;* put Russell even more at ease in regards to their intentions.

The first of these women had appeared on deck of the classic-looking sailboat that was anchored on the calm side of the island. She looked to be perhaps in her mid to late thirties, like the man on the catamaran, and like him she seemed at ease aboard a boat. Her tan, athletic body added to her image as a competent sailor and she was quite attractive, with short, but sexy blonde hair that just touched her shoulders. The other two females that greeted the day a bit later were much younger, in their early twenties, Russell guessed. One had the outdoorsy, at home on the boat kind of look and the other looked like she could have been a fashion model in a previous life. It was this one that Russell zeroed in on, unable to take his eyes off her, as he watched her ever move in fascination. It had been too long since he'd seen other people at all, and *way* too long since he'd seen a girl that looked that good.

Her oversized T-shirt and baggy shorts couldn't hide what he was sure was a perfect body, and her long brunette hair was pulled back in a ponytail, allowing him to see even at a distance that she had a face to match the rest. What were the odds of a girl like her ending up here? Russell didn't know, but he was certainly not going to object. He noticed too that there was a young man about the age of the two younger women as well. This one was clean-cut, still making the effort to shave apparently; something few men bothered with these days. There was one more man who emerged soon as well, and Russell guessed he could be in his mid to late forties. The final crewmember he saw was a young girl in her early teens, bringing the grand total from the two boats to seven. Russell figured one of the older men was the girl's father, and the blonde woman was no doubt her mother. Whatever the case, it didn't really matter. He had seen enough that he was sure they were all sailing together. Why the other boat ended up on the safe side of the island, unlike the catamaran, Russell didn't know, but he figured it was because the catamaran got their first. It make sense, because he knew catamarans were faster than boats like the other one.

Russell had been watching from behind a clump of bushes and cacti on a slight rise that overlooked the entire end of the island the boats and their crews occupied. As soon as all of them were out for the day, there was much walking back and forth across the island between the two vessels, and what appeared to be lots of discussion among their crews. Russell had no doubt it was in regards to getting out of their predicament. The next thing that happened was that they began offloading the gear and supplies aboard the stranded catamaran. Russell could easily guess what they were doing—trying to lighten the load. Maybe they were going to try and refloat the boat when the tide came in and sail it around to the other side where the other vessel was anchored. One thing he was sure of, they had *lots* of stuff. His mouth watered as he began to fantasize about foods he had not tasted in weeks. Surely they would share some with him when he explained his situation. Russell decided it was time to make an introduction. He would simply walk up to them and tell them the truth, that he was alone there, a castaway who had barely survived his ordeal, and if they were indeed ordinary, mostly good people as he was now confident they were, they would have pity on him and help him out. In exchange, he would help them with their boat problem. Maybe they would even give him a ride. That was what he *really* wanted, a ride and the opportunity to meet the beautiful girl with the long dark hair. Russell got to his feet and stepped out in the open, calling out to the strangers before approaching any closer.

The man he'd seen first was passing things from the deck of the catamaran to the other two men in the water, who were in turn handing them to the three women and the girl. They had a system going to get everything to the beach as quickly as possible, and Russell figured he could join in and help them, if only they'd give him something to eat so he would have the strength to work. His shouts clearly startled them—all seven of the strangers immediately stopped what they were doing and turned his way to look. Their first reaction was anything but welcoming. The women moved closer to the boat and the guy on deck reached for something through the closest hatch and seconds later had a shotgun in his hands.

"It's okay!" Russell shouted. "I don't have a gun, only this!" He held the fiberglass pole spear out to one side so they could see it. It wasn't much of a weapon against someone armed with a shotgun. "I'm not looking for trouble, I just need help! I'm hungry!" He hesitated before walking any closer.

"Where did you come from?" the man with the shotgun yelled back. "We didn't see another boat on the island. Are you alone?"

"Yes I'm alone! I don't have a boat! I'm stranded here and barely surviving!" Russell stood there waiting for a reaction while the surprised boat people talked amongst themselves, apparently trying to decide what to do about his unexpected appearance.

"Stay where you are!" the man with the gun yelled back. "We'll come talk to you."

Russell saw the man go below into the cabin again, and when he reappeared, he had two more long guns, both of which looked to be assault rifles. He passed one to each of the other two men and then walked to the bow of the catamaran and jumped off into the shallow water. Russell knew that if he'd misjudged these people, he was screwed. He was powerless to defend himself against them, and even if they didn't have guns he couldn't have done much against three men who all looked to be fit and healthy while he was underfed and weak. And so he stood there and waited, trying not to appear nervous. He resigned himself to the reality that if they killed him now it wouldn't matter much anyway. He couldn't go on like this forever and he knew that eventually something would happen to him here alone, and that would be it. Maybe he would step on a stingray or get bitten by a shark, or maybe the next time he got sick he wouldn't recover his strength, and would spend his last days lying there in his miserable hut, unable to get up and forage for food, wasting away until he died of starvation. It wasn't an attractive option, and even if he'd tried to hide, these people probably would have found him. If they decided to shoot him on the spot, then so be it. He would know soon enough if they were going to do so.

"I just saw your boats this morning," he said, as the three men walked towards him, stopping when they were some twenty paces away. They were close enough to talk in a normal tone, but far enough that they knew he couldn't try anything.

"How did you get here?" the one with the shotgun asked. "This island is a long way from anywhere."

"I was on a sailboat with some people I met in Nassau. They agreed to give me a ride to Staniel Cay in the Exumas. I have an old friend that lives there. I thought we were in the Exumas, but now I'm not so sure. There's nothing here and I have no idea which cay this is. We dropped the anchor nearby for what they said was a stop to do some spearfishing, but they left while I was off swimming, too far from the boat to catch up. They abandoned me here with nothing but this pole spear and my mask, and I haven't seen another boat until you guys showed up."

"You're a long way from the Exumas," the man with the shotgun said. "If they told you that's where you were, they lied. So why would they do that? Did you give them a reason to want you off their boat?"

"No, of course not! I was doing my part, helping them with everything aboard. I didn't really know them well. I'd just met them not long before the blackout. They were a Canadian couple, from Toronto, they said. They had an awesome boat, a Pacific Seacraft cutter. When the power went out they didn't know where they were going to go. Nassau was getting dangerous. There were riots and people from ashore were stealing boats to get out of there. It was getting *bad* let me tell you. The food ran out in the stores. There was no fuel at the docks or in town. But there were a lot of people living on boats there at the time, like always. I had done a bottom cleaning for these folks about a week before it all happened, because that's what I did for work. They asked me where I thought they should go, considering the situation, since it was their first time in the islands, and we talked about it several times before deciding to leave together for the Exumas. I didn't know what I was going to do until then. At first I thought about trying to get back to Florida, but more and more boats kept coming through the harbor at Nassau and the stories we heard about Florida made it sound even worse than it was here in the islands. So I remembered this buddy of mine and thought I should try and get to his house on Staniel Cay. He had told me that it was completely off-grid, with generators and solar panels, so I figured it would be a good place to go."

"So you didn't even know that you weren't in the Exumas when you anchored here with those folks? How is that possible?"

"They were doing the navigating. The GPS wasn't working, of course, but they had charts and a compass and they said they wanted to stop on the way to Staniel Cay and do some fishing at an island some other Canadians had told them about. I thought it would be a good idea to stock up on food too, and since they said the island was part of the Exumas, I figured it couldn't be much out of the way. And I figured it they made it all the way to Nassau from Lake Ontario, they probably knew what they were doing, so I just let them do their thing while I took my turns at the helm and on watch. Navigation is not my strong point, but I know boats from stem to stern, especially anything to do with maintenance and repair.

But look man. I'm hungry! I've been living off whelks and conch and a fish here and there, whatever I could find on the reef. I've been about to starve, and I was sick for the last two days. Today was my first time out since I got ill. I'd appreciate it if you could give me something... anything at all... some pasta or a little rice... anything you can spare man! I'll work for it. I'll help you get your boat back to deep water. I could tell it was aground. Is there much damage to the hulls?"

The men were looking at each other and back at him as Russell stood there awaiting their answer.

"Go back and ask Casey to put some water on the stove for oatmeal. We all need to eat some breakfast anyway," the man with the shotgun told the younger one. Then he turned back to Russell. "What's your name? I'm Larry Drager. This is my brother Artie, and that's my friend, Grant."

"Russell. My name's Russell. I'm so glad to meet you Larry. All of you. I thought I was going to die here."

"What have you been doing for water? Did you find an old cistern or a well on the island?"

"Yes! There's a big cistern near the middle of the island. The water's dirty and full of bugs, but at least it's fresh. There must have been a farm here a long time ago. There are goats on the island too, but I haven't been able to catch one."

"Yeah, I know about the goats. I've seen them before."

"You've been here before? What is the name of this island then?"

"Green Cay. It's about 40 miles west of the Exumas. Either your Canadian friends sucked at navigation or they flat out lied to you."

"I don't know. I thought they were pretty cool, but I guess I was wrong about them."

"It sounds like they didn't care if you lived or died, dropping you off here. I'm not surprised you haven't seen any other boats. Not many stopped here even in normal times. It's not on the way to any of the popular cruising grounds and the anchorage is no good in bad weather. Besides, it's too shallow for most of the big boats cruising the islands these days."

"Well, today is my lucky day then! I can't tell you how glad I am to see you guys! Man, I appreciate the grub and I'd love to catch a ride off this rock. I can work for it! I'll help you get your boat off the reef. I can help you fix anything that's broken. Whatever you need man! I've been working on boats most of my life. I'm good with tools and I'll do anything I can to help. I just want out of here!"

CHAPTER 6

THE NEWS that the Dry Tortugas were sealed off by the U.S. Navy changed everything for Scully. If no boats were allowed there, then Larry wouldn't be there as they'd planned when they had all set sail to cross the Gulf. And his hopes of catching up with Artie, Grant and Jessica aboard the *Casey Nicole* there were doomed as well. All he could do now was to try and find his friends in the Bahamas, assuming they made it to the remote chain of cays where Larry wanted to layover for a while. And if they *were* there, Scully could only hope they would hang around long enough for him to get there, and not give up on him.

Scully hadn't intended to get involved in the problems of others, and could have just as well continued on his way without interfering when he came upon the scene of the attack on Thomas and Mindy. But the advantage had been so clearly in his favor that he saw little reason to paddle by such a tragedy without doing something. He knew as soon as he saw what was going on that the young couple would be dead without his help, and Scully had seen enough such evil since the blackout that he hated to see those two thugs get away with such a crime unpunished. Killing them had been easy, and now he was glad he'd chosen the path he did. Not only had he saved their lives, but he'd saved himself many days of what would have been a futile effort to paddle to the Dry Tortugas only to be turned away when he arrived. Scully had no reason to doubt the story Thomas and Mindy told him of the navy blockade. The incident at Cape Sable made more sense now because of what he'd just learned about what was going on out there. But more importantly than the time he'd saved, he now had a sailboat under him again—a reliable means to reach the Bahamas—even the far outer reaches of the archipelago where his friends planned to go. Sure, it was a little boat; far smaller than what most would consider adequate to sail any distance, much less the hundreds of miles of open water that lay between him and the Jumentos Cays, but Scully knew a good boat when he saw one. Thomas had told him the design was famous for many long voyages undertaken in *Intrepida's* sister ships, but even if he hadn't, Scully could see that the lines of the hull were right, and the construction and rigging solid.

The chubby little 17-footer would be far slower at sea than the sleek *Casey Nicole* or even Tara's *Sarah J.*, and it would be quite crowded with three on board for that length of time, but it would get them there. If not for meeting this young couple, Scully knew he would have attempted the crossing to the Bahamas in the kayak, because what other choice did he have? That would have been possible too, but a lot more could go wrong on such an expedition. With no sails or other back up to the paddle, if he became incapacitated for some reason, he could be swept away from the islands by the Gulf Stream before he was across its strong currents. The sailboat, small though it was, had every advantage in this case, and seeing how it was rigged, Scully knew it could sail to weather too.

When he'd proposed to help Thomas and Mindy cross over to the islands in their little boat, he'd half expected them to say no, even though they said they really wanted to go there. After all, the boat was too small for three adults, and they were an intimate couple that would have to share their living space with a stranger for an indefinite time. If not for what he'd done for them, Scully knew his appearance alone might have kept them at a distance. Despite his friendly grin, many of the white tourists he'd met in the islands shied away from approaching too closely. Then, as now, his wild dreadlocks, unshaven face and lack of shoes or even clothes save for his cut-off camo army pants, kept most at bay. And if appearance alone were not enough, there was the fact that he was a black islander who spoke English with an accent barely recognizable as the same language spoken in America. But Thomas and Mindy didn't let any of that bother them after learning of his predicament. They had reason enough to trust him after he saved them from death when he could have just turned the other way.

To Scully it was a wonder these two had survived this long, and he knew the only reason was because they had the boat. With no weapons or even knowledge of how to use firearms, they were victims in the making, living on luck until killers like the two he'd dispatched found them. Even when he'd shot the man pointing the pistol at Thomas, the clueless young man hadn't thought to pick up the fallen weapon to defend himself. It was as if he was afraid of it, even though it was inert and useless without a hand to pull the trigger. But Scully had met people like them before, all of the tourists on holiday in the islands. It was no wonder so many people in America had already died just because the lights went out. To Scully, it was a shame, but that was the price they paid for the Babylon they'd created.

Scully understood that by joining these two aboard their little boat he would essentially be taking responsibility for them. They knew how to sail and navigate among the closely spaced islands of the Florida Keys, and had even made it to the Dry Tortugas and back, but from hearing Thomas talk, Scully gathered they were both afraid of the sea. He didn't know how they would react in a serious storm or serious boat crisis, but he had to assume it would be about the same as the way they'd responded to the men who'd attacked them—with helpless resignation.

What they would do after the three of them got where they were going was another question all together, but Scully wasn't going to let that be his problem. They couldn't stay with him and his friends, because their little boat could never keep up and besides, the last thing they needed was two more adults with little in the way of skills to look after. Larry would never tolerate it. There was only one reason he'd taken on Tara and Rebecca, and all of them knew what it was. Scully figured Thomas and Mindy would last a while, but not indefinitely. The odds were simply stacked too high against them, but their time might be stretched a bit longer in the Bahamas than if they remained here. At least while he was with them, their odds of dying were greatly reduced. Scully didn't know for sure, but from what he'd seen so far, he doubted things were going to be much different in the islands, other than the simple fact that Larry's choice was so remote the bad people might not have arrived yet.

One asset that Thomas and Mindy possessed in addition to their boat was a decent selection of fishing equipment. As they sailed away from the scene of the shooting, Scully felt confident that they could catch enough food to keep them going, especially once they crossed to the islands where the reefs were rich in marine life. All he had in the way of tools and gear aside from the kayak was his machete and the AK-47. And the only food he carried was the stash of green coconuts he'd gathered from the palms at Cape Sable just before he'd gotten separated from the *Casey Nicole.*

Scully didn't know how many more of those patrol boats might be out there, cruising the coast with their machine guns, but Thomas and Mindy had not had any encounters since they'd left the Dry Tortugas. This gave him hope they could get out of these waters and out to the high seas without incident. The only issue was that they were north of the island chain and would have to pass under at least one bridge to reach the Atlantic and freedom. Scully was leery of sailing under those bridges since that first time he'd done it with Larry and Artie on the way to New Orleans. Someone on the roadway high above had tried to hit them with large rocks dropped over the rail, to what end none of them new. They were lucky to slip under without getting hit, but now Scully feared if anyone saw them they would be using bullets instead of rocks. It made him uneasy to think about it, but if they could get out of these waters before daylight, he figured their chances of avoiding trouble would be better. They would be setting out to cross the Gulf Stream without a weather forecast, but once he could see the sea state and read the sky in the morning light, Scully could assess the situation then and decide if it was a go or no-go day. If not, they would have to find another place to hole up until the conditions improved.

The little boat responded well to the light, nighttime breezes and the long two-seater kayak riding on the tow line astern created little fuss in the wake and no significant drag to slow them down. Scully estimated they were making four and half to five knots on a reach, and Thomas assured him the boat could average at least that on a long crossing. It was slow compared to what Scully was used to, but still better than paddling at three knots, and working constantly to maintain even that. At least on the sailboat they could rotate watches and everyone could get a bit of sleep.

But that would be later, when they embarked upon the actual crossing. Right now Scully's greatest worry was getting as far away from the scene of the shooting as possible, while it was still dark. While he had voiced some concern that the dead attackers might have friends, he was more worried about any unwanted attention the sound of gunfire might attract. There could be other bandits unrelated to those two, or there could be another patrol boat like the one that had driven away the *Casey Nicole* from Cape Sable. Scully didn't know what to expect in these waters, but he knew that a sailboat with its rig up would be much more visible from a distance than his stealthy kayak. At least *Intrepida* had the tanbark-colored sails that were popular on such traditional cruisers. In low light the dark red color would be less visible than white Dacron, and leaving unseen was their best chance of survival. There weren't many boats they could outrun in a heavy-displacement 17-footer, no matter how well she sailed.

Thomas and Mindy were still shaken up from their close brush with death and were huddled together in the cockpit while Scully steered. Thomas had his chart book for the Florida Keys open beside him, and he confirmed that the elevated section of the bridge they could see on the dark horizon ahead was indeed one of the channels to the Atlantic side of the Keys.

"Not to worry mon. Soon we sailin' in de open ocean. Leavin' dis Babylon an' de evil killers in dat place in de wake. Your boat she a good one, mon. She gonna take us to de island, no problem."

"No problem thanks to you, Scully. I know she's a good boat, but it's been hard to work up the courage to go that far."

"Dem seh bettah you wait on de land an' wish you sailin' on de sea, den be out in de storm wishin' you on dry land, mon."

"Yeah, better safe than sorry, I guess."

"Except now," Mindy said. "Now we know it's not safe to be on land around here or even anchored anywhere near it. I'd rather go out there and drown than have to face men like that again."

"I agree," Thomas said, putting his arm around her and pulling her closer to him. "I'm just glad you're okay. I can't tell you what an awful feeling that was, knowing I couldn't do anything to stop them. But we're never going to be in that kind of situation again. We're going where we won't have to worry about men like that. You'll see."

Scully said nothing, but wondered just where Thomas thought such a place might be as he steered for the pass under the distant bridge. If he knew the answer to that question, he would have told Larry and the others a long time ago. But all that mattered to him now was simply finding them again. They would figure out where to go from there then, if the reunion he hoped for actually happened.

CHAPTER 7

JESSICA WOKE in her bunk aboard the catamaran that first morning on Green Cay and realized that things were going to be quite different now that they were reunited with the rest of their friends and her voyage with Grant and Artie was over. Casey was back in the picture now, and she had practically leapt into Grant's arms the moment she laid eyes on him as he waded through the surf to carry an anchor to the beach. He seemed equally ecstatic to see her again too, as if he'd already forgotten Jessica's embrace and kiss he had at last opened up to in those hurried moments in the waters off Andros. Jessica had thought he was at last coming around to wanting what she did, but all that seemed to change again when he saw Casey. Seeing this, Jessica was surprised that he even returned to his bunk aboard the catamaran, or that Casey didn't come with him. But everyone was exhausted after all the hard work of securing the catamaran, and they only had a couple hours to get some sleep before beginning the long day of work Larry said was ahead of them.

Jessica didn't want to harbor anger or jealousy towards her friend and former roommate. It was hard to suppress those feelings, but they were all stuck in this situation together for the long-term, and she knew that Casey and Grant had been friends long before she'd met him herself. Casey already had a crush on the older grad student before the three of them left New Orleans together. But the more time Jessica spent in his company, especially the week the two of them were alone together in the swamp after Casey went missing, as well as their recent voyage on the catamaran, she couldn't help it if she was attracted to him. Grant was calm, intelligent and capable, not to mention fit and handsome. That he found her appealing too she had no doubt; Jessica rarely met a man who didn't. It wasn't her fault she was born with that gift, and that she was now in her prime and able to turn the head of any male with a pulse. She didn't know how this situation was going to resolve itself, but she could feel trouble brewing because of it and arriving here where Casey and the others were brought it back to light.

She didn't want to think about it this morning though, and hoped she wouldn't have to. Larry said they all had a lot of work ahead of them. The *Casey Nicole* was damaged, but before they could even begin fixing the boat and making it ready to sail again, they had to get it unloaded and up onto the beach. From what she'd gathered from listening to Larry talk, they were going to be stuck here on Green Cay for at least a few days, and maybe even longer.

Green Cay was a beautiful tropical island, Jessica realized, when she first saw it in the daylight that morning. It was the kind of place romantic fantasies were made of, and if it were she and Grant alone there, it would be perfect. That was her dream and her only real hope now, to simply be in a place like this with Grant. It was all she had left after realizing she might never be able to go back to her old life or even return to the mainland for an indefinite length of time. She missed her parents and other family and friends in California, but there was simply no way of knowing if they were still alive or not. All she had was this, and the hope of something more, something *much* more, with Grant. It was this dream that kept her going; that saved her from falling into depression and despair, but now, seeing how happy Grant was to be with Casey again, she felt that hope begin to fade.

The work of unloading the *Casey Nicole* began shortly after everyone was awake and moving about. Larry said that the boat had to be lightened as much as possible by removing her stores and gear. They did this by passing things from the deck to the beach, stacking it all above the high tide line. The next step, after that was done, Larry said, was to get the catamaran out of the water as well. Jessica wasn't sure how that could be done, but she knew if anybody could do it, Larry Drager could. He had built the boat, after all, with Scully's help and his own two hands.

The work was strenuous and monotonous, and Jessica

would have preferred to wander off and explore the lovely beaches of the island alone with Grant, but that wasn't going to happen anytime soon. At least she was near him, even if he was on the deck with Larry and Artie while she, along with Casey, Tara and Rebecca were wading back and forth with the things they handed overboard to them. As she worked beside her, Jessica was bothered a bit by how her thoughts of Casey had changed. It made her feel bad, knowing inside she would have preferred if Casey were not there at all. She should be glad to see her friend again, but now Grant was a wedge driven between them, and Jessica feared it would only push them farther apart. She found herself thinking this way more and more and couldn't help it. It made her want to physically keep herself between Grant and Casey as much as possible, as if that would change things. The feeling was so strong that she realized she was moving more stuff to the beach than Casey, simply because she wanted to be the one he handed things to more often than her. If Casey had been on the deck with him instead of in the water with her, Jessica would have been furious. She tried to remind herself she had gotten closer to Grant than Casey, at least as far as she knew. He had opened up to her and returned her kisses, but still...

Her thoughts of this dilemma were interrupted when the stranger appeared later that morning; surprising them all after thinking they were alone there. She watched and waited in the shallows beside the catamaran as Larry, Grant and Artie went to meet him, keeping him at a distance until they determined whether or not he was a threat. Jessica certainly hoped not. She'd thought they'd put all that behind them once they left Florida and the rest of the U.S. astern. The point of coming here to the Bahamas in the first place was to find a refuge from the violence that seemed to be everywhere back there. Jessica hoped none of them would have to use their guns again, but she was glad they were all well armed when they walked up the hill to greet the guy.

Jessica judged him to be not much older than her or Grant, maybe in his late twenties. He was shirtless, wearing only surfer shorts and sandals, and was carrying nothing but a fishing spear. The guys talked to him for a few minutes, and then Grant returned to the boat, saying they were going to give him some food.

"He says his name is Russell. I don't think he's dangerous. He's just stranded here and he's hungry. Larry told him he could join us for breakfast. The guy's been living off whelks and raw fish for weeks. He doesn't even have a way to start a fire."

When Larry and Artie returned to the boat bringing Russell with them, Jessica thought he seemed friendly enough upon first introduction, but she could tell he had an obnoxious side too. Maybe it was just that he'd been alone here for so long and was so starved for conversation that he wouldn't stop talking once he started, but it seemed to be more than that. Maybe it was the way his eyes locked on hers for a long, intense moment and then quickly took in the rest of her body, whether he was conscious of it or not. Jessica was used to men looking at her that way, it was just a fact of life for her because so many of them found her attractive. She saw Russell checking out Tara and Casey too, but he *had* been alone for a long time so it was understandable that he must have dreamed about girls the way any normal young man would. But even as he looked at them and wolfed down the oatmeal Casey gave him, he talked and talked and talked, rambling on about every detail of his ordeal there and asking endless questions about their boats and where they'd come from and what they knew of the situation.

"That's sick, man! You mean it's really that bad way up in New Orleans? And all the way down to St. Thomas? Shit, man, I was hoping it was just a small area, like maybe the Bahamas and south Florida? Do you really think it was just a solar flare? I know that's what everybody's been saying, but the more I hear about it, the more I think it wasn't. And then what you said about those ships. I've been suspicious that's it's something our own government did. Maybe they've been planning it all along. Break everybody down with this and then set up the new system they've been preparing for."

Larry waved this off and tried to change the subject, but Russell was persistent.

"Look, man. They can totally do something like that! I've read a lot about it! They may even have some kind of weapon in orbit we don't know about. Some way to send an EMP pulse that could wipe everything out and make it look like a natural event. Natural solar flares aren't strong enough to do the damage that's been done. Not to kill all the cars and everything! After what you've told me about the ships being there, I'll bet that's what it was! They waited until a real solar flare happened before they pulled the trigger, so they could blame it on a natural event, then they did it. Just like that! Then they just sat back and waited long enough for things to break down so they could come in and mop up. Finish the job and establish their New World Order! I've been thinking about it a lot while I've been here. I already had it figured out, and now with what you've told me, I *know* I'm right! It all makes sense. That's why I wouldn't go back to the U.S. now for *anything!* Anyone who doesn't go along with the program is going to be slaughtered."

"That's crazy," Grant said. "There's no way the government would do something like that, even if they could. People are dying by the thousands, maybe tens or hundreds of thousands, because of this."

"Don't put it past them!" Russell said. "That kind of thing has happened before."

Jessica didn't say anything, but she thought it was crazy too. Russell had been stranded here alone for too long. Maybe all the sun and solitude had made him crazy. Maybe he was already crazy before any of this happened? He seemed obsessed with his idea though, and looking at him, she figured he'd probably done a lot of drugs in his day and would now if he had them. Just as she was thinking that, he finished his breakfast and immediately turned to Larry with another request.

"Hey man, you haven't got a joint you could spare have

you? I haven't had any smoke in over a month! It's crazy! But I *know* you've got weed on the boat."

"Nope!" Larry said. "No weed on board. I've never allowed it on any boat I sail. I'm a professional skipper and can't risk it. I might burn one now and then ashore with my Rasta buddy, Scully, but we don't bring it on the boat."

"Man, that sucks! I was *really* hoping when I saw the two boats. Are you sure you're not holding out on me? I'm not asking for much. Just a toke or two would be awesome!"

"Sorry, but I'm not kidding. There's nothing to smoke on the *Casey Nicole*."

"If you say so man, but I still think you're holding out. What about the other boat? Somebody's got a stash on board that one, I know it!"

"No," Tara said. "The *Sarah J.* belongs to my retired parents. They don't smoke marijuana, and I don't either."

Jessica saw that Russell looked completely dejected. It was like he wanted a joint worse than he wanted food, after being stuck here all this time without it. He reminded her of her stupid ex-boyfriend Joey, who was the same way about beer. And as if reading her thoughts once again, alcohol was the next thing Russell asked for.

"What about a shot of rum... or whiskey? Brandy? Or *anything*? I know you've guys have to have a liquor cabinet on board!"

"Look, Russell. We've got our hands a bit full right now. As you can see, the tide is already starting to come in. We've got to finish unloading this boat so we can get set up to haul her out when it peaks. You're welcome to the food we gave you and you can eat with us again too, but nobody's interested in drinking at this hour."

"It's cool, man. Sorry! I've just been stuck here so long! You have no idea how glad I am to see you guys!"

Jessica felt his eyes sweep her entire body again and lock on for a moment as he said this. It gave her the creeps, but she looked away and pretended not to know he was staring at her.

"What can I do to help? I'm ready to work! Just say the word, man, and I'm on it."

CHAPTER 8

LARRY HAD TOO much on his mind this morning to give this Russell guy much thought. He didn't mind sharing a little food with him, since it was obvious he was indeed a bit desperate and was telling the truth about being stranded on Green Cay. Anyone could look at him and see this was so. Even though Russell looked like the perpetually skinny type, you could see that he had been living even leaner for a few weeks. Larry could tell too that Russell had probably always been a bit of a pain in the ass. It was understandable that he was starved for conversation and human contact, but it was more than that. Larry pegged him as the type that was always running his mouth, telling anyone who would listen about everything he'd ever done and offering his opinions whether they were solicited or not. Larry didn't have time to hear any of it right now, and the last thing he needed was a drunk underfoot all day when they had critical work to do. He wouldn't give in to Russell's request for a drink until that work was done, but figured he would probably share a bit of rum with him tonight if all went as planned.

It took another hour and a half, but once they had everything off the boat that could be removed without tools, Larry was ready to begin setting up the tackle to haul her out. That he considered it doable at all was largely because of the ideal slope angle of the beach above the tideline, and the fairly good tidal range for these latitudes, judging by the high water marks on the nearby rocks. There was just enough room on the powdery sand of the beach directly ahead of the *Casey Nicole's* bows to accommodate her full length, which would get her high hulls high enough to dry out at low tide. All he wanted to do was fully inspect them and lay up some fiberglass reinforcements over the cracked and damaged areas. It was important to keep the water out of the plywood core under the fiberglass, so these kinds of breaks in the sheathing had to be dealt with as soon as possible.

"Is it going to work?" Casey asked him as Larry double-checked the set of his anchors on the high ground beyond the beach while they waited on more water.

"You can count on it, Casey. She'll come out the same way she went in. Once we start winching her up, she'll have no choice. We'll put the big fenders under the bows and then more under the keels as she goes. It'll take a lot of fiddling back and forth and we'll have to go slow, but we'll have her high and dry before the tide goes out again."

"That's good to hear. I'm so glad the damage wasn't worse."

"Me too. The reefs just a bit to the north would not have been as kind to her."

"I wish Scully was here, Uncle Larry. I don't like the idea of you sailing back to Florida after what my dad said about that gunboat."

"I don't like it either, Casey, but you know I've got to find him. Scully is like a brother to me. I'm not leaving him behind, but I'm not going to put any of you at risk to look for him either. I'll do it myself."

"How? You can't go back there all alone! You know that. I'll go with you if you like. You're gonna need help sailing the boat."

"No, Casey. You've *got* to stay here with your dad. We've put him through enough worry already. Practically all he's been doing since the grid went down is looking for you. Now that you two are together, you are *staying* together! I can do this alone. All of you can wait right here on Green Cay."

"What about this Russell guy? He gives me the creeps. Jessica said the same thing."

"Yeah, I know, but I'm pretty sure he's harmless. I've seen his type at every marina and boatyard I've ever been to. Typical know-it-all boat bum. Likes hanging around boats but has never managed to own one. I'm keeping an eye on him. I don't know yet what we'll do about it, but we'll deal with that later. I'm sure he's hoping for a ride off the island."

"Right now it sounds like all he wants to do is get high," Casey said. "And he's had an eye on Jessica since he saw her. He was looking at me and Tara too."

"Well, you can't blame him for that," Larry grinned. "He *has* been stranded on a desert island for weeks, you know." As he said this, Larry saw that Russell was sticking as close to Jessica as he could, while she was in turn doing her best to make sure she was following Grant with every move he made. Casey wasn't oblivious to that either, and had to comment to her uncle about it:

"I gather that Jessica would have preferred to keep sailing with Grant. I see she's doing her best to pester the hell out of him."

"Well, from what your dad said, he had every opportunity if she was what he wanted, Casey. They've been at sea together long enough. I don't see him hanging all over her the same way though. I think he still likes you better."

"Maybe. I just wish Jessica wouldn't act so stupid sometimes."

"Women!" Larry laughed, touching Casey's shoulder as he did. "*Some* women. Not you! I guess Tara's happy to see that I've got my own boat back. I'm sure she was just elated that I wasn't on board the *Sarah J.* last night."

"If so, it's her loss, Uncle Larry. But I think she's forgiven you by now. Maybe you two are just too much alike. Do you really think two captains with two boats can ever agree on anything?"

"Hell no! But I would have enjoyed making up after

the fights! Maybe the two boats part would have made it work. We wouldn't have to deal with each other until we made port. Then when the fun was over, we could set sail again!"

"It's a nice fantasy Uncle Larry. I'm sure the two of you would get along better that way. Maybe it could still work out?"

Larry didn't get a chance to answer before Russell made his way into the middle of their conversation, hitting Larry with half a dozen questions at once about the design of the catamaran, while at the same time telling him what he would have done differently if he had built it.

"I don't like that idea of tying the beams to the hulls. That looks pretty sketch to me. I would have glassed them in and made it all one piece. And dude, you've got all that deck space. Why not build a big main cabin over it? Think of all the room you'd have! If the beams were glassed in, the deck cabin could open into the hulls. Most catamarans I've seen are like that. Every been aboard a Gemini?"

Larry did his best to ignore Russell's questions and comments. He'd heard them all before when he was building the big Wharram cat on Culebra. Most people didn't get it, but he didn't care about that. He had his reasons for liking the design and the last thing he had time for was discussing the intricacies of multihull parameters with a typical boatyard know-it-all.

"If the hulls were round-bottomed, it'd be a lot easier to haul her out. She would draw less with centerboards that could be lifted than with those deep Vs. It's going to be hard to get her up on the sand, the way they're going to dig in. That's why they got damaged on the reef in the first place."

"We'll get her out, don't you worry," Larry said.

"Yeah, and I'm going to help you do it. I'm just sayin'. Could be a lot easier with a few small changes. That's just the way I would have done it. And it's what I'll do when I build *my* boat."

"Sounds like you've got it figured out then," Larry said.

"Yeah, man. I've been around boats all my life. I've seen all kinds come and go. Got a feel for what works and what doesn't. That's what I've been doing; studying them and keeping the best ideas I've seen in my head. I didn't want to compromise with my own boat, so I've been biding my time until I'm ready. When I build one, it's going to be the best! Then, I'll circumnavigate on her. That's always been the plan."

"Is that so?" Larry asked. Russell's spouting off was going in one ear and out the other. Larry didn't care what his plans had been or what he thought of the *Casey Nicole* or anything else for that matter. But as long as he stayed out of the way and maybe provided a bit of extra muscle when they began winching her out, he could tolerate his presence to a degree.

"Looks like we're about ready, little brother," Artie said, checking the taut anchor lines that were in place.

"Yep. When the tide peaks, in less than a half hour,

we'll start cranking the big winch and see if we can make this happen. If you and Grant don't mind, you two can help me with that. We can spell each other when we get tired. I'm still working with one arm, you know, Doc."

"Yes, I *do* know. And if you'd listened to your doctor and kept it in a sling to give it more time to heal, you'd be farther along the way to recovery than you are now!"

"Probably. Kinda hard to do though, you know, the way things have been... gunfights... storms at sea... getting beaten up by an angry mom...."

"Dude, somebody nearly cut your arm off!" Russell said, noticing the long scar where Artie had sewn up the gaping machete wound that had indeed cut nearly halfway through his arm just below the elbow.

"Nah, it's just a scratch."

"Right.... Hey, I can work a winch handle. But I'm still so weak from the last two days of being sick. And not having enough to eat for a month."

"Don't worry about it. We've got enough muscle between the three of us to do the grinding. You can help the girls with the fenders as she comes out. It'll probably take two people on either side of each hull to hold them in place until they get some weight on them. It's going to be slow, but slow is better than nothing."

Larry looked at the gentle waves lapping at the rocks and decided it was time to get started if they were going to make this work.

"Okay, if everybody's ready, let's do this."

Grant was already in the cockpit, standing behind the centrally mounted winch that served as the anchor windlass when it wasn't needed for the sheets. Larry gave him the go ahead to start cranking even as he and his brother were still climbing aboard.

CHAPTER 9

RUSSELL WAS QUITE content to stay on the beach and work with the girls on the placement of the fenders. He followed Jessica, the brunette that had caught his eye from a distance, seizing the opportunity to talk to her by offering to help her. The other girl, Casey, and the blonde named Tara, who owned the other boat, were busy getting their half of the fenders ready for the other hull.

"So where are you from, Jessica?"

"L.A." She said, without asking him the same.

"Wow, you are a long way from home then. How did you end up on a boat in the Bahamas? Were you in L.A. when the pulse hit?"

"No, I was in New Orleans. Casey and I were roommates there."

"Cool! I *love* New Orleans. I used to go every chance I got! It's a party town."

"Not anymore, it isn't."

"No, I guess not. I didn't realize until I talked to Larry that the effects of this thing went that far. What about the West Coast? Have you heard from anybody back home?"

"How would I?" Jessica asked, giving him a look that suggested she didn't want to talk about it.

"Sorry, I guess that was a stupid question. Nobody's got a phone that'll work. I just thought you might have gotten word somehow."

"No, and I'm just trying not to think about it. I don't know what will happen to my parents and my other family and friends out there, or if something already has. I'm afraid it's as bad as New Orleans, or worse."

"Yeah, big cities are the worst in something like this. That's why I didn't want to go back to Florida when it happened. Some people living on boats in Nassau said that's what they were going to do, but I knew it was crazy. We'd already heard from others who'd arrived from Ft. Lauderdale since it happened and they said things were insane on the mainland. I wanted to stay the hell away. That's why I waited until I could find a ride with somebody going to the out islands. I knew it would be better to be somewhere with fewer people and where the fishing was good. You guys did the right thing, coming here."

"We never planned to stop here. It was just dark out and we didn't see the island."

"Maybe it was just fate then," Russell grinned at her. "I've been waiting all this time for a boat to show up, and now, there are two. What are the odds of that?" When Jessica said nothing, Russell went on.

"I hope I can get a ride with you guys. I'm a good sailor. I can help Larry with everything. You think he'll agree to that? I've got to get off of this freakin' rock. Wherever you guys are going is fine with me. I don't even care. I've just got to get back on a boat. It's in my blood and at sea is where I belong. I'll sail *anywhere*, just as long as I'm moving, I'm happy."

"You'll have to ask him. All I know is that our boat is already too crowded as it is. We never planned to sail with another boat, but he wanted to help Tara out because she was alone with her daughter, and she had her own boat. But they didn't plan to stop here at this place anymore than we did. Larry only did because they had engine trouble."

"I can help him with that, no problem. I'm a good mechanic; gas engines, diesel engines, all of them. I've never run across one I couldn't fix! I'll help him get it going just as soon as we get this catamaran out of the water. I'll show him what I can do. He's going to want me as crew when he sees, believe me."

Russell was excited. So much was happening in one day after all those days of nothing. Now, not only was he no longer alone on the island, he had the prospect of a ride off of it. And on a sailboat with Jessica, at that. Russell had a hard time keeping his eyes off of her as he stood there in the knee deep water beside the hull, waiting on the boat to start moving. He heard the clicking of the winch on deck above and saw the main anchor rode from the bow begin to vibrate as it went taut. Before starting this phase of the operation, Larry had taken his biggest anchor some one hundred feet from the water's edge and buried it in a pocket of deep sand among the rocks. The lead of the rode was as straight as possible off the bow, so that there would be no binding as the winch ratcheted up the tension.

Larry had said the catamaran was light for its size, and Russell believed him, because he knew all catamarans and trimarans had to be lightweight to sail at the speeds they did. He still thought the design was too minimal though, and like he had told Larry, he would have built more cabin space onto it if it were his boat. It just seemed a waste to leave all that deck area open like that. But he would sail on it, no question about that. He didn't care if it was a raft if it was a way off this island and a way to go wherever Jessica was going.

The hull beside him began to move, and Russell followed it, wading forward to the point where the keel curved upwards in a gentle sweep to the bow stem. He held the line attached to the big inflatable fender in one hand as it floated next to the hull. Larry wanted them to stuff the first fender under that forward rocker area of the keel, so that the hulls would lift up over the sand as the boat was winched forward. Russell aligned the fender perpendicular to the bow and passed the rope attached to the other end to Jessica, who was across from him on the inner side of the hull. He could see that Tara and Casey were doing the same thing on their hull. It took some effort to force the fully inflated fender into position, because of its buoyancy, but with Jessica pulling and pushing from the other side to help him, at last it was done.

"Watch your fingers, Jessica!" he warned as they fina-gled it in place. He was staring at her again, trying to make eye contact, but she quickly turned away. It didn't matter. Russell was sure she was interested. How could she not be? She obviously liked boats and he was a boatman. He was a survivor too, and she would be impressed the more she learned about how he'd managed to make it here on this island all alone for so many weeks. Girls like Jessica *needed* survivors in this new reality. She might not have looked his way back in her old world before the grid collapse, but she couldn't ignore him now. Those college boys from that other life were probably all dead now and what she needed was a man. A *real* man who could *do* things! Russell grinned at her again as the hull began to lift onto the fender.

Larry said that if they used enough of them to distribute the weight, the heavy-duty inflatable fenders could completely support the catamaran out of the water. He had a lot of them, enough to put four of them under each of the twin hulls, but it was going to be a slow process, getting them all in place. Jessica was hidden from view now on the other side of the hull as the boat steadily moved forward, pulled onward by the inexorable force of the winch. As the weight of the keels forced them down onto the hard sand bottom, the first two fenders were squeezed and distorted, but seemed to be holding up. Russell grabbed a second one off the beach while Tara and Casey did the same on their side.

"It looks like it's working," Russell said, smiling at

Jessica as she stepped forward to help him when the time was right to place the next fender in front of the first.

"Of course it is. Larry knows what he's doing. He'll have it fixed and back in the water in no time too."

"It's still going to be tricky, getting back out through these reefs to clear water from this side. It's a wonder you got through them coming in without a lot more damage. Your friend Grant should have been keeping a better watch."

"Anybody could have made the same mistake. Larry said so himself. Grant was doing the best he could."

"Maybe. But running right into an island is not very good sailing."

Jessica ignored him and Russell didn't press it. As soon as she got to know him, she would see the difference between a man like him and a boy like Grant. She was obviously going to defend his actions because he was her friend. He may even be her boyfriend for all Russell knew, but if so, it was because he was the only one among them close to her age. That and he was a college prick that probably had money and a nice car before the collapse. None of that mattered now though, and Russell didn't see what use he could be to anyone out here. *What an idiot, to run a boat right into an island!*

The catamaran inched along as Artie and Grant took their turns at the winch. By the time they had four fenders under each hull, the keels were barely touching the water from amidships forward, and the sterns were only halfway submerged. When the tide went out again, they would be completely dry until the next high cycle. Russell heard Larry tell Grant to stop winching and then he jumped down from the deck to have a look.

"We could go a good bit farther," Russell said. "She's still going to get wet at every high tide."

Larry ignored him and walked into the water between the hulls, going back and forth to feel along the keels and get a better look at the damaged areas. Russell was right behind him, step for step.

"If you try to do the repair like this, your epoxy is going to get wet before it cures. I think we ought to pull her up another eight or ten feet."

"I've got fast-drying hardener for the epoxy," Larry said. "We'll have plenty of working time between the tides. It'll take several cycles to get it all done, but I don't want to be any farther out of the water than absolutely necessary. The way things are, you never know when you're going to have to make a quick escape."

"You're being paranoid man. Nobody's coming here. Like I said, I've been on this island for weeks and there hasn't been a boat in sight until you guys came. It would be safe to stay here from now on, but not the way I did it, with nothing to my name and all alone."

CHAPTER 10

NO MATTER how many times Larry and the others assured him that any of them could have made the same mistake, Grant still felt all this inconvenience was his fault and his alone. He had been the one at the helm, after all, even though he and Artie had worked together to plot their course. He was the one who failed to recognize the sound of surf in the dark in time to do something about it, so how could it be anyone's fault but his? Now they were days away at best from getting the repairs done and leaving again. It would not have mattered so much if all of them were accounted for, but Scully was missing. Every day that went by could be crucial for him and might determine whether or not they ever found him. Larry would never be satisfied until he could sail back to Florida to look for him, but he wouldn't do it until the damage to the boat was taken care of.

Like Casey, Grant had offered to go with him when he

sailed, arguing that he was the best choice despite his error in nearly wrecking the boat. But Larry wouldn't hear it, saying he didn't want to keep dividing their group. Besides, they now had this Russell guy to deal with and since he wanted off the island, Larry said he would take him to Florida. Russell could help him with the steering and watch keeping on the way over, and if things went as planned, Scully would do so on the way back. It didn't take any of them long to discover how obnoxious Russell was, and even though he didn't think he was dangerous, Larry thought it best if they got rid of him as soon as possible. He didn't want to leave him there for everyone else to deal with, so taking him to Florida seemed like the best solution. He would be a pain in the ass to deal with on the boat, even for that short trip, but Larry said he would have to do as he was told or he would drop him off somewhere along the way. Russell might not like it, but that was going to be his only choice, and Grant was relieved to hear it. Russell's interest in Jessica especially, was making her uncomfortable, and Grant knew if it continued, he was going to have to say something to him about it.

They were all exhausted after a full day of work with little sleep the night before. After unloading the *Casey Nicole* and moving her most of the way out of the water, they worked with Larry to scrub the hull bottoms when the tide fell later that afternoon. With the green film of marine growth cleaned away, the repairs could begin tomorrow with the next low tide. A closer inspection once they were clean revealed numerous cracks and scrapes and a couple of places where the reef had punctured the plywood core near the keel of the starboard hull. Larry assured them that none of the damage was serious, but fixing it would take longer and be harder without grinders and other power tools to prepare the surfaces for new layers of glass and epoxy.

Russell was in the midst of the discussion the whole time, and no matter what Larry said, he had to add his two cents, usually to offer a differing opinion. Grant was about sick of hearing his mouth, and he knew Larry was, but just as he'd shown them through all the trials they'd already been through, their captain had great reserves of patience, even when dealing with an asshole. Russell even had the audacity to argue in the face of Larry's generous offer of a ride off the island.

"Man, going back to Florida now would be crazy!" he said, as they all sat around the evening cooking fire they'd built on the beach, overlooking the catamaran. "We'd never find your friend now," Russell continued. "From what you said about those ships and from what your brother and Grant and Jessica said about the smaller gunboats, he's got to be either dead or in a prison camp somewhere. If we go there, the same thing is going to happen to us. I know he's your friend, but that's the harsh reality of it, man. We should all just go to the Exumas. We can anchor near my friend's house and we'll be safe and have everything we need."

"I wouldn't be so sure that it's any safer there than it is in Florida," Grant said. "From what Larry told us back when we were first talking about the Bahamas, the Exumas are probably the one place that thousands of boats from Florida headed to after things got bad."

"We are *not* sailing to the Exumas," Larry said, flatly.

"But dude, it's just *stupid* to sail to Florida now!"

"Look, Russell. You said you wanted a ride off this island, right? Well, I'm offering you a ride, but that ride's going to Florida! You can sail with me, or you can stay here from now on or until you have a better offer. The choice is yours."

Grant could see Russell fuming, staring down at the sand between his feet before turning to look at Jessica, hoping to catch her eye and get some sympathy for his cause. She ignored him, of course, and looked at Grant instead. Grant knew from the look in her eyes that she wanted him to say something to get this guy off her back.

"You need to go with Larry," Grant said. "He's offering you a ride and you'll have free food too while you're on the passage. If you've been stuck here as long as you say you have, I don't see why you wouldn't jump at that opportunity."

"Because going to Florida is a death sentence. It would be worse than things were here when I was alone. *You're* not going there. Neither is Jessica or Tara or anybody else. Larry here is going just because of his friend. There's no other reason to risk it. I'll just wait here with all of you then and go with you when you finally *do* leave to sail some- where sensible."

"That's not going to happen," Larry said. "We've already got enough people to take care of."

"I'm talking about going with them on the other boat—the monohull—when you don't come back. Because if you sail to Florida, you *won't* be coming back."

"And if he doesn't, you still can't go with us," Tara spoke up. "I'm the captain of the *Sarah J.,* and she is much too small to take on any more crew, especially if Larry doesn't come back. There will already be six of us aboard her."

"*Damn!* You people are some cold! I thought I'd finally caught a lucky break when I saw two boats here this morning!"

"You did," Larry said. "At least we didn't shoot you on sight like a lot of people would these days."

Russell muttered something under his breath and then, as if nothing ever happened, started running his mouth again about how useful he was around boats. He could work on engines, do rigging work, electrical repairs, fiberglassing... not to mention clean and cook. He would be their greatest asset, and they would never regret taking him on as crew. It was if he hadn't heard what Larry and Tara just told him and he still thought he could convince them to take him where he wanted to go. Grant just rolled his eyes. The sooner this guy left with Larry, the better, as far as he was concerned.

He excused himself from the fire and walked across the island to the point overlooking the calm waters where the *Sarah J.* was anchored. He wanted a few minutes of peace and quiet, but when Casey joined him he welcomed the opportunity to talk to her alone. Jessica had been doing her best to stay between them since they'd arrived there, and so far he'd not had any real time with Casey. She sat down beside him on a big rock, and as if reading his mind, Jessica was the first thing she brought up.

"It seems like my former roommate has taking quite a liking to you, Grant, though I can't say that I blame her."

"It's not what you think," Casey. "Yeah, we had a lot of time together on the voyage, but it wasn't like it was a romantic cruise or something."

"It's none of my business if it was. I just want all of us to be happy. I'm glad you're here safe, Grant."

"Me too." He took her hand in his and looked into her eyes so there would be no doubt that he meant what he said. "I missed you the whole time you were on the other boat, Casey. I didn't like the idea of splitting up like that, but I understand why Larry wanted to do it. Tara seemed perfect for him, but from what I heard, it didn't work out so well between them."

"No, it didn't. But I wouldn't say there isn't any hope that it still might. I can understand why Tara got so pissed at him, but it really wasn't his fault."

"Do you think Rebecca will try anything like that again?"

"No, I don't think so...."

Before Grant could ask her to elaborate, he heard foot-steps and looked up to see Jessica approaching. She just couldn't stand the idea of him having even a few minutes alone with Casey. It was a problem Grant was going to have to deal with soon, but he wasn't looking forward to that.

"Hey guys," Jessica said. "I don't mean to interrupt, but that Russell is just creeping me out. He won't stop staring at me. I had to get away for a minute."

"Yeah, that's why I left," Grant said. "I got sick of his mouth."

"Unfortunately for us, he had to be stranded on the one island in all the Bahamas on which we ended up!" Casey said.

"Speaking of the devil... here he comes."

"I'm not putting up with any more of his crap," Grant whispered, before Russell was quite close enough to hear.

"I wondered where all of you went off to," Russell said, as he walked up to the rock like he was one of their life-long friends. "I guess you guys just wanted to get away from the older crowd. I can *definitely* relate! That Larry seems like a hard-ass, and Tara's not much better."

"My uncle is just being realistic. We can only do so much to help the people we meet. In an ideal world, we could do more, but it's far from an ideal world right now."

"I was hoping you guys could put in a good word for me or something to the others. I'd love to hang with all of you. The more you get to know me, the more I'm sure you'll want me to. I just don't want to go back to Florida and fall into the hands of the people who caused all this. I *know* it was all a conspiracy, all right? If you'd read as much as I have about the stuff that really goes on in the U.S. government, you'd believe me."

"Look, man. We've seen a lot more places since the power went out than you have. Trust me. This wasn't some conspiracy! No government or any other human entity could have caused a disaster of the proportions we've seen."

Russell tried to argue his point further, but Grant got to his feet and started back to the fire, ignoring him and asking Casey and Jessica to come with him. He knew Russell had been drinking, and he wished that Larry had not given in to his constant requests for rum or whiskey. Alcohol wasn't going to improve his personality, and Grant didn't want to spend any more time around him tonight. He stormed on ahead, expecting the girls to be right behind him, but then he heard Jessica cry out:

"Get your hands off me, you creep!"

Grant wheeled and saw Jessica backing away from Russell in the other direction.

"I was just trying to tell you something!" Russell was saying."

But even as he tried to explain himself, he continued his advance and reached for her hand again, completely oblivious to her warning or Grant's watchful eyes. Grant had seen enough and he was through. He closed the gap in three long strides and shoved Russell back with the heel of his palm against his chest, focusing his energy into more of a strike than a simple push. Russell stumbled backward and tripped over a rock, landing hard on his back in sand.

"You heard what she said! Don't let me see you put your hands on her again!"

CHAPTER 11

"WHAT THE HELL, dude? I wasn't doing anything, I was just trying to talk to her!" Russell couldn't believe that Grant had pushed him like that. If he hadn't already hated the guy because it was obvious Jessica liked him, he surely hated him now. What Russell wanted to do was get up and beat the living crap out of him. But despite his pretty college-boy face, Grant was no scrawny-looking bookworm. He had a solid muscularity about him and after feeling the force in that simple push, Russell doubted he could take him in a fair fight, especially as weak as he still felt after being sick for two days. And even if he could, he would still have to deal with the know-it-all captain and his brother, both of them even bigger than Grant. So instead of tempting his luck he just got to his feet and backed farther away.

"Why are you people so freakin' uptight? Shit man, just

relax, you're in the islands! You've got a couple of boats and everything you need. I was just hoping you would make room for me and let me go along for the ride. Geez! It wasn't like I wasn't willing to do my share of the work too!"

"Look, Russell. This isn't about that! You haven't taken your eyes off Jessica since you crawled out of whatever hole you've been living in. She's not interested, and she made that clear already, but you didn't seem to get the message."

"Okay, okay! I've got that she's your girlfriend, dude. But I was just talking to her. No harm in that!"

"She's *not* my girlfriend," Grant said, "but she's not going to be yours either! Look, Larry offered you a ride. I'd say you ought to be grateful and take him up on it."

Russell noticed that Jessica seemed to wilt at Grant's words. Was it true that she wasn't his girlfriend? She seemed upset by what he said and quickly walked away, heading back to the fire where the others were, while the other girl, Casey, stayed put. Why would Grant pick her over a smoking-hot fox like Jessica? Russell didn't know, but he did know Grant was a prick and an idiot. He had no doubt that if the two of them were around each other long enough, a fight would be inevitable whether he wanted it or not. But he wasn't going to push it tonight. He was tired from helping them with the boat, and the two shots of rum he'd had made him feel like what he really needed was sleep.

He ignored Grant and turned around to walk back to his camp on the other end of the island. Maybe they would change their minds and maybe they wouldn't, but there was nothing else to do tonight. Grant didn't want him around because he was competition for the attention of the girls. Even if the punk wasn't into Jessica as much as Casey, he still didn't want another guy hanging out with her. Probably because he wanted her for himself whenever Casey got tired of him. *Fucking prick!*

Russell awoke the next morning with a headache he couldn't shake. It had to be the rum, and he figured it was only because he'd been so long without a drink until last night. He felt like he could use another one right then to treat that awful hangover feeling, and he was hungry as well. He didn't want to see Grant, but he needed to talk to Larry again and maybe his brother, Artie, who might be more reasonable than the others. So he made his way back to where the catamaran was beached and found Larry and Artie standing there beside it. The tide was up so they couldn't do anything below the waterline at that hour.

"Morning, guys! What's the plan today?" They both turned his way but Russell could tell Larry wasn't particularly thrilled to see him. "I'm here to help. Whatever you need...."

"We could use an extra hand," Artie said. "Larry has decided that while we have the boat on the beach, we might as well unstep both masts and finish up some rigging jobs we didn't have time for when we rushed the launch in Puerto Rico."

Russell looked up at the twin masts. They were tall and massive and looked heavy. He didn't see how they were going to get them down and back up again without a crane.

"I don't understand the thinking on building a cata-maran with two masts. Why not just have one taller one, like most catamarans?"

"The schooner rig has its advantages," Larry said.

"They look heavy as hell to me. I don't see how we're going to get them down."

"Looks can be deceiving. They're made of wood, but they're hollow on the inside. And it's lightweight Doug fir. We'll get them down the same way we got them up."

"I wouldn't have used wood. I know a lot people are into that retro old-school stuff right now, but dude; carbon fiber is where it's at! That's what *I* would have used if it was *my* boat."

"Yeah? Well it isn't, so you can just keep dreaming about that boat of yours, Russell. Or you can help us get the *Casey Nicole* seaworthy again so we can sail her to Florida, if you really want to get off this rock. Your choice."

"Not much of a choice—stay here and eventually starve to death or sail to Florida to end up dead or in prison...."

"It is what it is. You'll just have to decide."

What an asshole, Russell thought. Larry was as much a prick as Grant, but worse because he was a know-it-all boat captain who thought he was the shit. Russell was silent as he stood their staring up at the two wooden masts. Yeah, he would help them take them down, because as he stood there looking, a new idea dawned on him, a brilliant idea really, and one that he was surprised took so long to come to him. He smiled as he turned his gaze back to Larry and Artie.

"Okay, captain. When you put it like that, I see your point. I'm all in! So, where do we start? How do we get these two beauties down without dropping them on our heads?"

Russell worked without complaint and when Grant the two girls and Tara and her daughter joined them, he made it a point to stay as far away from Grant as possible and avoided even looking at Jessica. Now that he had a plan, it wouldn't do to arouse any more mistrust or hard feelings. The important thing was that they get those masts down. Once that was done, and once the tide went out again late that afternoon, it would be hours at the bare minimum before the catamaran could get underway again, and that was exactly how Russell wanted it.

Once he saw Larry's methods, Russell had to admit the man knew what he was doing. Using just the central cockpit winch and the four-part mainsheet tackle, Larry set up a leverage system that allowed them to unstep both masts, working each in turn by degrees until finally both were lying horizontal, supported on the main crossbeams. Like Larry said, they weren't overly heavy for their size, but they were long and awkward to handle at over 40 feet each. As soon as they were down, Larry set to work with his rigging bag to improve and finish the hastily done splices at the upper ends of the stays and shrouds. It was work he planned to complete over the coming days in between low tide cycles while they had drying time on the epoxy and fiberglass work.

Russell hung around until mid-afternoon, when the

tide had fallen enough to begin work on the hulls again, then he excused himself, saying he was feeling weak again from being sick and that he needed to go back to his camp and sleep for a while. Larry thanked him for his help before he left, and invited him to come back that evening to join them for dinner if he felt like it. Russell said he would, but he had no intention of doing so.

It was clear to him by now that these people were not going to change their minds and decide to take him with them deeper into the islands. He knew now that Larry meant what he said when he told him it was Florida or nothing. But that was fine. Russell didn't need their help, now that he knew what he had to do. He started back to his camp and continued along his usual path to the other end of the island until he was out of sight among the trees and scrub, then he stopped and doubled back to watch.

Everyone from the two boats was there working on the catamaran except for Tara's daughter, Rebecca. Like a typical teenager, her enthusiasm for the work had waned even sooner than Russell's and she'd asked to go back to the other boat, the one that belonged to her mom. Tara had rowed her out there in their dinghy and returned to where the others were working, and now Russell wondered how long it would be before Rebecca was off the boat again. He hoped it was soon, because the afternoon breeze had filled in nicely from the east and was perfect for what he had in mind.

He figured he had a little while to wait before someone went back to get the girl, so Russell continued on to his pathetic little hut and collected his mask and the pole spear. They were his only possessions on the island other than the bits of rope and other junk he'd found washed up by the tide. There was nothing to leave behind here but the memories of his misery. He kicked one of the support poles of the shelter so hard that the whole thing collapsed and turned to go back to a place where he could watch and wait.

When he got there, he saw that the dinghy had not been moved and that Tara was still busy at work with the others. Rebecca was nowhere in sight, so that meant she had to be still aboard the other boat. This wasn't part of Russell's plan, but as he contemplated the situation, he realized there was little choice. The girl might sleep the rest of the afternoon and still not come ashore for dinner. If he waited to see, it would be too late. By then the others would be done for the day and would be building a fire on the beach like they did last night. They would then be in full view of the anchored boat, and even in the dark they couldn't help but notice if it began moving from that vantage point. Russell couldn't risk that. He had to act now while all of them were busy with the catamaran and out of sight of the anchorage. The wind was perfect for a quick getaway, and the tide wouldn't be back for several hours. But even if they could get the catamaran back in the water in a hurry, both masts were down and the rigging was in total disarray. Russell couldn't help but smile at his good fortune. It would be even better if it were Jessica aboard the boat instead of the girl, but oh well; he would take what he could get. *Fuck you, Jessica! And fuck you too, Grant! It is what it is, right Captain Larry?* Russell circled around through the trees to the beach just east of the anchorage and waded into the water, pulling on the dive mask as he did. From there it was just a short swim to the boat.

CHAPTER 12

LARRY WAS PLEASED at the way things were going as he mixed another batch of epoxy and added the thickening agents that turned it to the consistency of putty. Using a small handsaw and his razor-sharp chisels, he had neatly cut away two small sections of fractured plywood and made replacement parts that fit into adjacent surfaces with beveled scarf joints. The hulls would be good as new once the epoxy holding them in cured and a few layers of fiberglass were laminated over the wood for sheathing and reinforcement. That would come tomorrow, on the next low tide cycle. The important thing today was that the parts were in place and well saturated with clear epoxy that in the warm, tropical air, would be cured before high water returned after midnight. He would spend the morning reinforcing and tidying up the rigging, checking off a few items on his never-ending to-do list that had been bugging him since they'd first set sail from Culebra with Scully.

Every time he thought of his best friend his anxiety and impatience returned. He should be sailing Florida waters even now, cruising through the Keys and along the Everglades coast searching for any sign of the kayak. Scully could be in serious trouble, or something bad could have already happened to him. He didn't discount completely Russell's comments that his friend could already be dead or that he could be detained somewhere by the authorities, but Larry knew Scully was a savvy survivor. If anyone could evade the police or military and avoid detection while traveling a restricted coast, it was Scully. He had plenty of experience as a younger man back in the day, when smuggling ganja was an enterprise he'd tried for a few years until Larry came along and offered him more legitimate, if less lucrative work delivering yachts.

The problem was that it would be equally hard for Larry to find him as for those who might wish to do him harm. Scully would be laying low in the mangroves if he couldn't travel, and if he could, Larry knew he might already be en route to the Bahamas himself. Larry didn't discount the idea that Scully could cross the Straits in the kayak, and he knew that he certainly would if he had no other option. All of these factors were going to conspire to make finding his friend as much a matter of luck as anything else. But Larry had to try. The others would be relatively safe here while he was away, and he was taking the loud-mouthed bum they had the misfortune of sharing the island with along with him, so they wouldn't have to worry about problems with him. Larry wasn't looking forward to sharing his boat with the guy even for a short trip, but it *would* solve the problem of getting him away from the others—especially Jessica. She had told him about their altercation the evening before, and Larry knew it was just a matter of time before Russell would screw up again and someone would get hurt—probably him if he tangled with Grant.

As they worked that morning to lower the masts, Larry was glad to see Grant display maturity and restraint by keeping well clear of Russell and avoiding interaction with him as much as possible. He noted too, that Russell made an effort to avoid getting too close to Jessica. Maybe that simple push that landed him on his ass taught him a lesson that would stick. Time would tell, but as it turned out, they were all relieved when Russell complained of being too tired to continue working and left to return to his camp and rest.

Jessica had been working close at his side as he made the plywood patches, and he could tell something was bothering her. It didn't take a genius to figure out that it was more than Russell, because Jessica was avoiding Grant and Casey almost as much as she had the stranger before he quit for the day.

"I would go with you to look for Scully," if that idiot wasn't going."

"I appreciate it, Jessica, but even if it weren't for him, I'd hate to put you in that kind of danger. You'd be better off sticking with the group. We already know what all this splitting up has gotten us."

"Yeah, but you're about to do it again."

"You know I have to. I can't leave Scully behind."

"Maybe he's already on his way here? Maybe he will get here before you leave? That would be perfect."

"It would, Jessica. But it's not likely. I know I said he would make his way to the Bahamas eventually to look for us, but the chances of him finding us here on Green Cay are probably zero. First of all, he would try to go to the Dry Tortugas because he knew that's where you guys were going to look for us. If he made it there and got turned away like us, he would probably go the Ragged Islands and Jumentos if he were able to make the crossing. But that would be extremely dangerous in the kayak. It's practically dead to windward and there's nowhere for him to stop, to break up the crossing to rest. I think he'll be smart enough to wait a bit longer before he tries something that desperate. He knows I won't leave and go somewhere else we hadn't talked about without doing everything in my power to find him. So I've got to believe there's a good chance I'll find him in the Keys."

"I hope you do. I just wanted to help, that's all."

"I figured you might want a break from sailing after being at sea so long. This is a pretty nice cay to hang out on for a while. It'll be a lot better when I leave with Russell."

"I don't know if it will or not," Jessica looked away. Larry could tell she was upset about something.

"What's the deal, Jessica? Is this about my niece being back in the picture?"

Jessica wouldn't say, but Larry already knew. He knew

from what Artie told him of the voyage that Jessica had clung to Grant the whole way. It was understandable that she didn't want to share his attention with Casey when they were all reunited here. Larry had seen this coming for a long time. He didn't know when, but there was going to be a blow-up between Jessica and his niece over Grant. It was simply inevitable, although he also believed that if Grant were truly more interested in Jessica than Casey, his niece would be far more likely to accept it and let it go than Jessica. Jessica was used to getting her way, and Larry knew why. He would do his best to keep things smooth among his crew, but it would probably have to wait until he returned from his trip to Florida.

Jessica was about to say something else when they both heard Tara scream, followed by shouting from Casey as well. The two of them had put away their tools and gone ashore to gather more wood for the evening fire. Artie and Grant were still in the water, finishing up their work on the other hull.

"MY BOAT! REBECCA!"

Tara's voice was hysterical. It was just like the night she'd come on deck during the Gulf crossing and discovered Rebecca was missing. Larry bolted to the beach with Jessica right behind him, and saw Artie and Grant doing the same out of the corner of his eye.

"THE *SARAH J.* IS UNDERWAY!" Casey screamed as they all ran to meet her.

Larry saw that Tara was racing for the dinghy, which was tied up high above the tide line with the oars in their locks. He took in the scene in the anchorage and his first thought was that Rebecca was pulling another stunt like her last, but then almost as fast as he thought it, he dismissed that idea. Her attitude had changed completely since her ordeal in the Gulf and besides, he doubted she could get the anchor up and set the sails by herself anyway. The *Sarah J.* was already more than a quarter mile south of where she'd been anchored, the mainsail full and drawing and the jib flogging as a figure in the cockpit worked to wrestle the sheets under control. He could now see that it wasn't Rebecca and he knew immediately what was going on; it had to be Russell! *That sneaky bastard!* Rebecca was nowhere in sight. Larry scanned the water as he ran to meet Tara but didn't see anyone swimming or anywhere in sight along the beach. Tara was already dragging the dinghy towards the water as fast as she could.

"WAIT TARA! I'M GOING BACK TO GET A RIFLE!"

"I'll get it, Larry! I can run faster than you. Go ahead and help her get the dinghy to the water!"

"Ok, thanks!" Larry said, knowing Grant was right. He needed to get that dinghy launched as fast as possible. But with the *Sarah J.'s* sails filled with a favorable wind that would rapidly carry her away from the island, he wondered how they were going to catch up. Tara's face was set with grim determination when Larry reached her side and grabbed the gunwale opposite her to help her carry the boat to the water. The finely crafted lightweight dinghy was designed for efficient rowing, and there was a sailing rig for it too, but unfortunately, the mast and the sail was still stowed aboard the *Sarah J.* where it had been since Tara's parents last used it. With the rig, they would have a better chance, but what Larry really wished for was a Zodiac with a powerful outboard.

"Rebecca's still on the boat! She's got to be!" Tara's voice was frightened, but she was somehow holding it together.

Larry agreed. There was still no sign of the girl in the water or anywhere else. Russell must have swum out to the boat and boarded it while Rebecca was below in her cabin.

"He must have hit her or threatened to or she would have screamed," Tara said as they neared the water with the dinghy. Artie and Jessica and Casey had caught up by now too and all were helping. "I'm going to kill that son of a bitch when we catch him!"

Larry knew that once again, he'd screwed up. It was obvious from the minute they met him, that Russell was going to be a pain in the ass. But he'd misjudged his capacity to pull a stunt like this. He shared Tara's sentiment, but wondered how they were going to catch the 37-foot sailboat that was already underway with a fair wind in its sails.

Grant sprinted across the island with two rifles in hand, one of them the lever action carbine he'd used so effectively in his first gunfight on Cat Island. "Let me go with Larry. We'll catch them."

"No!" Tara said. "I'm going. That's my baby out there! You can't leave me here!"

Larry took the rifles and put them both in the dinghy. It wouldn't do to argue with Tara now. It was her daughter out there after all, not to mention *her* dinghy and *her* sailboat that had been stolen. But there was room for Grant too, and he could row faster than either of them, considering Larry's injured arm. The only real hope they had was that Russell would screw up and run aground on one of the many shoals Larry knew were scattered to the south of the cay, or that he would give up and stop if they fired a few rifle rounds across his bow. Larry doubted the latter, and shooting directly at him wasn't an option because Rebecca was on board and there was no way of knowing just where. There was no way Tara would let him risk a shot like that, and Larry wouldn't take it even if she did.

Grant pulled at the oars for all he was worth and the dinghy was soon up to its maximum cruising speed. The Tartan 37 was slowly gaining distance on them though, and Russell now had the jib trimmed so the gap would widen rapidly. Tara was standing in the bow of the dinghy, screaming at Russell to stop and calling out her daughter's name. It was heartbreaking to hear the desperation in her voice, and it brought back all his memories of that awful night in the Gulf when Rebecca had gone missing overboard. This time they knew exactly where she was, but she was just out of reach. Russell managed to slip through the shoals, whether by sheer luck or because he could still read the water depths by color in the late afternoon sun, it didn't matter. He had also found time to look around down below, judging by what happened next. Larry didn't notice the first small splash next to the dinghy until the sound of a rifle report reached his ears. He grabbed Tara and pulled her to the floorboards just as several more shots followed the first. Grant immediately stopped rowing, letting the dinghy drift.

"Dammit! He found the SKS!" Larry said, looking around to make sure Grant and Tara hadn't been hit. "We've got to fall back. The bastard's gonna get lucky if he keeps trying long enough!"

"NO!!!!" Tara screamed "We can't let him just sail away like that with my baby on board! We can't let him get away!

Tara got back to her feet and refused to get down, striking Larry's arms away when he tried to grab her again. He gave up and let her stand there, screaming into the wind as they drifted. The shooting had stopped, but the *Sarah J.* was nearly out of rifle range anyway. They would have never caught up in the dinghy even if Russell hadn't fired on them and Larry knew it. He felt like a helpless fool; an idiot who had truly screwed up again even worse than he had that night when he'd taken a brief nap while letting Rebecca have the watch. If he'd even guessed for a minute that Russell would pull something like this, he'd have shot him dead when he had the chance. What a fool he'd been to not see this coming. Tara collapsed into a sobbing heap in the floor of the dinghy when Grant started back for the beach and Larry didn't know what to say or do to comfort her. But he knew what he was going to do about it. And he *would* do it or die trying.

CHAPTER 13

THOMAS ALLEN FELT a huge sense of relief once *Intrepida* cleared the bridge span of the Overseas Highway and the Keys were finally astern in the wake. By daybreak they were three miles south of the chain and making a steady five and half knots in the morning breeze. Scully felt good about the conditions and said it would be best if they continued on while the wind was good. He said it might strengthen later in the day out in the Atlantic, but he read no sign of a storm in the skies and didn't think they would have trouble making the passage to the islands.

Thomas hadn't slept all night, but he was still so wired from his near-death experience that he didn't have the slightest inclination to try and get some rest. He was always that way when under stress or worry, which had been much of the time since they'd left their apartment and moved aboard *Intrepida*. Mindy, however, amazed Thomas with her ability to put worry aside—at least her worry about those things that did not require immediate attention or were beyond her control. Because of this, she'd gone below as soon as they were under the bridge and were relatively safe from the threats of land. Now she was sleeping soundly in the V-berth despite the heeling motion of the boat under sail. Thomas wasn't sure how that was going to work out once they were in the open sea, however. Maybe she could do it, but he didn't really expect to find out what it was like. The truth was, he usually felt queasy when he went below if there was much motion at all, so he figured he would be spending most of the offshore passage in the cockpit with Scully.

"So, what do you think? Do you still think this boat can handle the crossing, Scully?" he asked nervously as he stared at a chart of the Florida Straits and then out at the open ocean that stretched endlessly before them.

"Not to worry 'bout de boat, mon. De boat, she's good. Now we need only workin' out de navigation. If you pass me dem chart, an' take de helm, I doin' dat now, mon."

"Sure, no problem. I hope you can estimate about how long it will be until we can anchor somewhere again."

Thomas wanted to be in the Bahamas already. Getting there was the part he was less than enthusiastic about. As he steered the boat while Scully plotted their course, he scanned the horizon for any signs of other boats—especially Navy ships or other gunboats. But they were alone for now. If they could just get out to International Waters and into the Gulf Stream, he hoped they would be home free. When they reached the outer reefs that separated Hawk Channel from the open Atlantic, Thomas steered through a well-marked pass that led to deep water. On a normal day, scores of fishing boats and dive boats would be hanging around the reefs up and down the Keys, but all that had changed now. Gone were the recreational vessels that dotted inshore waters, as well as the freighters and cruise ships that would normally be coming and going out in the Straits.

"I wonder why there are no Navy ships off this part of the coast? Seeing how they had the Dry Tortugas locked down and then what you said about the Everglades. It's strange."

"Probably dem not havin' enough ship. Maybe only put de one dem got in de main place de traffic comin'"

"Yeah, you're probably right. I'll bet they have their resources in the Miami-Ft. Lauderdale area if they have them anywhere. Those are major ports. Probably several places farther north up the coast too. Any big ships coming in from other countries would go in there or enter the Gulf west of the Dry Tortugas." It made sense that the blockade was mainly there to intercept bigger ships. Maybe they were concerned about foreign military vessels trying to enter U.S. waters in light of the crippling effect of the solar flare. Kicking recreational boats out of the anchorage at Ft. Jefferson might have simply been a drill or a matter of wanting the area to be exclusive to their operation. He didn't know what they would have been doing in a remote place like Cape Sable, where Scully said his friends had been driven away with warning shots, but Thomas figured they must have had some need to secure the area. Whatever the blockade was about, it was a tremendous relief to get out of Florida waters unchallenged. Thomas had been worried about that ever since he and Mindy left Fort Jefferson. They weren't ready for the Bahamas crossing then, but he'd certainly wanted to have the option when they were.

He thought there was a good chance they'd be stopped by Bahamian officials as well, but when he asked Scully about that, the islander said he wasn't worried. Larry told him the Royal Bahamas Defense Force was spread thin even in normal times, and it was rare to see them in many parts of the islands, especially in the more remote places like their destination. He said that if they were even operating at all, they would likely have their hands full dealing with a huge influx of American boats seeking refuge in the more popular parts of the archipelago—like the Abacos, the Berry Islands and the Exumas.

"Not passin' dem places where we goin'," Scully said. He held the chart so Thomas could see while he steered. "I t'ink we cross to de closest point of de big island, dis Andros here," he pointed. "Larry said not many boat going to Andros. We sailin' down de west side all de weh to de bottom. Lots of reef but no problem in de small boat. We go in places most boat, dem can't, an' den work our way down and den sail southeast to de Raggeds."

Thomas followed the route Scully's finger traced and contemplated the voyage ahead. It was a *long* way to the Ragged Islands. Even after they got to the south end of Andros, they would only be about halfway there. Thomas had never even considered that part of the Bahamas when he'd dreamed of sailing there. The Ragged Islands were closer to eastern Cuba than they were to any of the more popular cruising destinations of the Bahamas. But the fact that they were so far from Florida was reassuring too. Such a remote place *had* to be safe. He couldn't imagine that it would be otherwise. The people with bad intentions like those two men Scully had killed were going to be found in places with a good supply of potential victims. They wouldn't make the effort to go someplace as remote as the Ragged Islands. At least that's what Thomas told himself.

They were well out of sight of all land by midmorning, and sailing over water that was the prettiest shade of blue Thomas had ever seen. Scully said they were now in the Gulf Stream, and seeing nothing different about it other than the color of the water, Thomas felt silly for fearing the notorious stretch of ocean for so long. There was certainly nothing to fear there now, sailing under sunny skies in steady winds that were between 10 and 12 knots. At last he was able to relax, and when Scully took over the helm again, Thomas napped on the leeward cockpit seat until Mindy woke and came back on deck from below.

Thomas' smug feeling that they had defeated the odds and were in control of their destiny vanished again that afternoon, though, when heavy clouds began to gather out of the east, the sky darkened by an approaching line of squalls from dead ahead.

"We've got to turn, Scully. We can't sail through that!"

"Where we gonna turn to, mon? Can't run from every

cloud, mon. Thunderstorm comin' most every day dis time in de year."

"I thought you said you felt good about the weather," Mindy said, in a voice only slightly less nervous than Thomas'.

"Not to worry, only little rain, mehbe lightning, an' de strong wind. Soon pass, mon."

But what Scully called "a little" was an afternoon of terror for Thomas and Mindy. They sailed directly into what appeared to be an impenetrable wall of dark clouds. The color of the sea changed from the tranquil deep blue of the morning to a cold and opaque, steely gray. Thomas helped Scully reef the main to the deepest row of reef points after they dropped the jib completely and stuffed it in its bag to put below. Scully assured him they could ride out what was coming, as long as they didn't have too much sail up, but that didn't relieve the twisting knots of anxiety Thomas felt in his stomach. Were his worst fears about the Gulf Stream about to come true? What if the wind turned against the current? How would their little 17-foot boat possibly stay upright in the mountainous seas he heard so many sailors report in those conditions?

Thomas heard the fast-approaching rain pelting the water in sheets just before the first band of the storm swept across. When it reached them, the big drops stung as they hit from a near horizontal angle. Scully steered so that the boat fell off the wind, running before gusts that at times heeled it to the rails even with both reefs in the main. They were all drenched in a matter of seconds. Thomas had given Scully one of his extra T-shirts, since he had no shirt at all when they met him, but there were only two cheap plastic rain jackets on board before the blackout and they were already torn and leaking from before, making them practically useless.

"We're going to die!" Thomas muttered, after *Intrepida* was pushed so far over in one gust that he was sure just another few degrees would capsize her. Mindy squeezed his hand as they huddled together, but Scully was still grinning wildly through it all, apparently having fun.

"She's a good boat, mon! I told you she a good boat. Not to worry 'bout de wind mon. Storm soon pass!"

And pass it did, first the strong wind, then the rain, and finally even the clouds in time for them to witness the sunset. Scully estimated their approximate position and said that they might have gone a bit farther north in the current than he would have liked, but that Andros was such a big target, it would be hard to miss. The problem was that they would reach the banks sometime during the night, rather than in daylight hours. They would have to stay alert and watch and listen for any signs of shoals or reefs when they did, so it was going to be another long and sleepless night.

Thomas didn't care. He was just relieved to be out of that storm. It was the same feeling he had when the man pointing the gun at him had suddenly dropped dead—the feeling of knowing he was alive again when he was certain it had all been over. He wasn't sure which was worse, the fear of being shot or the terror of a storm at sea. But he'd survived both because of a man named Scully. Was it sheer luck he'd come along, or some kind of divine providence? Thomas wasn't sure, but wasn't about to question it. Come morning they would be sailing *Intrepida* through Bahamian waters. He had to squeeze Mindy tight to make sure he wasn't dreaming.

CHAPTER 14

ARTIE STOOD on the beach feeling totally helpless as he and the girls watched his brother and Grant and Tara set out in the dinghy in pursuit of the *Sarah J.* He didn't particularly like Russell, especially after seeing what a pest he'd become shortly after meeting their group, but the thought that he would do something this outrageous hadn't occurred to him. It was obvious from the beginning that he was a loud-mouthed know-it-all a bit of a bum and a con, but he hadn't come off as *this* irrational. Artie had been worried about how they were going to get rid of him but he'd assumed Russell would give in and accept Larry's offer of a ride to Florida, despite his strong objections to going there. He realized now that maybe it was because of Larry's continued refusal to take him anywhere else that he'd decided to take matters into his own hands and leave without warning. Whatever the case, they had all seriously misjudged him and now Tara's boat and her daughter were gone with him. It was a nightmare for them all, but Artie was afraid it would absolutely destroy Tara if they didn't stop him before he got away.

"I don't think Grant or anyone else could row fast enough to catch him," Casey said. The *Sarah J.* may not be as fast as the *Casey Nicole,* but she still sails well and the wind is good."

"God! I can't believe that bastard did this!" Jessica said. "What a low-life creep! I wish he had gotten back up when Grant pushed him now, so Grant would have beaten the crap out of him. I wish *I* had beaten the crap out of him!"

"Tara will, if she ever catches up. She'll probably half kill him. But I don't think they're going to. Look!"

Russell had gotten the jib under control and now with both working sails set and trimmed, the *Sarah J.* was bearing away quickly to the southeast on a beam reach. And if that were not bad enough, they heard rifle shots echo across the water.

"He's shooting at them!"

"Oh my God! GRANT!" Jessica screamed.

The sailboat was too far away to make out any details in the cockpit, but Artie knew the girls were right. It had to be Russell doing the shooting because he could clearly see that it wasn't Tara or Larry. Grant instantly slowed his rowing pace and Artie knew that it was because they were under fire. He could hardly watch, expecting any minute to see his brother and the others collapse into the dinghy or fall overboard.

"They've got to turn back! They're going to get shot!"

"They will!" Casey said. "Uncle Larry won't shoot back because Rebecca is still on the boat. All they *can* do is come back. Russell must have found the rifle Larry left on board."

"They've stopped," Artie said, confirming what Casey said would happen. The shooting had stopped as well. Maybe Russell wasn't trying to kill anyone, though he might make an exception for Grant after their altercation last night. The devious thief had what he wanted—a ride off the island and now so much more—a boat that would take him anywhere, along with loads of supplies and other goods. But he also had a captive 14-year-old girl. What he might do with her, Artie didn't want to think about. But maybe he would simply drop her off at his first stop, wherever that might be. Artie doubted taking Rebecca was part of his plan, but then again, he didn't know that. Whatever the intention, he feared that if she fought back, Russell might do anything, including throwing her over the side. And after what Casey told him about the incident in the Gulf, Artie knew Rebecca might jump overboard voluntarily if she thought she had no other option. It was a terrible situation no matter how anyone looked at it.

"What are we going to do?" Jessica asked. "We've got to get Rebecca back! Tara's boat too! But our boat is on the beach!"

"Yeah, and that bastard knew that too," Casey said, utterly disgusted. "He probably figured that with the catamaran grounded for repairs, and especially with both the masts down, we'd never be able to catch him."

"And he would be right, but I think he's underesti-mated what lengths Larry will go to." Artie said, as he stood looking out there at the tragic scene. The dinghy was simply drifting now, as the wind bore the *Sarah J.* steadily away from Green Cay, her sails growing smaller on the horizon with each passing minute. Artie could see that Tara had fallen to a kneeling position in the floorboards of the dinghy and that Grant and Larry were trying to comfort her, but how could they ever?

"I feel so awful for Tara," Casey said. "You cannot imagine what she was going through that night out there in the rain and dark when we discovered Rebecca was miss-ing. And now this!"

Artie *could* imagine, because he was a parent too, and he knew the hell he'd gone through to get back to his child after all that had happened. Casey was a grown young woman, but he didn't think of her that way all the time, especially during those long weeks when he wasn't sure he'd ever see her again. Like Casey was to him, Rebecca was Tara's only child. And it was worse that she *was* just a teenager, helpless at the mercy of a man they now knew was capable of anything.

"Larry's going to be so torn," Jessica said. "He was dead set on sailing back to Florida to look for Scully. We were just talking about it when we heard Tara scream. I told him I would go with him if he wanted me too."

"He wants to find Scully, of course," Artie said, "but he's not going to be torn. There is no contest. It's an easy choice. Scully is a grown man and a survivor who can take care of himself. Rebecca is still a child. And besides, we need Tara's boat. I'd say we better get ready, because as soon as Larry gets back to the beach, we're going to be working our butts off to get the *Casey Nicole* ready to sail."

Russell whooped and hollered as he stood at the helm of the beautiful Tartan 37, the main and jib curved into perfect airfoils as they pulled him away from that wretched little cay where he'd spent so many weeks hungry and alone. He stared back at its desolate shores, receding in the distance, and at the pathetic little rowing dinghy he could barely see by now, making its way back to the beach. The SKS rifle he'd used to drive away his pursuers was lying on one of the cockpit seats beside him, and Russell was almost as thrilled to come into possession of it, as he was the yacht itself. He'd been instantly transformed from a starving, desperate beachcomber to an armed mariner with a ship of his own command. Life was about to be good again—*really good!*

He laughed to himself as he reflected on how easy it had actually turned out. He had seized the opportunity when it presented itself and pulled it off without a hitch. What an idiot that know-it-all Captain-Larry-whatever-his-name-was, had turned out to be! A light bulb had flashed on in Russell's mind as soon as Larry started talking about taking down the rig of the catamaran. With the boat not only aground, but dismasted as well, Russell would have plenty of time to sail so far they'd never have a hope in hell of finding him. It was an opportunity he recognized in an instant—a one-time opportunity that would only last a day or two—and Russell was determined not to miss it. When he noted that the wind was right that very afternoon for what he had in mind, he knew he couldn't afford to hesitate.

It wasn't ideal that the teenaged girl was on board, but that couldn't be helped and he considered too that her presence might be an advantage later. He could order her off the boat before he left, giving her the option of swimming ashore, but if Larry and the others came after him, it could be handy to have a hostage to keep them at bay. And besides, he was tired of being alone. He would rather be taking Jessica instead, but that just wasn't going to happen.

Russell knew teenagers well enough to know that the girl was probably shut up in her cabin and would not come out until her mother insisted, when it was time for dinner. As long as he could get on board without her knowing it, she wouldn't be a problem. He'd been correct in thinking he could do just that. When he swam out to the boat, he approached it from the side opposite the island, just in case one of the others ventured away from their work on the catamaran and glanced that way.

The Tartan 37, with its relatively low freeboard, was easy enough to board from the water. Russell pulled himself up and crawled under the lifelines, keeping low as he peered inside through one of the port lights. The girl wasn't in the main salon, so that confirmed his hunch she would be in her cabin, probably reading or sleeping. He eased down the open companionway, dripping water onto the teak steps as he went, until he could see that the door to the forepeak was indeed shut. Russell glanced around the salon until he found a small coil of spare line hanging on a bulkhead hook, then he crept forward to the door. It was a simple matter to lash it shut from the outside, as there were convenient tie-down hooks on the adjacent bulkhead. The girl didn't even know it was happening, and when she figured it out, it would be too late. A strong man could probably kick the teak door apart, but Russell doubted this skinny 14-year-old could.

With the door secured, he went back on deck and quickly made his way forward to the ventilation hatch over the V-berth. It was easily big enough for even a full-sized adult to exit through, so he had to secure it too before she discovered what was going on. When he reached it, he could see her lying on the bunk with a book obscuring her face. He quickly reached into the opening and loosened the lock-down knobs on the hatch supports. The hatch was design to be dogged-down from the inside, not locked from outside, but he would figure something out. Rebecca either heard his movement or sensed his presence this time though.

"Hey! What are you doing? What's going on?"

"Don't worry about it, sweetie. Just getting ready to go for a sail, that's all."

"What? A sail? Where's my mom?" Rebecca put her book aside now and was climbing out of her bunk, reaching for the hatch. Russell slammed it shut just before she put her fingers onto the coaming.

"Hey! That's not funny! Open it back up!"

Russell stood on it instead. She wasn't going to budge it while he scanned the immediate decks around him for something with which to secure it. A long piece of quarter-inch Dacron that had been used to lash the dinghy in its deck chocks would do the trick. Russell kept a foot on the hatch while he reached for the coiled line. One end was already tied off to one of the chocks. It was a simple matter to pull it across the hatch and pass it around the nearest lifeline stanchion. From there he crisscrossed the hatch cover several times, pulling the slack out of the line with each pass until it was good enough. If she had access to a knife, she might be able to push it up enough to get at the rope, but he doubted she did, and he would keep an eye on it until they were out to sea.

Russell's next step was to haul in the anchor. It was slow work with the manual windlass on the foredeck, and he was afraid someone on the island would see him before he was done, but at last he had it up in the roller and then he rushed to the mast to haul up the mainsail. He had just cleated the halyard and jumped back into the cockpit to haul in the sheet when he heard the first scream from the beach. It was Tara, the girl's mother, and he knew he didn't have long before they would do their best to reach him in the dinghy. Russell cleated the mainsheet and worked to get the jib up. By the time he had it set, the dinghy was coming his way with Grant at the oars and Tara and the captain on board with weapons. Russell had noticed the SKS secured in a rack on the main bulkhead when he'd gone below before. He climbed down quickly to retrieve it and was delighted to find it loaded. He wouldn't shoot to kill, unless they fired back and he had to. All he needed was to buy a little time by slowing them down, and a few rounds fired in their general direction did exactly that.

CHAPTER 15

GRANT PUT his back into the oars and made for the beach, glad he was facing aft so he didn't have to see Tara falling to pieces in the bow while Larry tried to comfort her. Seeing her boat sailing away with her daughter aboard in the hands of a lunatic like Russell had to be devastating. But as soon as they all realized that they could accomplish nothing by sitting there adrift in the dinghy, watching the sailboat grow smaller on the horizon, Grant set to work to get them ashore. Larry was determined to catch this guy, and Tara would pull herself together as well. She would have to because it would take all of them. They would get the *Casey Nicole* into the water as fast as humanly possible and they would find the *Sarah J*.

Grant grew more and more furious as he rowed. What he would give to have another face-to-face encounter with this Russell character! He would have beaten him to a pulp last night if he'd had the slightest inclination to believe he would pull something like this. *What a lying, worthless, sack of shit!* And after they'd shared food and drink with him, and even offered him a way off the island! He was going to pay for this. Grant was as determined as he knew Larry and Tara were.

He ran the dinghy onto the sand and they all leapt out. Artie and Casey and Jessica were all there waiting, and without hesitation helped pick up the dinghy and carry it across to the other side of the island where the *Casey Nicole* was beached. It would be needed to carry out the anchors they would use when the time came to pull the catamaran back into the water, and they would take it with them of course, when they sailed. When they put it down next to their other gear and supplies, everyone looked to Larry for orders on what to do first and how to do it most efficiently.

"The tide won't be in for another five or six hours, but we don't have to wait for the peak going in. We'll have gravity working for us this time. We need to get the rig up first while we still have daylight to see. All I've got to do is finish the new splices on the upper ends of the shrouds. The other stuff I wanted to do can wait until next time."

"What about the hull repairs?" Artie asked. "Don't we need to finish the fiberglass over the new patches?"

"No time. The cracks are filled, and the plywood patches glued in place are solid. The epoxy will be fully cured before the water reaches them again. There's no time to glass over them. We'll just have to haul out again somewhere else and finish it then."

"It's going to be tricky getting back out over the reef in the dark though, isn't it?" Jessica asked.

"A little. But it's doable. I know where the cuts are now after swimming out there yesterday. And we won't have the squalls like the night you guys came in. I think this breeze will calm down quite a bit after midnight. We can't afford to wait. The tide will be highest around 1:00 a.m. Even though it'll be harder to see, that will give us a better chance of getting out to deep water without touching the reefs again."

"I just hope we can find him," Casey said. "He's getting a heck of a head start. And we have no idea where he's going."

"I've got a pretty good hunch though, Casey. He kept talking about the Exumas. That's where he wanted to go, and he left here sailing east after he tacked. Of course he could have changed course after he was out of sight, but there aren't a lot of options. I don't think he's a good enough sailor to beat to weather any length of time singlehanded. He'll fall off to the east or northeast because that will take him directly to the middle of the Exumas on a beam reach. I know that's what I would do if I were him."

"He must know we'll be coming after him though," Artie said.

"Yeah, but he probably figures it'll be hard to find him with so many possible anchorages over there. He'll think he's got time to go somewhere else before we can come after him. He knew it was his chance to pull this after he helped us take the masts down, the sneaky son of a bitch! It may not be easy to find him, but we will. And he's going to pay dearly when we do! That bastard is keeping me from going back for Scully."

Grant felt sorry for Scully, but finding the *Sarah J.* and Rebecca had to take top priority. Hearing Larry talk, he didn't doubt that they could do it. Before this experience, Grant had no idea how much of a role the prevailing winds played in determining routes through these islands. He'd always assumed boats could go most anywhere at a whim, but now he knew it wasn't so. Even under power it would be uncomfortable bashing a long distance against the wind and accompanying waves. The good thing about this revelation though was that it narrowed down the list of possible escape routes and destinations, leading Grant to believe that they really did have a chance of finding the *Sarah J.*, in this trackless expanse of water and far-flung cays.

Tara Hancock didn't have a lot to contribute to the discussion. She was clearly experiencing a range of emotions, but as they worked she said little about it. She just wanted to get going as fast as possible, and to that end she was working to help Larry finish sorting out the standing and running rigging. When it was time to step the two masts again, the entire crew was needed. The girls were stationed on the beach on either side of the boat holding the halyards as steadying lines while Grant and Tara took turns at the winch and Larry and Artie manhandled each mast high enough off the deck to get them in position to hoist to vertical. The process worked in reverse the same way it had during the unstepping. First they raised the foremast and then used it as a crane for hauling up the mainmast aft. It took a good hour for Larry to adjust and inspect the tension on all the shrouds and stays, but once everything was tightened up, the two masts were in column, properly raked and looking good.

Their work was hardly over though. The next job was to move anchors and mooring lines in preparation to reverse the haul-out operation. The two biggest anchors were buried ashore now, but they needed to move them out to seaward as far as the longest rodes would reach and set them so they could use them to pull the catamaran backwards into the water. This took another hour and half of hard work using the dinghy, but when they were done the two anchors were approximately 200 feet off the sterns at slight angles, and all the gear that needed to go back on board was stacked on the beach near the bows. They would begin loading it as soon as the boat was afloat again.

"It's going to be a lot easier going back in than it was coming out."

"Gravity is on our side this time, right Uncle Larry?"

"You got it. All we're waiting on now is the tide. We should eat while we have a chance, because we're going to be plenty busy until we get well away from this island and all its reefs."

Tara was the only one among them with no appetite. While they were cooking fish and waiting on the tide, she paced back and forth across the island between the beached catamaran and the spot from which she'd last seen her daughter and her parents' boat.

"She's been through hell already," Larry said. "I hope this doesn't send her off the deep end."

"She looks pretty determined to me," Grant said. "After she broke down once in the dinghy, she's been holding it together pretty well."

"That's because this is different than when Rebecca was missing overboard at night. That was horrifying because the weather was so awful, it was pitch dark out, and Tara knew very well the odds of finding someone out there in that were slim to none," Casey said.

"Yeah, that's a fact," Larry said. "That we did was a bit of a miracle."

"She has more hope this time because it's not the merciless ocean that has her daughter. It's a man she can put a face on."

"A man who ought to be *shot* in the face!" Jessica said.

"And he probably will," Grant said. "If one of us doesn't, Tara might."

The tide was sufficiently high to begin the process of relaunching the *Casey Nicole* about an hour after sunset. Going in backwards, more care had to be taken with the placement of the fenders to keep the rudders clear of the sand. As when they hauled out, Grant did most of the grinding on the winch, with Artie taking a turn here and there to give him a break. Larry was in the water with Tara and the girls this time, helping with the fenders and checking progress. Once the catamaran was afloat, the next step was to spin it around 180 degrees using the anchor rodes and a couple of extra long mooring lines Grant and

Artie handled from the beach. It took some time to accomplish, but Larry said it was essential because of the reefs they had to get through. He wanted to go out bow first, using the anchor lines, but with the boat in position to sail away as soon as they were clear of danger.

"It sure would be a good time to have that outboard that got lost," he muttered.

Grant said nothing. Jessica was standing right there and he knew the outboard went to the bottom of the Pearl River when Scully rammed the boat it was mounted on. Jessica's ex-boyfriend, Joey, likely drowned there when it happened. Scully didn't know for sure, but they'd never mentioned the incident to Jessica.

They left one stern anchor ashore after the turning was complete and Grant stayed behind with the dinghy to pick it up and bring it out to the boat when he came. He was also going to pick up the last bow anchor once Larry cast off the final rode and sailed out to deep water. It made him nervous to watch the catamaran slowly pull away from the beach. If they got it stuck on the reef at high tide, getting it off again would be nearly impossible. He trusted Larry's judgment, but he knew it was risky to attempt this in the dark. He understood that they needed to go after Russell as soon as possible though, so the risk was worth it. It wouldn't do to give him more of a head start than he already had, even if the catamaran was a much faster boat than Tara's monohull under most conditions. Even though Larry was relatively confident of the direction Russell would go, Grant knew there was always a chance he would do something really radical or unexpected. If he did sail straight for the Exumas like he wanted to do, he had to know that they would be coming after him as soon as they could relaunch the catamaran. He wouldn't stay anywhere long, even if he believed it would take them several days to get underway and on his trail.

Grant stood there waiting until the catamaran was as far out as it could go while still tethered to the beach. The rode off the stern was 250 feet in total, most of it five-eights-inch nylon rope. Larry didn't want to risk getting it caught on the reef or some other bottom obstruction, so dropping it astern and letting Grant retrieve it in the dinghy was the safer option. Grant first pulled the anchor out of the sand and loaded it aboard, then piled the 25-foot length of chain on top of it and began pulling in the nylon until he had it all coiled on the floorboards. As he did this, he was watching the *Casey Nicole* as Larry and the crew pulled her out to the farthest anchor he'd set off the bow. So far it appeared they were in the clear. The mainsail and jib went up, and Grant held his breath as she slowly gained way and moved away from the island.

He slid the dinghy into the water and jumped in, rowing hard to catch up. Larry had attached a small fender to the bitter end of the last rode so Grant could find it. He spotted it bobbing in the swell once he was well away from the island and adjusted his course to pick it up. It took him another ten minutes of hard work to pull the second rode into the dinghy and hoist the heavy anchor aboard, but once that was done, Grant was anxious to join the *Casey*

Nicole. Larry was tacking back and forth approximately a half-mile north of the island to hold position well clear of the reefs, and now as Grant neared, the catamaran was hove-to and waiting. Grant put his back into the oars and made a beeline for the ship. They were free of Green Cay, and ready to begin their pursuit of the *Sarah J.*

CHAPTER 16

RUSSELL HAD no doubt that Larry and Tara would do everything in their power to launch the catamaran and come after him as soon as possible. How soon that would be, he wasn't sure, but the fact that both masts were down and the tide was out when he left was reassuring. He knew they couldn't set sail immediately, and doubted they could until late the next day, probably longer. That would give him time to get far from Green Cay, but now he had to decide where to go. He wished now he had not mentioned his friend on Staniel Cay to Larry or anyone. Richard wasn't really a close friend, more like an acquaintance, but he had told Russell to stop by if he ever visited the Exumas. That was before the grid collapse, of course, but Russell still thought the invitation might stand. Richard was a diving instructor who knew the Exumas like the back of his hand. He would know the best anchorages in which to hide out for a while and he was already self-sufficient even before all this happened—living in an off-grid bungalow powered entirely by solar energy. It would be nice to find him and get his help, but now Russell deemed it too risky to go anywhere near Staniel Cay. When Larry and the rest of his crew on the catamaran set sail, they would go there first and they would search every possible anchorage deep enough to hide the 37-foot sloop. The catamaran, with even less draft than the keel-centerboard Tartan, could go anywhere he could and more.

Russell had left Green Cay with the southeast wind close on the port bow until he was well clear of the island and its surrounding shoals and reefs. After the dinghy in pursuit had turned back to the beach, he had remained on that tack for another mile or so, and then he came about to sail east. He was sure Larry and the others were still watching at that point, and that it would convince them he was indeed heading to the Exumas. The wind was favorable for a reach to the middle of the popular chain and they would certainly believe that was his destination. But now he knew he had to think of an alternative. Russell really wanted to stay in the Bahamas, as he was convinced that was the best place to be considering the situation, but he did not want another encounter with that crew. If they caught up with him after what he'd done, it was not going to end well for someone, and he was greatly outnumbered. He needed to buy some time to think, and that meant going somewhere he wouldn't have to worry about constantly hiding out, at least for a few days until he could figure out a better option.

The great thing about this well-kept Tartan 37 was that it had a powerful diesel engine. Larry said they had stopped at Green Cay to work on some minor problem with it; something about the cooling system, but that didn't bother Russell. If it would run at all, he would use it if he needed it. If it overheated, so what? He'd either fix it later or do without it. But the main thing was that in the short term the engine would give him the ability to go into the wind, in a direction his pursuers would not be expecting. He would work out where as soon as he had time to look over the charts.

There was also the matter of his female crewmember, confined for now in the forward cabin. Russell was going to have to talk to her at some point, to inform her of how it was going to be now that he was in charge of the *Sarah J*. He had no doubt that she would come around eventually, but now was not the time to argue. She could stay where she was until she had time to think about her lack of choices. Once they were in a place he felt was sufficiently remote that she would have no possibility of escape, he would give her a little more freedom. At just fourteen years old she couldn't be too hard to persuade that her life going forward had to be in accordance with what he deemed best. That she still had hope of life at all she would eventually come to recognize was due to his mercy and protection. She would come to see him as her provider and surely realize he had been right all along to bring her with him.

Russell figured the girl had been spoiled by a life of ease before the collapse. He didn't know where her father was or why he wasn't with them, but he could guess that Tara had probably cheated on him and then cleaned him out in the divorce. That was what all women like her did and Rebecca would have grown up thinking it was normal, probably doing the same herself one day. Tara was obviously spoiled by rich parents as well. The fact that they owned the yacht and cruised it to the Bahamas every winter proved that. She probably grew up thinking she was better than everybody else, especially guys like him, and Russell was used to being snubbed by women like her. But he'd shown her now. In this new world, her daddy's money meant nothing, and Russell had used his brains to outsmart her and her egotistical boyfriend who thought he was such a hotshot sailor and boat builder. Russell couldn't help but chuckle to himself as the thought about the two of them now, and how they must be absolutely freaking out trying to figure out how they were going to get that big plywood catamaran back in the water with the tide out. It was an image he found hilarious, and he would have given anything to see their faces and hear what they were saying —especially what they were saying about him right about now.

And then there was Grant, that asshole who had shoved him. Russell wondered if Jessica still thought he was so great now, after seeing him fail to catch Tara's boat and then turn tail and run back to the beach at the sound of a few shots that Russell wasn't really aiming to hit anyone with. Russell knew he was a spoiled dickhead too, the kind of college boy whose parents had plenty of money. That was why Jessica liked him. And she was too stupid to even realize that none of that mattered any more. It was just as well that she was back there on Green Cay with him. The last thing Russell needed was a shallow, materialistic bitch that was in no way mentally or emotionally equipped to deal with the reality of the world as it was now. Thinking of all this, he realized he was much better off in the long run with Rebecca as a companion. She was still young and malleable enough to adapt; young enough to not think that she already had all the answers like those smug college kids who thought they were smarter and better than everyone else. No, Rebecca would get a *real* education. Russell would see to that. He was willing to bet she'd be eager to learn too, but if she weren't, it would be easy enough to rid himself of her if it became necessary.

One of the first things he would have to teach her was some respect. She had cursed and screamed at him when she realized what was going on, and had called him names he'd never even thought of before. That had lasted about a half hour, until she'd finally either grown tired of it or had yelled herself hoarse. It didn't bother him too much anyway as long as he was at the helm with the companionway shut. He knew she would start up again when he tried to have any kind of interaction with her, but he was determined to set her straight and put a stop to it when she did.

By the time the sun neared the horizon astern, Russell decided it was time to stop and study the charts so he could make some decisions. He didn't want to be sailing blind into the night. He'd already learned from a quick glance at the chart book he found down below that there was a long line of shoals and reefs just to the north that stretched between Green Cay and the Exumas. But the color of the water around him told him he was in the clear and still in water too deep to anchor. He turned the bow up into the wind so he could simply drop the sails. He figured he had plenty of room to drift for an hour or so while he worked out a plan. He was hungry too and was looking forward to going through the provisions he knew were on board. Suddenly coming into possession of a large food supply was as huge as having the boat itself; especially considering how deprived his existence had been on Green Cay all those weeks alone.

Russell knew the basics of how to make a sailboat go where he wanted it to and that was about all he cared about. Let the rich yachties and racer boys worry about all the finer points of sail trimming and tweaking. Dropping the sails to the deck was as easy as heaving-to, in his opinion, especially since he'd never learned how to do the latter. He wadded up the jib and strapped it down with a bungee cord someone had left on the bow pulpit, probably for that purpose, and likewise wrapped a piece of spare line around the main to loosely secure it to the boom. The wind was only ten knots or so and the sails weren't going anywhere.

This done, Russell stared over the side into the turquoise depths. He felt free again at last, out here in deep water far from the island that had been his prison for too long. The change was so abrupt that Russell almost had to pinch himself to make sure it was real. He was on a seaworthy, comfortable sailboat, out of sight of any land and free to go wherever in the hell he pleased. He made his way down the narrow side decks to the cockpit and then descended the companionway steps into the teak cabin he could now call home. Rebecca heard him enter and started screaming at him again through the forepeak door, ruining the pleasant ambiance of orange sunset light on vanished wood and polished brass.

"LET ME OUT OF HERE! WHAT ARE YOU DOING? WHERE ARE WE?"

Russell walked forward to the door. She had opened the latch and was pushing against the rope that held it in place, but was only able to crack it about an inch.

"When you chill out and calm down, I'll let you out. But right now I've got my hands full."

"This is my grandpa's boat! You'd better turn it around and take it back to my mom right now. Captain Larry will kill you if you don't! Don't think he won't. He's killed other people already!"

"Captain Larry isn't going to do anything, because his boat is on the beach with the rig down. You can forget about Captain Larry! *I'm* your captain now, Miss Rebecca, and we're going to find ourselves a nice island where we can hang out on for a while and chill. You'll be glad when you see, just wait."

"I will kill you myself, if Larry doesn't! Just wait until you let me out of here!"

"Why would I do that then?" Russell laughed. "If you're going to kill me, I'd better keep you locked up for a while. I'm not ready to die today! This has been my luckiest day in a long time. I wouldn't want to ruin it by dying. Now, I'm going to make myself something to eat. If you're hungry, I'll push something through the crack. But I'm not going to risk letting you out so you can kill me," he laughed some more.

"Screw you! Captain Larry should have shot you dead the minute he first saw you!"

Russell smiled at that astute observation. *Of course he should have!* What an idiot he and the rest of them were, to trust a total stranger in times like these. But if they had simply treated him better, none of this would have happened. If Larry had offered to take him aboard as crew to wherever they were going—*not Florida*—and if Jessica had just been a little nicer to him and given him a chance.... Oh well, in the end, he'd simply seized an opportunity when it presented itself. Anyone with half a brain would do the same. It was simply a matter of survival.

CHAPTER 17

IF THE GIRL didn't want to eat, Russell wasn't going to force her. She'd get hungry soon enough and then she'd be asking for food. As the boat drifted under bare poles, he rummaged through the cabinets and cubbyholes in the galley and in the lockers under the bunks, taking a brief inventory of the stores. Compared to having nothing while stranded on the island, it was a windfall. Most of it consisted of canned goods and other non-perishables such as rice and oatmeal and several varieties of pasta. There were two large aluminum propane bottles mounted on the stern rail that supplied the gimbaled two-burner stove and oven, and when he tried the manual pump at the sink fresh water flowed into the cup he held under the tap. He downed the water but what he wanted was a drink to calm his nerves after all the excitement. Further searching yielded an unopened bottle of Scotch whiskey and two fifths of brandy squirreled away in another locker that contained engine spares and tools. He hoped that measly stash wasn't the sum of the ship's liquor stores, but deeper digging could wait until he found a good place to anchor and hide out for a while.

Rebecca had gotten quiet after her last outburst of screaming and kicking the door to her cabin. It was solid teak and was mounted on sturdy hinges, but he still worried she might break if she kept it up. He didn't want to have to do it, but if she got out and went crazy he knew he might have to grab her and tie her up to keep her from interfering with the operation of the boat. He hoped it wouldn't come to that and figured the best thing he could do was ignore her as long as she stayed quiet and calm.

He twisted the cap off one of the bottles of cheap brandy and poured himself a double shot. Then he opened a family-sized can of chili with beans and dumped it onto a pot that was already on the stove, held in place by adjustable pot clamps. Hot food and a drink was just what he needed to prepare for sailing through the coming night. When the chili was warm he carried the whole pot and a spoon up to the cockpit and sat there looking at the chart book spread out beside him as he ate.

The sun was already down and the light was fading fast. As he studied the options to going straight east to the Exumas, where Larry and the others on the island thought he would go, Russell was becoming intrigued with the idea of heading southeast instead. That way was directly into the wind, which was just the way he needed to go to throw off his pursuers when they came after him. It was also the direction of the Jumentos Cays and Ragged Islands. Until he'd heard Larry mention that was where they were headed, he'd never realized how big an area those remote little cays actually covered. Looking at them on the chart now, he could see why Larry would want to go there. It was a lot farther from where he was now than the Exumas, but also a lot farther from civilization in general and certainly off the beaten path to anywhere. It would be difficult to sail there, as it was practically dead to windward and would require lots of tacking back and forth, but with the engine on the *Sarah J.,* he wouldn't have to. The wind was not much over ten knots and he figured it might drop some more after dark. He could easily motor into it at a pace that wouldn't work the diesel too hard. Russell knew that prolonged running of the engine without the water pump would eventually damage the exhaust system and probably warp or crack the heads, but it would take a while. Marine diesels were more rugged than most people realized and could stand a lot of abuse. He would run it dead to windward until it got dangerously hot, then shut it down and sail until it cooled enough to start it again. The process could be repeated as necessary and would certainly be faster than tacking back and forth the whole way. If the engine would just last long enough get him safely beyond reach of his pursuers that was all he would ask of it. It might be nice to have it later, but if Larry and the others on that catamaran found him first, there wouldn't be a later.

They would never expect him to go in that direction because they wouldn't expect him to take the most difficult

route since he was single-handing. They would also probably assume he wouldn't use the engine, since they themselves wouldn't take the risk of doing irreparable damage to
it. They might sail to the Jumentos sometime later, after
they gave up searching for him in the Exumas, but he
planned to be long gone by then. Where to, he would
decide when the time came. He figured heading there
straight away would buy him at least a week, maybe more,
while they worked to get the catamaran ready to sail and
then wasted days looking in all the anchorages in the
vicinity of Staniel Cay.

This decision made, Russell washed the dinner pot
over the side and went below to ready the engine, keeping
his fingers crossed the battery had enough charge to start it.
He pulled the dipstick to make sure the oil level was good,
then reinstalled the cover, turned the key to the start position and pushed the button. The battery was indeed strong,
and the old Yanmar turned over rapidly and fired right up.
Rebecca screamed at him again as soon as she heard it come
to life.

"You can't run the engine, you idiot! Larry hasn't fixed
it! He said we couldn't use it until he did!"

Russell just laughed as he climbed back up to the cockpit. Rebecca was kicking the door again, but once he closed
the companionway and revved the diesel to half throttle,
the noise was barely a bother. He left the sails as they were,
sloppily bundled on deck but tied well enough that they
wouldn't flap around, and put the boat in gear to bring it
around to his new southeast heading. The compass had an

L.E.D. light that was working fine off the ship's battery, and Russell found a small flashlight on the chart table with which he could read the charts. Flipping the switches on the control panel revealed that the 12-volt navigation lights were all working too, but Russell turned them off immediately, knowing it was wiser to run dark even if no one was in pursuit just yet.

There was nothing out there to hit on his new course, and by his rough estimates from the chart, he knew he could run all night and most of the following day before he had to worry about nearing land. As it grew darker, the clear weather revealed a bright starry sky, with enough ambient light to spot any vessels large enough to be a collision risk. Russell knew he couldn't let his guard down long, so he scanned the horizon every few minutes. It might be an empty stretch of seldom-traveled ocean, but if there were other vessels sailing it at night they would likely be unlit as well, considering the circumstances.

As he stared onto the empty horizon surrounding him, Russell pondered all that Larry and the others had told him about Florida. He didn't care whether they believed him or not, he was certain that all of this was a deliberate action planned and implemented by the United States. They were likely in collaboration with a few other select governments working with them in their master plan to break down society and reboot it according to their desired New World Order. There was no way he was going back to Florida or anywhere else on the U.S. mainland, and he didn't trust that some of the nearby island nations in the region were not in on the scheme as well. Thinking of that kept him occupied as he steered to the southeast and he wondered if perhaps Cuba, which did not have a strong relationship with the U.S., might be the best place to go in the long run. It was worthy of consideration; because once he reached the Jumentos Cays he would be relatively close to the big island. As long as he didn't run into a navy or coast guard ship no one was likely to challenge him if he decided to take his chances and go there.

Russell was snapped out of these thoughts by a loud, obnoxious buzzer sounding from the cabin. Knowing it was the temperature warning alarm, he took the flashlight and went below to the engine compartment. It took him a few seconds to find it and then he yanked loose the sensor wire connected to the alarm and the maddening noise was silenced. There was a lot of heat coming off the engine block, but there were no unusual sounds as it hummed along at the steady rpm he'd set, running just a tad over half-throttle. Nothing seemed in imminent danger of burning up, so he decided to run it for another half hour. Then he would shut it down and get the sails back up. An hour or so of sailing as close to the wind as possible would give it time to cool down again. He would check the oil before starting it back up, since it would likely burn some running hot, but he doubted it would lock up as long as he kept it topped off and stopped to give it frequent cooling breaks.

The important thing was that every minute it ran, he was making headway dead to windward. That made it well worth the risk. He estimated his speed made good under power was around seven knots, so every hour he could coax it to run would get him farther from the path of likely pursuit. It was just under 100 nautical miles to the Jumentos by his rough measurements on the chart, so it wouldn't take all that long to get there even with all the stopping and tacking under sail. And so what if it did? The only thing that really mattered regarding his landfall was that he approached the low-lying islands in daylight. There were lots of shoals and reefs surrounding them, and the entire area looked hazardous to navigation, which was precisely why it was seldom visited and therefore such an excellent place to go in times like these.

A half hour later, he shut the diesel down as planned and opened the engine compartment to maximize cooling. The heat was extreme and it would make the cabin uncomfortable, but Russell was going to be on deck anyway. He rushed back up there to get the sails up, as he didn't want to lose any of the headway he'd made. To sail at all, he had to fall off to the southwest, but that was okay as long as he was making some southerly progress as well.

For a few minutes, it was blissfully quiet, with just the flutter of the jib leech and the rushing of water past the hull, but then Rebecca yelled from below again, this time her tone changed and her plea urgent:

"You've got to let me out of here! I've got to use the head! You don't have to leave me locked in here the whole way. Where do you think I'm going to go?"

Russell considered this and looked around. What could

she possibly do? She was right. There was nowhere to go, and he was sure she probably did have to go to the bathroom by now, after all these hours. He tied off the helm so the boat would hold course for a few minutes and went back below to let her out. If she tried something, he would smack the crap out of her. She was just a scrawny 14-year-old after all. There wasn't really anything to worry about now that they were at sea.

CHAPTER 18

"WE WOULD ALREADY BE on our way if he had just left that last anchor! You've got three more, do you really think we'll need that one too?" Tara was pacing back and forth on the deck as Larry stood by the helm, the catamaran hove to until Grant could catch up.

"I don't know what we'll need, but I do know I'm not leaving any gear behind. Grant will be here in just a few more minutes. It's not going to make a difference in the long run. Trust me, we're going to catch that guy."

"Trusting you hasn't worked out too well for me so far." Tara glared at him, then turned to watch Grant as he began rowing their way.

Larry understood Tara's impatience and frustration. He couldn't imagine what she must be feeling right now. Her boat was gone with her daughter on board, and the man that had taken it had nearly an eight-hour head start. Larry knew that wasn't near as much as Russell probably thought he would have, considering the condition of the *Casey Nicole* when he pulled his stunt, but even so, it was significant. Significant enough that Larry was worried about finding him. If he went where they thought he was going, that was one thing. But if he didn't... then all bets were off. But Larry couldn't let Tara know he was anything less than fully confident they would find her daughter. She had to believe that or she would totally lose it. He made sure there was no hint of uncertainty in his voice:

"With the wind favorable to sail to the Exumas, we'll get there not long after he does. Even on a close reach the *Casey Nicole* is faster than the *Sarah J.*, and especially in the light air we've got tonight. We may catch him before he makes landfall even if he doesn't stop. But he's alone at the helm and he was already weak from being stranded here with so little to eat. He may drop the anchor on the banks somewhere and sleep a while, thinking there's no way we could relaunch our boat so soon."

"I think Larry's right," Artie said. "I can't see him sailing all night through unfamiliar waters. I would think he would have sense enough to rest before approaching land exhausted like that." Artie had been standing there with them as they waited for Grant, not really knowing what to say to Tara. None of them did. All any of them could do was show her that they were willing to do everything in their power to catch up to her boat and her daughter. Jessica and Casey were standing at the stern boarding ramp, waiting to meet Grant and help him get the anchors and dinghy aboard.

Tara was actually holding herself together a lot better than Larry expected. She had snapped at him once or twice with suggestions this was his fault, but it wasn't with the outright fury she'd rightfully had when he'd fallen asleep on his watch, leaving her emotionally confused daughter alone on deck. If Rebecca had succeeded with what she intended when she slipped over the side and into the kayak, Larry didn't know how he would have been able to live with himself, knowing he'd allowed it to happen. Tara was correct that this incident was partially his fault too.

He'd misjudged what Russell was capable of and likely to do. Larry hadn't liked him much from the beginning and now he knew he should have trusted his instincts and put aside his desire to help a fellow human being in need. But offering the man a ride off the desolate island had not at the time seemed much of a stretch, particularly since he could use his help with the boat on the way to Florida. Russell's unappreciative attitude should have been enough of a red flag though. He had clearly displayed his disappointment at Larry's "take-it-or-leave-it" offer of a ride to Florida and nowhere else. Larry had thought he would sulk for a while and get over it. He hadn't considered that instead, the man would plot and scheme and then do something as rash and bold as stealing one of their boats and kidnapping Tara's daughter. Now Rebecca was in grave danger whether Russell intended to harm her or not. Anything could happen out at sea. They could have a navigational accident or hit bad weather, or encounter bandits that would not be deterred by the SKS Russell found aboard. And aside from all that, after what Rebecca had done in the Gulf in a moment of despair, Larry couldn't be sure she wouldn't do so again if she thought she had no other out. It pissed him off to no end, thinking about her going through all of this now after how far she'd come emotionally since that awful night. By the time they'd found her out there in the dark, Rebecca had decided she *wanted* to live. And during the many days and nights at sea after that, she and Larry had many long talks about life and hope and he'd seen a total turn around in her attitude. The last thing she needed at this point was for all that to be erased by the actions of one selfish idiot. Larry knew they simply *had* to catch up before that happened.

Even if Rebecca were not aboard the *Sarah J.,* losing the other boat would be a disaster at this point. Without two boats, Larry could not go back and search for Scully and it was too risky for all of them to return to Florida. Aside from that, stores were low aboard the *Casey Nicole,* while the heavier-displacement *Sarah J.* still had a decent supply of canned goods and other non-perishables. When Larry had first decided to help Tara and Rebecca after meeting them on Cat Island, he had not been thinking much beyond the passage to the Bahamas. Now, he had no intention of leaving them behind, even though his fantasies of what might have been with Tara were unlikely to work out. He had grown attached to Rebecca too, and abandoning the two females alone in these islands to fend for themselves was simply out of the question. But they had to have that boat back, just as they had to rescue Rebecca and then eventually, find Scully. Larry was used to having plenty to worry about as a professional skipper moving boats between islands and across oceans in all weather and all times of the year, but never had he found himself with as much worry as he had on his shoulders now.

When Grant reached the catamaran he and the girls with Artie's help made quick work of stowing the dinghy upside down on the forward trampoline and lashing it in place. Then Larry put the helm back over and set a course to the west. They first had to sail around the western end of Green Cay and then well to the south of it, steering clear of the reefs and shoals before they could set an eastward course for the Exumas. Thinking about the dangers in these shallow waters at night just made Larry angrier because he was leaving with unfinished repairs from the accidental grounding. He hated that Russell had made him sail before the work was complete. It would cause them to have to go to the trouble to find another suitable spot to haul out again later. It was just one more thing to fuel the fury he would unleash upon the sorry asshole when he caught up with him.

"We need to keep a sharp watch," he told Grant and Artie; as if it were something they didn't already know. "He could be anchored or adrift most anywhere, and it would be all too easy to pass him out here at night and never know it."

"It looks like we're going to have good visibility," Artie said, glancing up at the clear, starry skies. "That's certainly a blessing."

"Yeah, in more ways than one. Maybe he won't screw up and hit something on a clear night like this."

Getting Rebecca back and recovering the boat in whatever condition they found it was the goal, but if they could get it undamaged, that would be even better. Larry just hoped Russell had enough sense not to run the engine without the water pump. It would be a shame to ruin a perfectly good diesel that was well maintained and simple to keep going even in these circumstances. At least he knew about the problem with the pump, and he claimed to be experienced working on boats, so maybe that would make him think twice. The wind was favorable to take him to Staniel Cay, so if he were really going there, he wouldn't need the engine to do it and would hopefully leave it alone.

Tara spent the rest of the night standing watch as far forward as she could go, on the catwalk platform that spanned the gap between the forward beam and the forestay. She had no interest in taking a break from her vigil for any reason and was still there nearly five hours later as the eastern horizon began to lighten with the coming of dawn.

Just as Larry had predicted, the breeze died down to less than ten knots after midnight, and on a close reach their boat speed stayed in the upper single digits as well. He was disappointed that they had not spotted the silhouette of a sail on the relatively bright horizon they had all night. Either Russell hadn't stopped to rest or he had gotten far enough off course to his destination that they missed him if he did. Taking him by surprise would be best of course, since he'd already shot at them with the rifle. There was plenty of ammunition for it in the drawer under the chart table, and Larry had no doubt he would find it in his search for a joint or something to drink. If they could have spotted the boat anchored out on the banks in the dark, it might be possible to board it before he realized what was happening. Even in the daylight that tactic could work as long as he was below and asleep. But if they didn't find him before he reached the Exumas, Larry knew things were going to be that much more difficult. The biggest factor there was going to be all the other boaters he knew would be congregated there. That entire chain was a mecca for yachts of all types and sizes anyway, and he had no doubt that many Florida and other East Coast boaters with vessels seaworthy enough to get there would congregate in what they would consider a safe island haven.

After what they had already seen in the Caribbean and along the northern Gulf Coast, Larry wasn't inclined to go sailing boldly into any of the popular Exumas anchorages, even if Russell already had. To do so without some kind of reconnoitering effort first would be putting his ship and his crew at risk of attack or ambush. And even if that were not a worry, if Russell was there and on deck when they arrived, he would surely recognize the distinctive catamaran from a distance and have ample time to prepare his defense.

Tara wasn't going to like it, but Larry was determined to take the careful and smart approach even if it cost them several extra hours. With this in mind, he studied his

Bahamas charts in the gradually increasing daylight and considered the options for making his landfall. The main anchorage at Staniel Cay was definitely out of the question. The sizable town ashore there probably already had its share of problems, and he had no way of knowing how the local authorities may have responded or if there were even any present at all.

A short distance to the south there was a better option. Bitter Guana Cay was uninhabited (at least in normal times, though maybe not now) and there was a semi-protected anchorage near the beach on the west side. He felt okay about sailing there, but would approach with caution and an eye out for the masts of other vessels that might already be there. If he could find someplace reasonably remote to secure the boat, he had an idea of what he would do next to find Russell and the *Sarah J.* It was going to take a little bit of work to get ready, and he was certain too he would catch some flak from Artie and the rest of the crew, not to mention Tara, when he laid out his plan. He already knew how Artie felt about splitting up, but dammit, sometimes these things just couldn't be helped.

CHAPTER 19

WHEN REBECCA first realized something strange was going on, she thought it was some kind of a joke. She had been reading in her bunk to pass the time while her mom and the others worked on the catamaran, and the last thing she expected was to see the weird guy that had been living on the island suddenly aboard their boat. When he closed the hatch over her head, she was sure that he was just messing with her and that he would open it right back up. But when she asked him what he was doing, he said he was going for a sail. That didn't make a bit of sense because she knew there was still a lot of work to be done on the other boat before they could go anywhere.

She tried pushing the hatch up but he was standing on it and wouldn't budge. He wouldn't move either, even when she yelled at him to get off of it and open it up. When she tried to open the door and go out into the main cabin, she discovered that it wouldn't open either. Pushing on it with all her might, Rebecca was able to open it about an inch; just enough to reveal that it was lashed shut with rope. When she turned back to the hatch, he was still standing on it and pulling a length of rope back and forth over the top of it to lash it shut as well. Why he would keep doing this after she told him to stop, and why he didn't want her to get out of her cabin, she did not understand. If it were a game, some of the others would be in on it too, but when she called out to Casey and Jessica and Grant to see if any of them were aboard with him, no one answered.

Despite that, she was still convinced it had to be some kind of joke until she heard the clanking of the anchor windlass over her cabin at the bow. She could see enough through the hatch to see Russell bent over it, working away with the long handle to crank in the rode. The slow rattle of chain falling down the hawse pipe and piling up in the chain locker was unmistakable proof that he was weighing anchor. Had her mom or Captain Larry really asked him to move the boat closer to the beach or something? Was he just doing that and having a little fun at her expense by joking around in the process? It was possible, but he had said going *sailing*, not just moving the boat. She didn't believe for a minute that her mom would let a stranger like him take the *Sarah J.* out for a sail, especially not with her alone on board with him. She felt the boat slowly moving forward in the direction of the anchor and tried desperately to see what was going on.

There were two small port lights in her cabin, one on the starboard side and one to port. She could see out of both of them, but since they were so small her field of view was limited to what was directly abeam of the boat on either side. Since the boat was being pulled up to the anchor, which was dead to windward and away from the island, she couldn't see in the direction of the beach where her mom had landed the dinghy. All she could see was open water to starboard and the far end of the island to port.

She tried kicking the door to see if she could break her way out but the rope he'd tied it shut with gave enough with each blow to absorb most of the impact. She knew it was a solid door and she could see enough of the rope to know it was the good kind, the same kind used for all the running rigging that controlled the sails. There was no way the rope was going to break and she didn't have anything in her cabin with which to cut it. If she had her shoes she thought she might be able to break the wood itself, but she'd left them on the cabin sole on the other side of the door and kicking it with her bare feet was too painful to keep up for long.

When the sound of the windlass stopped and all the chain was aboard, she could hear Russell running back and forth across the deck, working to get the sails up. A few minutes later, she heard the sails flapping in the wind and felt the boat heel over and begin moving. He really was taking the boat sailing, but where to and why? Her yelling of these questions got her no answers, but she could hear the sound of water rushing past the hull as the boat picked up speed.

The next thing she heard was the sudden crack of a

rifle fired from so close that it made her ears ring. She knew then that something really bad was happening. Russell was stealing the *Sarah J.* and her mom and some of the others on the island must have seen what was going on. Now he was shooting at them!

"MOM!" she screamed at the top of her lungs, as the shooting continued. She counted five shots before it stopped but she kept up her screaming until he answered.

"Nobody got shot!" he yelled back at her. "They turned around and went back to the beach. Just chill out and relax. I'm not going to shoot anybody and I'm not going to hurt you!"

Rebecca didn't know whether to believe him or not. She had her faced pressed to the port light and now Russell had changed course enough that she could see. The dinghy was drifting several hundred yards from the island and she could see there were three people in it, one she was sure was her mom. She watched as one of them began rowing and saw it moving slowly back towards the beach. She couldn't be sure, but it didn't look like any of them were hurt. She had not heard any other shots other than the five Russell had fired, and was kind of surprised no one had shot back at him. She thought that maybe Larry and whoever was in the dinghy with him and her mom didn't have a gun with him or that they were simply too far away. Whatever the reason, it was too late now, and it was obvious that they weren't going to be able to catch up to the *Sarah J.* She knew the catamaran was in no condition to sail and she wondered what was going to happen to her now if

Russell didn't turn around and take her back to the island. She assumed he was taking the boat because he wanted to get off the island after all that time he was stuck there, and he didn't want to go to Florida with Larry, but why was he taking her with him? Was it just because she was already on board? Did he think he needed her for a hostage or something? Or did he have something even worse in mind for her?

Rebecca had not paid much attention to Russell since he'd surprised them all by walking to their end of the island that morning. He'd been hanging around the catamaran ever since, but he'd not been aboard the *Sarah J.*, nor did she seem all that interested in it. She knew he was getting on Larry's nerves and that he'd been bothering Jessica with his constant leering at her. Grant had put him in his place over that and Larry had said no to his continued pestering as he begged to join them as part of the crew when they eventually left to go wherever they were going. Even though Rebecca had little interaction with him, from what she had seen and what her mother and Casey and Jessica said, Russell was a stoner and a drunk looking to get by doing as little as possible. Her mom said he didn't get that way just since the blackout either. It was a way of life for him and probably all he'd ever done.

Larry offered to take him to Florida, but that wasn't good enough. So now he'd stolen her grandpa's boat and taken her along for the ride. She kicked the door again as hard as she could in frustration, wincing at the shock of the impact transmitted through her bare heel. She wasn't going to be able to get out of there on her own, and he continued to ignore her pleading to let her out. Rebecca yelled so much it hurt her throat, then she curled up and began to sob.

Why were so many bad things happening to her? All she'd wanted to do was simply stay home in Gulfport and go to school with her friends like every other normal person she knew. Why did the lights and phones and everything else go out and make them have to leave home on a stupid sailboat? When they met Larry and the others on the catamaran, it was even worse, because he convinced her mom they had to sail all the way to the Bahamas to find someplace safe. She had wanted off the boat so bad she'd decided it wasn't worth living any more if life was going to be like that.

But she'd made a terrible mistake. Leaving the boat and being out there on the dark, scary ocean at night was a lot different than she thought it would be. She was floating on the kayak, and though she wanted to drown, she couldn't bring herself to slip over the side and let it happen. It was going to be all together too slow and too frightening. So she clung to the tiny plastic boat even after the wind tore the paddle out of her hands and the hours passed by with no end to the terrible night in sight.

Captain Larry had found her in spite of the conditions and after her rescue he gave her renewed hope and convinced her that life *was* worth living after all. But now this had happened despite what he said. He'd been wrong about it being safe in the Bahamas because now after all she'd been through, she was taken captive by a stranger who lied to Captain Larry and her mom and everybody else. There was no telling where he was taking her and no telling what he would do next. He would probably kill her if she didn't do everything he told her to, and there was no way she would because she knew what that would probably be. She'd rather kill herself than let that happen, even though she'd promised herself she would never think that way again after her failed attempt to drown in the Gulf.

As she lay there crying, with these thoughts running through her head, she could tell by the motion and the sounds that the boat was sailing at a steady speed, taking her far away from those who loved her and could help her. The light streaming in through the Lexan hatch and ports eventually changed to the reddish color that told her it was nearly sunset, and finally Russell stopped the boat, taking the sails down to let it drift. She knew he was eating because he'd offered her food, but she didn't want anything from him. Darkness fell and he started the engine, even though she told him that Larry said it was broken.

It seemed to be running fine anyway, and the longer she heard its relentless throbbing, pushing the boat on and on into the night, the more desperate she became. How would anyone ever find her now? If the motor kept working, Russell could take her so far away they wouldn't even know where to look. Rebecca decided right then and there that she had to do something to save herself. She couldn't depend on Captain Larry to do it this time. She knew that what she had to do was take the boat back from this pirate who'd stolen it. She thought and thought as she lay there, coming up with all kinds of crazy schemes, but none of them seemed possible. As the hours passed, she finally had to go to the bathroom so bad that when Russell shut the engine off to sail for a while, she begged him to open the door so she could. After all her thinking and planning, the best idea that she could come up with was to simply trick him into thinking she would go along with him. It was the only way, as she was too small to fight him and overpower him, even if he didn't have the gun he'd fired to make her mom and Captain Larry turn back. She would play along, pretending to accept her fate, and when the time was right, she would do what she had to do.

CHAPTER 20

SCULLY HAD KEPT a reef in *Intrepida's* mainsail through the night, even long after the thunderstorms that had given them a thrashing had cleared out the wind dropped. The boat was slow even under full sail, but he wanted to sail slower still as they neared the dark coast of Andros Island in the dark. There were plenty of shoals and reefs close to the island to worry about, so he was content to sail at four knots until daybreak. Thomas was asleep on the leeward cockpit bench and Mindy was curled up down below. Both of them had been terrified during the storms, but after the weather passed their worries went away and getting no sleep the previous night when they were attacked, they both passed out in a deep slumber.

Scully watched the kayak trailing behind on the towline as he sat there at the helm, fighting his own drowsiness. Looking at it clipping along in the wake, he knew that if he were paddling he would be going even slower than this little 17-footer under reduced sail. He would not have been able to take a break of any length while crossing the Gulf Stream current and he would likely be completely exhausted by the time he made it to this side, if he ever did. It was a good decision to help the American couple, saving him from a major expedition he might not survive.

When dawn came and the coast of Andros was in sight, Scully's next task was figuring out exactly what part of the huge island he was looking at. Andros stretched nearly a hundred miles from north to south, but the convoluted shoreline and its shallow bights that cut across it made for many more hundreds of miles of coastline. As he spread Thomas' Bahamas chart book out in the cockpit and studied the area, Scully considered all the feasible routes. According to what Larry had said, it was even possible to cut across the big island by sailing the bights, if one had a shallow draft boat such as the *Casey Nicole* or *Intrepida*. But as tempting as such a short cut might be, Scully didn't think it was worth the risk. The creeks and estuaries were mostly uninhabited, but there were small villages that such a route would take them quite close to. And he knew that many islanders by now might have relocated to isolated places like the bights to find better fishing and safety from the violence that now pervaded human settlements both large and small.

That left the other two options: going north, in the direction away from where they needed to go to sail around that end of Andros to reach the established routes that led down island, or following the coastline south until they were clear of it and then beating to weather to make the required southeasterly heading. Looking at the chart, Scully could see that either way would require extensive sailing to weather, it was just a matter of where they were starting from that would determine which made more sense.

He closed on the coast while comparing what saw before him to the charts, and then after finding a channel marker to confirm it, determined their position to be just south of Gold Cay, the westernmost point of the island. They had done well on the crossing and managed to avoid being swept farther north than necessary. Thomas woke as Scully sailed closer to land, the morning sun on his face becoming too bright and too warm to ignore any longer. Mindy soon came on deck as well, and both of them were visibly thrilled to be in the Bahamas and close to land.

"So that's Andros?"

"Yes, mon. Biggest island in all de Bahamas."

"There's nothing there," Mindy said.

"I've heard it's mostly wild," Thomas said, "just a few small settlements, but nothing like the more popular tourist islands over here."

"It might be a safe place to stay for a while then. Look how clear the water is here! It's amazing! Even clearer than it was at the Dry Tortugas. I'll bet there's plenty of fish to catch!"

"De fishin' good all in de Bahamas." Scully said.

"Then if we could find a good little hidden place to anchor, we *could* stay!"

"You know we can't do that, Mindy. We promised Scully we'd give him a ride to the Jumentos Cays in exchange for helping us get to the islands."

Scully studied Mindy's face as she considered this. He didn't know if she was having serious second thoughts or not. If so, he would gladly leave them here if that's what they wanted and go on in the kayak. It was still a long way to the Jumentos, but he was closer now than he was before he met them. He could make it, he was sure, but he was glad it didn't come to that.

"No, I know we can't really stay. Of course we have to take Scully where we promised. It's just wishful thinking, that's all. It's so beautiful here, and I was so scared out there in those storms yesterday. I just want to be somewhere quiet and peaceful like this."

"It's gonna be de same where we goin', and maybe better. Dat Larry he know de best place in de island to go. Not to worry so much."

"So how do we get there from here?" Thomas wanted to know.

Scully pointed out where they were on the chart and then showed him and Mindy the options. He said he thought it made sense to turn south and follow the coast as closely as they could. They would be sailing in mostly smooth waters in the lee of the island, but far enough out to avoid the shallows and to find a good breeze. They could roughly parallel the coast until they cleared the south end and then it would be an open water passage across the banks to the Jumentos.

Because of its shallow draft and small size, the Montgomery 17 was the perfect vessel in which to sail down west coast of Andros. Twice along the way, they entered into shallow tidal estuaries where there was nothing around them but sand and scrub forest. These remote anchorages made it possible to catch up on their sleep, and each evening they caught enough fish to have a filling meal on the beach. Although there was no sign of human presence, Scully slept in the cockpit with the AK-47 in easy reach.

During the daylight hours as they sailed the length of the island, they saw several small boats in the distance, most powered by sails or small outboards. Scully could tell they were local native craft, and according to Larry, the inhabitants of Andros had a reputation as skilled wooden boat builders. The people in the boats they saw were all occupied with fishing; none of them seemed threatening, but Scully steered well clear of them all so that they had no close encounters.

The last evening before they set sail from the southern tip of the island for the crossing to the Jumentos, Thomas told Scully he'd been thinking about the guns and that he wanted to learn how to shoot them. They were cooking fish on a barren little cay close to the boat, and Scully felt quite sure they were alone, so he agreed that it was a good idea. He took stock of what little ammo they had. He'd fired three rounds from the AK, so he knew he had 27 more in the single magazine that was the only one he'd been carrying when he got separated from the *Casey Nicole*. The two men who'd attacked Thomas and Mindy had even less between them, and their weapons were in rough condition. But since Thomas was genuinely interested in learning, Scully cleaned them as best he could. The pistol was a 9mm semi-automatic with the name Hi-Point etched on the slide. Scully had never heard of the make but it looked and felt cheap and was certainly no Glock or Colt. The magazine held only 10 rounds, but it was full, as he had killed the owner before he had a chance to use it on his intended victims. The other gun that had fallen into the water when he shot the second man was a lever-action hunting rifle made by Marlin. Unlike the pistol-caliber Winchester that Grant had used so effectively on Cat Island, this one used a rifle cartridge in the .30-.30 caliber. Scully knew it was an old and effective round, but because of the longer cartridges the built-in magazine's capacity was only five rounds. Both of the weapons were rusty due to exposure to salt air. The complete dunking of the Marlin in seawater made it worse than the pistol, but they would both still function, at least for a while. Scully didn't have much use for either of them as long as he had the AK, so he eventually planned to give them both to Thomas and Mindy anyway, especially if he found his friends. There were plenty of weapons and ammo aboard the *Casey Nicole*.

Scully first showed the young couple how to load all three weapons and how the safety mechanisms for each worked. Then he instructed them on how to hold and aim each of the rifles and the pistol. With so little ammunition available, they of course could not learn and practice shooting skills through the use of live fire. He compromised by allowing Thomas one shot with the 9mm pistol and then one round for each of them from the AK.

"That's awesome!" Thomas exclaimed when he saw what the rifle round did to a chunk of driftwood that he was able to hit on his first try. "I wish we had two more of these," he said, handing the AK back to Scully.

"Dat Thirty-thirty hit de same, mon. Just can't waste de shot. Only five, but if you aim true, dat's five bad guy givin' you no mo' problem!"

"Thank you for showing us," Scully. "I hope we'll never need to shoot anybody where we're going. I hope we've seen the last of the bad guys," Mindy said.

Scully said nothing. He would give them the guns when he left them, and that was all he could do. Maybe they would be of help in their survival, or maybe they would not. The guns might even get them killed sooner, but that was out of his hands.

They left early the next day, after Scully worked out a course and planned the passage so they could avoid bashing hard into the wind the whole way. His course took them far to the south in the direction of Cuba, and once they'd reached the latitude of the northern end of the Jumentos, they came about to the starboard tack and sailed that course directly to landfall. This route nearly doubled their total passage distance, but *Intrepida* was close-winded enough to make it possible. After 30 hours at sea, Scully heard the sound of breaking surf in the dark and knew they were near land once again. He sailed away to the north a bit and hove-to until dawn, then they returned to a long line of reefs through which he found a pass a few miles northeast of a tiny cay they could barely see in the distance.

"There's *nothing* here, is there?" Thomas observed as they turned to the southwest to sail in the direction of the deserted cay.

From what he could tell on the chart, Scully figured they were looking at one of the many little cays in the Jumentos that were only a few feet above sea level. There were bigger ones that were more what Larry had in mind when he described them, but even more of these little ones spaced here and there in between. Most, like this first one they'd come to, would have nowhere that a normal-sized cruising boat could anchor, but even so might provide enough protection for them to drop *Intrepida's* hook and get a few hours of rest. After they caught up on their sleep, they would explore more of the island chain, checking all of the possible hideouts where the *Sarah J.* and the *Casey Nicole* might be holed up. Scully was sure they would find them. It had only been a little over a week since he'd been stranded on Cape Sable, so he wasn't really that long overdue and maybe not that far behind the *Casey Nicole*, if Artie and Grant and Jessica had managed to find their way all the way out here. And if they hadn't, Larry would be waiting for them as well, and surely they would find him. Scully knew his friend had to be stressed because of the separation of the two boats. He was the one who'd made the decision to sail with the woman and her daughter on the monohull, so he had to feel that it was his fault. But things were going to be better soon. If Scully found Larry before Artie did, he could tell him what happened and they would at least know where to start looking if the *Casey Nicole* didn't show up soon. But he was confident that wasn't the case. As soon as he and Thomas and Mindy got a little rest, they would set sail again and soon find all of his friends. Scully was sure of it.

CHAPTER 21

ARTIE WAS surprised that his brother would consider splitting up yet again, but when he explained his reasoning, he had to admit it made sense. Larry didn't want to go boldly sailing into the crowded anchorages of the Exumas for two reasons: One, there was no telling what kind of reaction they'd get from the people on the other boats already there. And two, if he were indeed anchored in one of those places, Russell would easily recognize the unusual Wharram catamaran approaching, even from a distance. What he had in mind would be a lot stealthier, but it would take a little more time to implement.

They had dropped the anchor close to a gorgeous deserted beach at a place called Bitter Guana Cay. It was not really an anchorage, especially in bad weather, nor was it deep enough for most cruising boats to approach. But it was a secluded spot to secure the catamaran and allow them to keep a low profile while they worked. And it was still close enough to Staniel Cay to make the next part of the plan feasible.

What Larry had in mind involved Tara's beautiful, handmade wooden sailing dinghy—the same one they used in their unsuccessful attempt to catch up to the *Sarah J.* when they discovered Russell leaving. When Artie reminded him that the sail and other parts of the rig for it were still aboard Tara's yacht, which of course was why they couldn't use them when they tried to catch Russell, Larry said it didn't matter.

"The dinghy already has a built-in centerboard. That's the hardest part to improvise. An oar lashed to the gunwale for steering can replace the rudder, and I'll step the *Casey Nicole's* spinnaker pole for a mast and use the storm jib for a sail. It should sail just fine like that."

"But won't it still be just as risky as sailing into those anchorages in the big boat? What's the point?" Tara asked.

"No. For one, a dinghy won't attract as much attention as a new cruising boat coming into a harbor. People who see it may think it's just someone off another boat that's already there or maybe someone who lives on the island or one of the nearby cays. The main thing is that if Russell is there and sees it approach, he won't recognize it until it's too late, especially since it will be coming in under sail."

"You're going to need someone to go with you then, in case he is there. You know he's armed. It's not worth trying to take him alone," Grant said. "I'll go."

"No, you need to stay here with Artie and help him look out for the *Casey Nicole*. This boat is all we have left until we find the *Sarah J.* All of you need to stay here. There's no room in the dinghy anyway, especially trying to sail it. I'll need to move my weight around for ballast. It'll be better if I go alone. I'll be well armed. Don't worry."

"You're not going without me," Tara said. "It's my dinghy, my boat and my daughter. Everything that matters to me in my life is at stake. *I'm* going!"

Artie didn't see how Larry could argue with that if he insisted on going through with this plan. He hated to see the two of them leave, but he could certainly understand why Tara wouldn't want to stay here on the catamaran when Larry might be so close to finding Rebecca and her parents' boat.

"Look, I'm not talking about taking on this guy from the dinghy. I just want to do some scouting around and see if he's even here. The dinghy can skim over the sandbars and take shortcuts. I can cover a lot of ground and find out if he stopped here or not. If he did, I'll come back immediately and then we'll make a plan to take him out before he knows we're here. Maybe we'll sail up onto him where he's anchored in the middle of the night and take him totally off guard. I don't know yet. All I know is that it's essential to do some scouting first.

"And Tara, it is precisely because it *is* your daughter and your boat at stake that I don't want you to go. I know that if we see him, you're not going to want to wait or to come back for help. *Please!* Just let me do this my way. I won't be gone long, and if am gone longer than a few hours, then you all can do what you like and come look for yourself."

"In that case then, take me," Jessica said. "I'll do whatever you say if we see him. I just don't want to be stuck here waiting. You might need some help, even if you think you don't."

"Don't be ridiculous, Jessica! Why would you get to go instead of me? If you think it's hard for you to sit here waiting, imagine what it's like for me. That's my *daughter* with that lunatic!"

"And like I was trying to say," Larry interrupted, "it's precisely *because* it's your daughter that I'd rather you wait here. It's too emotional for you and there's no way you're going to be able to keep your cool. Especially with me in the same boat with you. We already know how that worked out before."

"It wasn't because *I* was the asshole," Tara glared back at him in disgust.

"We're wasting time arguing about this. I've got to get the rig set up if I'm gonna do this. But you're right. It *is* your dinghy. If you don't want me to take it I won't. And you can come up with your own plan. But that's the best I've got. Now please, let's just work together on this, okay?"

"He's right, Tara," Artie said. "Let's just help him make it happen and we'll find Rebecca. You can count on it." Artie could feel her pain just by looking at her. He knew exactly what she was going through, although he knew it was probably even worse for her than it had been for him. He would do all he could to help her through it. All of them would. But he knew too that if they failed to find her daughter in time there would be little any of them could do for her. He couldn't let himself think about that though. He agreed with Artie that it would be better if she waited on the catamaran with them. He and Casey would help her through the anxiety somehow, and hopefully, Larry would return soon with good news and they could move into action.

Finally, she relented; persuaded by all of them that Larry's plan was the best anyone could come up with. Larry also stressed that anything could happen out there and that her chances of getting Rebecca back were better if she stayed on the boat with the rest of the group. With Scully missing, she was also the most experienced sailor among them after Larry, and would be her daughter's best hope if something happened to him.

Larry set to work and as always, Artie was amazed at his brother's knowledge of all things nautical and his ingenuity when it came to repairing, rigging and sailing boats. With just what he had on board, he converted the 10-foot dinghy to a simple sloop, with a steering oar lashed to the stern quarter, Viking style. Artie knew the boat was already designed to sail, and that the center-board that was already there made the job easier, but still... his brother had put all this together in little over an hour. When he was ready to go, Tara still expressed her doubts.

"Look, it's not like I'm going to be gone long. I'll be back this afternoon. The dinghy should be pretty fast when the breeze picks up later this morning. I can cover a lot of ground and find out quick if he's here or not."

"If you're *not* back this afternoon, I'm not waiting," she said. "If I stay here on the *Casey Nicole,* I want it understood that if you're not aboard, *I* say when and where she sails."

Artie nodded when she looked at him, and so did Casey, Grant and Jessica.

"Fine by me," Larry said. "That's exactly why I want you to wait. You'll be the skipper if I don't come back. But don't get any ideas that's going to happen, because I *will* be back. And way before dark too!"

"What about me?" Jessica asked. "There's no reason for every single one of us to stay here. Let me go with you. Then you'll have another set of eyes to look for him. Please?"

"He said there wasn't enough room," Grant said.

"I don't need a lot of room. I'll stay in the front out of the way when you have to tack. I'm not going to be doing anything but looking for Tara's boat."

"Okay, fine," Larry said. "Fill up a couple of water bottles and I'll grab my binoculars and the shotgun. We need to get going though. The morning's already half over."

Tara didn't try to argue anymore and Artie figured it was because she was satisfied knowing that if Larry and Jessica weren't back soon, she would be able to make the call as to when they would go on without them in the catamaran. Artie was a little surprised that Larry agreed to let Jessica go, but he was also glad his brother wasn't going alone and he figured it would probably do Jessica good to get off the boat for a while. Everyone aboard could sense the tension over the Jessica and Grant situation, and Artie began to get the feeling Jessica didn't want to be around Casey or Grant any more than she had to right now. He didn't know exactly what happened on the beach that night when Grant shoved Russell, but something was said that caused a visible change in Jessica's mood.

They stepped down into the dinghy and Artie held the bow painter while Larry fiddled around making final adjustments to his improvised rigging; then he cast them off. The storm jib for the *Casey Nicole* was cut from heavier material than what would be ideal for a dinghy sail, but the wind had picked up again to better than 10 knots so the little boat moved away at a good clip even with the overweight canvas. Larry and Jessica waved back to them as the breeze carried them north, skirting along the edge of the rocks close to the shore of the desolate island.

"It looks like it's working pretty good," Grant said, as they watched the dinghy sail away.

"Of course it is. Uncle Larry is an expert when it comes to sailboats. But you know that by now."

"I think that once again, he had the right idea. No one is going to pay much attention to a small boat like that, and if Russell is there he'll never make the connection if he sees it sailing instead of being rowed. He's going to find her, Tara. We're going to get Rebecca back and your boat too, I'm sure of it. Russell won't dream that we could have followed him here so soon. He'll be totally off guard for at least another day or two."

"Maybe so," Tara said. "But what if he isn't even here? What if he went somewhere else instead? The guy was crazy. That was obvious from talking to him just the little I did. Somebody like that is capable of doing anything."

"Yeah, but like Larry said, the wind has a lot to do with his choices, and from where he started, he didn't have many. The Exumas were the logical destination," Grant offered.

Tara didn't look convinced. Artie and Casey put their arms around her. They all watched until Larry and Jessica disappeared around the north end of the island and were gone from sight.

"Let's cook something and eat," Artie said. "We have to keep our energy up. When they get back we're probably going to be getting underway immediately."

"Sounds like a plan to me," Casey said. "I'll make some coffee too. We're getting low, but I could use some this morning after staying up all night."

CHAPTER 22

RUSSELL WENT BELOW and made his way forward to the forepeak cabin in which the girl was secured. He untied the multiple half-hitches in the Dacron line he'd passed through the latch, keeping his weight against the outward opening door until he was finished.

"Okay, I'm going to open this door. You can use the head, and you can even come up on deck if you want. But I'm warning you; if you try anything stupid you will wish you hadn't. I don't care if you *are* a girl. I'll knock the crap out of you if you test me. Do you understand what I'm saying? I'm *not* playing games!"

"I understand," the girl answered through the door. "I'm not going to try anything. I've just got to get out of here."

Russell stepped back and opened the door halfway. Rebecca was sitting on the edge of the V-berth, glaring back at him as soon as she saw his face in the darkened cabin. It was natural that she was unhappy with him right now, but he was sure she would get over it and be in a better mood eventually.

"I'll be waiting right out here until you're done in there," he said, indicting the head. "Then, if you want to come up on deck, you can come. If you don't, you can go back to your cabin again. I've got my hands full with sailing this boat and you're going to have to stay where I can see you or stay locked up, your choice."

"I already *told* you, I'm not stupid! I'm not going to do anything! Just let me go to the bathroom and I'll come up on deck."

Russell waited until she came out, then he restarted the engine for another run of perhaps an hour to make some headway before it got too hot again. He had stashed the rifle in one of the cockpit lockers and secured it with the padlock that was on the latch. The key that had been hanging from a hook on the bulkhead over the Nav station was in his pocket now. He didn't expect to need the rifle in a hurry out here, and he sure didn't want her to get her hands on it while he was messing with sails or something, because it was loaded and ready to use. He didn't know what she was capable of, but he knew she was plenty pissed off and it wasn't worth taking a chance.

It was only a couple of hours until dawn now, but he was wired and didn't feel sleepy at all, especially now that she was on deck and he had someone to talk to. He was thrilled that she seemed to be breaking so soon, already making the transition from trying to kick the door down and screaming to sitting there quietly just a few feet away from him in the cockpit. He was happy to give her a little freedom because he figured it would help convince here that they were going to get along just fine and everything was going to work out for the better in the end.

But she wasn't being very talkative. She just sat there on the starboard cockpit seat with her shoulder against the bulkhead, staring out at the dark horizon with a blank expression. She ignored him as he attempted to educate her about solar flares and how he knew that there was more to this event that shut down the grid than a mere natural occurrence. It was somewhat disappointing that he couldn't get her to engage in conversation with him about it, but he figured she would in time. When it was time to shut the engine down again, he told her he needed her help if she wanted to stay on deck. Maybe that would get her involved and serve to break the ice between them.

"You can take the helm and hold our course while I get the sails back up. Steering makes the time pass faster anyway."

"Where are we going?" she asked, seeming barely interested in getting an answer, as if she didn't believe he'd tell her anyway.

"We're going to the same place you guys were planning to go before—to the Jumentos Cays. After I looked at them on the chart, I understood why Larry wanted to go there, and I agree with him. It's a good place to go."

"He's going to find you there, or wherever you go. And he's probably going to kill you when he does."

"Well, I'm sure he would like to, Rebecca, but he'll have to be lucky to do it. You might not realize it, but finding a small boat in the middle of thousands of square miles of ocean and small islands is not as easy as you think. And besides, we're not staying in the Bahamas for long anyway."

"It doesn't matter. He will still find you. He knows every sailboat harbor in the world."

"Yeah, right. Hey, can you just take it and keep the bow into the wind while I go up forward and get the jib up? If you don't want to be confined down below, I need your help."

To Russell's surprise, Rebecca actually complied, taking the helm and holding the bow into the wind as he asked. He took it as another good sign that she would come around to his way of thinking even sooner than he expected and cooperate with the plan. But really, what other choice did she have? She had to know by now that pitching a fit and fighting wasn't going to work.

Russell made his way to the bow pulpit and crouched to untie the straps holding the jib down. As soon as the sails were back up, he'd shut down the engine again and let it cool. The wind had decreased a bit from earlier but it was still strong enough to sail. What was aggravating though was that they were now getting lifted and tossed by large ocean swells that were coming from somewhere far away rather than created by local conditions. The swells made the boat very uncomfortable, especially up on the bow where the motion was greatest. He was crouching low to maintain his balance but as he struggled with the flogging jib the boat suddenly turned hard to port as it was coming off of a wave and he felt his feet go out from under him. He fell backwards into the lifelines and would have tumbled over the top of them if he hadn't already been in a low stance when it happened. Grabbing a stanchion, he pulled himself to his feet and yelled at Rebecca.

"WHAT ARE YOU DOING? I SAID KEEP IT INTO THE WIND!"

"I'M TRYING! THE WAVES ARE MAKING IT HARD!"

Russell wasn't sure if she was telling the truth or if she'd intentionally put the helm over in an attempt to dump him over the side. When he returned to the cockpit he dug through the lockers until he found a couple of inflatable PFDs, the kind that had the CO_2 inflators and the built-in safety harness to prevent just such a man-overboard incident.

"I'm putting one of these on. You should wear one too at all times when you're on deck. Especially at night."

"I'm not wearing one. I'm not planning on going forward. I won't fall overboard as long as I'm holding onto the wheel."

"Maybe not, but you're not going to put me overboard with it either. So if that's what you had in mind, it was a nice try, but it didn't work and it won't."

"I didn't do that on purpose."

"Yeah? Well, I'll bet you wouldn't have turned around to come get me if *had* gone over, would you?"

"Nope. I wouldn't be able to find you anyway, even if I

wanted to. Nobody could find a man overboard out here at night. If you're really a sailor you would know that. So you'd better be careful!"

"I know you wish I would drown or something right now, but you're going to thank me later. You're going to see that I did the right thing."

"The right thing? Stealing my mom's boat and kidnapping me? After all we did for you? We gave you food! And Larry was even going to take you to Florida! But this is the thanks we all got."

"I'm telling you, Rebecca, just like I told Larry. It would be crazy to go to Florida! If Larry had gone back there looking for his friend, he would probably never come back. You would have all been waiting and waiting on Green Cay for him to show up and he never would have. At least this way he's not going to go missing, because they're all going to waste their time looking all over the Exumas for you. It won't do them any good, but at least they'll all be alive and all be together, so there's that."

"Why did you take me? You wanted the boat. You should have let me go before you left."

"Well, for one thing, the only reason they didn't shoot me before I got out range was because you were on board and I'm sure they were afraid of hitting you."

"So I was a *hostage*. I figured that much out. If that's the case, then you don't need me now. You can just drop me off at the first little island we come to and I'll be fine. Take the damned boat. But leave me alone!"

"That would be crazy! You might think you'd rather do

that, but let me tell you from personal experience, you have no idea what it's like to be stranded on one of these little islands with no way off. It's intense! Most people wouldn't have lasted half as long as I did on Green Cay. But I'm a survivor. I'm a good diver and I was able to get fish and shellfish. I built my own shelter and foraged for edible plants. Could you do all that? What do you know about survival? Don't kid yourself. It's not like those reality shows on TV. It sucks, to be honest. I would never dump you off in a place like that and make you suffer that way. I wouldn't do that to anybody, unlike those Canadian assholes that did it to me!"

"Then you can dump me off where there are people. I don't care. Just let me go."

"I'm not *going* anywhere there are other people. Why would I? I've got this boat and everything I need is on board. Besides, what makes you think any other people are going to give a shit about you now, in times like these? Any people we meet are as likely to try and hurt you, or take advantage or you or even kill you as anything else."

"They wouldn't be as bad as you!"

"Oooh, that hurts my feelings, Rebecca! I'm really a nice guy. You just don't know it yet because you don't know me. But you will. You'll see."

Russell kept trying to make Rebecca understand, but she said she was tired and asked to go back to her cabin and sleep. Sleep was the last thing on his mind as he was still so wired and excited after all that had happened and his prospects ahead. He felt refreshed and wide-awake when morning came, despite being up all night. The near miss with the fall had released a surge of adrenalin that contributed to this feeling, and talking to Rebecca was energizing as well as he had been deprived of any conversation for so long while on the island. With her gone back to her bunk, he greeted the dawn alone with his thoughts. He still wore the PFD, and had no desire to take it off, as it was not uncomfortable and it made him feel better wearing it while out there alone. The thought of falling overboard without one really bothered him. Maybe it would only prolong his misery until he died if he did, but at least he felt it would give him a fighting chance. He didn't plan to find out, because it would be such a stupid thing to do, to fall overboard from the yacht he'd just had such good fortune to acquire. Based on his luck prior to the blackout, just such a thing would not be unexpected. But Russell was determined to change his luck now. Setting his course to the horizon aboard this fine vessel at the dawn of a sunny new day was the first step in doing just that.

CHAPTER 23

"YOU WOULD HAVE BEEN SAFER STAYING BEHIND on the boat. You know that don't you?" Larry asked Jessica as they neared Staniel Cay and what appeared to be a forest of aluminum masts that marked the anchorage.

"No, I really don't. Is there any place that's really safe any more? Or is that just wishful thinking?"

"I think some places are probably safer than others. Like where we were going before all this crap with Russell happened. I've got to admit it makes me nervous sailing into an anchorage like this. It doesn't matter whether we're in the dinghy or the catamaran, we're outsiders here. These people have probably been holed up here for weeks and are settled in. There's no telling what they've had to deal with, either. They're not likely to welcome outsiders."

"Well, if that's true it would be the same for that dumb-ass, Russell if he did get here, right?"

"You know as much as I do. All we can do is try to get a good look around. And hope we don't get shot in the process. I just wanted to make sure you know what you're getting yourself into, Jessica."

"I'm not worried as long as I'm with you. You know what you're doing."

"Thanks for your confidence. But since you said you could be my extra set of eyes, why don't you scan the anchorage with the binoculars as we close in on those boats. If you can spot the *Sarah J.* from a distance, it'll be to our advantage."

The anchorage area off the Staniel Cay Yacht Club and everywhere else in the surrounding waters with sufficient depths for anchoring looked about the way Larry expected—full of boaters that appeared to be hunkered down for the duration. Even more so than regular cruising boats, these vessels had the full-time, off the grid live aboard look about them. Most had laundry hanging all over the place in the rigging, and many had more than one dinghy floating in the water beside them, as well as various assortments of kayaks, paddleboards and other small watercraft. Some of these folks might have already been in the islands when the solar flares struck, but Larry figured most were refugees from Florida who'd come here looking for a better place to ride out the aftermath. He was sure every anchorage up and down the Exumas would be much the same.

"I don't see it," Jessica said.

"It's a big area, there will be more boats farther north

around the point. We're going to have to sail all the way through to other side to be sure it's not here."

"There are people watching us from some of the boats. Some of them are using binoculars too. And I see a lot of guns."

"I'm not surprised about that."

"Do you think they're going to shoot at us if we sail in there?"

"I hope not, but I can't make you any promises. All we can do is not get too close to anybody that looks particularly scary. Do you still want to do this?"

"Of course. We've got to find Rebecca. I'm really worried about her being alone with that creep. We've got to find her as soon as possible."

"I agree." Larry glanced at the 12-gauge shotgun on the floorboards of the dinghy. He had thrown a couple of life jackets over it to make it less obvious, but it was close at hand and ready for instant use. He hoped he wouldn't need it, because as they drew closer, he could see they were severely out-gunned. The people on the boats seemed anxious and on edge, and Larry wondered what might have happened here in the weeks since the blackout. One thing was for certain; his hope that they could sail through in the dinghy without attracting a lot of attention was pure fantasy. Someone from almost every boat they could see was watching them. All Larry could do was steer a steady course and remain nonchalant, sailing among them like he belonged there. He didn't think they would draw any fire as long as they didn't act stupid.

He was looking at every boat for a Tartan 37 but saw no sign of the *Sarah J.* If Russell had come this way, maybe he decided to keep going after seeing how full the anchorage was. Larry knew *he* wouldn't stop in a place like this if he were looking for a place to lay low with a 14-year-old girl taken against her will. But despite his initial impression that Russell wasn't here, Larry knew they needed to be thorough and methodical in their search. If they didn't scope out every possible hole big enough to hide the *Sarah J.*, it would be pointless to move on to other islands in the chain. They had to completely rule out Staniel Cay first. When they passed within hailing distance of a bearded man standing on the bow of a steel schooner with an AR-15 in his hands, Larry yelled out to him that they were looking for a vessel named the *Sarah J.*

"Haven't seen it," the man called back. "You're the first stranger that's called here in nearly a week. I'd be careful if I were you! The last two fellows that came in here and tried to steal a boat ended up shark bait."

Larry thanked him for the warning and assured him they were just passing through, looking for their friends on the *Sarah J.*

"I hope we don't look like thieves," Jessica whispered.

"Everybody they see probably does to them. We don't exactly look like Sunday afternoon yacht club racers, you know? At least I don't. I don't imagine anyone's going to complain about your looks."

Jessica smiled. "So, what are we going to do now?"

"Sail on around the north end of the island. I want to

look for that house he described, where he said his friend lived. If he wasn't lying, it shouldn't be hard to find. He said there was a dock with a 21-foot Boston Whaler the guy kept there. If we find that and still don't see Tara's boat, we'll know he probably went elsewhere."

Larry was pretty disappointed because he'd really expected Russell to come here, at least for a short stopover. If the man he'd spoken with was telling the truth, it was almost guaranteed that he hadn't, because he would have been spotted right away. This left Larry at a bit of a loss as to where to look next. Staniel Cay was about in the middle of the Exumas chain, which stretched more than 100 miles north to south. Russell could have still sailed to the Exumas, but there was no way of knowing if he'd made landfall north or south of Staniel Cay. If they guessed wrong they could waste days looking in the wrong direction, giving him even more time to gain distance and disappear for good. Tara was going to flip out when he went back to the *Casey Nicole* and told her they had found nothing. She was going to blame him and she was going to make any decision he wanted to make next even more difficult.

Though they were sailing close enough to shore to clearly see all the waterfront houses, Larry didn't see one near the north end that fit the description Russell gave for his friend's place. Of course he could have been lying completely, or the guy he had said was a friend may have been lying to him. It was all so typical of boat bums like Russell. He may have met the guy in passing one day at the dock in Nassau and then created this elaborate delusion in his mind about him being a good friend who'd invited him to come visit. Who knew the truth? Probably no one and it didn't really matter.

Since he knew there was a cut to the east side of the island at the north end, Larry decided to sail on that way and run back down the other coast on the way back. There was a small chance that Russell could have the *Sarah J.* tucked away somewhere outside of the anchorage, but the main reason Larry chose this route was to avoid passing through the middle of all those boats again. A return trip might invite trouble, and it just wasn't necessary, as the dinghy was sailing well and they had plenty of time to circumnavigate the island and return to where the *Casey Nicole* was anchored by mid-afternoon. Besides, he was enjoying this time away from the others, especially Tara, and he was enjoying Jessica's pleasant company now that she wasn't aboard the same boat as Grant and Casey.

Once they cleared the north end of Staniel and were sailing south again, Larry steered the dinghy far enough from shore to avoid the moderate surf pounding the rocks on that side. There was no place to anchor a big boat here, and as long as they kept away from shore, no one to worry about.

"The water is so gorgeous here," Jessica said.

"It is that. Too bad we couldn't have come here under different circumstances. Thunderball Cave is an awesome place to dive."

"So what do you think? Are we going to go north or go south looking for him after we get back to the boat?"

"I haven't decided yet. When we get back, I'm going to study the charts and analyze the wind and current he would have had since he left Green Cay. Try to get into his mindset and see if I can figure out what I would do if I were him and decided not to do the logical thing and come here."

"Why would he do anything logical? There was nothing logical about that idiot!"

"You've got that right."

"Hey, can we stop for a minute on one of these little islands? I really need to go to the bathroom."

"Sure. It doesn't look like there's anyone around. I'll land on that beach straight ahead."

There were four little cays strung out south of Staniel on the way to Bitter Guana. The largest one had a deep cove near the south end and this was where Larry steered, easing the bow of the dinghy up to the edge of a narrow beach.

"I've got to go too," he said. "I'll meet you back here in a few minutes. Don't wander off too far."

"I won't. I promise."

Larry had brought a small Danforth anchor along in the dinghy and he carried it up onto the sand and set it with just a short length of anchor line out to hold the dinghy to the beach. Jessica picked her way through the coral rocks in the direction of the interior and Larry walked west along the beach to the end of the cove. Thinking they were alone there and not planning to go far from the dinghy, he left the shotgun where it was, still partially hidden by the life jackets piled on top of it. He immediately realized his mistake as two men carrying rifles stepped out of the scrub between him and the dinghy when he had turned to walk back to it.

"Hold it right where you are, mon! Don't make me shoot."

The two men were 15 or 20 yards away; both apparently local islanders, dressed in ragged shorts and T-shirts and carrying old, weather-beaten weapons that looked like bolt-action .22 hunting rifles. One was aiming his from the hip in Larry's general direction, and the other turned to intercept Jessica as she emerged on the scene to make her way back towards the dinghy.

"Hey, we don't have anything you want, and we're not here to make trouble. We were just stopping here for five minutes and passing on." Larry hoped this was all a misunderstanding and that the men were just reacting defensively to strangers.

"Got somet'ing we want, mon—de boat! You don't move, you an' de woman, you don't get hurt. Try to get in de way, you gonna get shot. You got dat, mon?"

Jessica was looking at him now from where she was facing the other gunman. Larry felt like a complete idiot for leaving that shotgun in the dinghy, though he also realized that if he'd brought it he might have gotten shot in the back before he even saw these two. He had no doubt they meant what they said. The one facing him looked to be in his forties, and the other perhaps a decade younger. Both were lean and hard, and had a desperation about them that told him they would stop at nothing to get that dinghy with its sail rig.

"So, you're going to take our boat, mon. And leave us stranded here on this rock with no way off, no water, no nothing..."

"Better stranded den dead, mon. Got a little dinghy on de other side. When we goin' you habin' dat one. But we need de sailboat an' we goin' now."

They directed Jessica over to the end of the beach where Larry was standing and the younger one waded out with the anchor and got in the dinghy while the other backed slowly away from Larry. When the one in the boat shouted with joy, Larry saw that he had found the shotgun and was waving it triumphantly overhead to show his buddy. Larry stood there beside Jessica, her hand in his, watching helplessly as the other one boarded the boat and the two of them sailed away.

CHAPTER 24

REBECCA WAS LYING in her bunk, thinking of her options as the morning turned to afternoon while Russell continued his routine of running the engine for a while, and then shutting it off to sail until it cooled again. She had to get rid of him and somehow take the *Sarah J.* back to her mom and the others before they left Green Cay. She knew that as soon as they could get the catamaran back in the water, they would set out to look for her, but she feared they would look in the wrong places. She had to get there before they left or they might never find her. She didn't know how she would sail the boat and find her way all by herself, but that was a problem she could figure out later. The first thing she had to do was get Russell off the boat, but she wasn't sure how she would do it.

She'd come close when she made the sudden turn and caused him to slip and fall, but the stupid lifelines had kept him from going overboard, and he wasn't going to be that careless again. He didn't know for sure that she'd done it on purpose, but realizing how easy it was to fall overboard had prompted him to put on the PFD harness.

Without making it obvious, Rebecca had looked for the rifle that she knew he had as soon as he let her out of the cabin. When she saw the padlock in place on one of the cockpit locker lids, she knew he'd probably put it in there, and her suspicion was confirmed when she'd checked the hook where her mom kept the key and found it missing. Russell wasn't completely stupid, and if she couldn't get her hands on a gun it was going to be hard to do what she needed to do, especially now that he was clipped into that harness whenever he went forward. It would be so much easier if he simply went over the side without her having to do anything, but now she doubted that was going to happen because it wasn't even stormy weather. She was going to have to make it happen, whenever the time was right, but she had to do it in a way that was one hundred percent certain, because she knew there would be no second chance if she failed.

At least he wasn't afraid to let her come up on deck. That was a start, and she knew the more she gained his trust, the better her chances would become. He was likewise trying to gain her trust, which was why he was giving her a little more freedom. Listening to him talk, she could tell that he actually thought he was doing her a favor by bringing her out here. He thought her mom and Captain Larry and all the others were idiots when they said they didn't believe the blackout was all planned and deliberate.

Like her mom had said after the first night he ate dinner with them, he was a know-it-all who thought he had the answers to everything. And the worst thing about him was that he wouldn't shut up. All he wanted to do was talk and talk and talk.

Maybe that's why he took her with him when he took the boat, just so he would have someone to listen to him while he ran his mouth. But Rebecca was also old enough and smart enough to know there might be a lot more to it than that. So far he hadn't tried anything or even suggested anything inappropriate, but she had no doubt that if she were on the boat alone with him for long enough, that could change. She was not going to wait long enough to be in the position to find out. Rebecca had never thought about killing another person before, even though she'd wanted to end her own life a few times even before that night she'd nearly done it. But now she didn't want to die and she thought she *could* kill if that were the only way for her to live, or the only way to keep this guy from doing what she was afraid he would try. If she could get him off the boat without killing him, that would be best, but if not....

Her thoughts were interrupted when he began yelling her name with great excitement in his voice. It was getting close to sunset, and somehow he was still awake and full of energy, not the least bit sleepy after all this time at the helm. And now he was practically jumping up and down out there as he had apparently found the way to the islands he was aiming for:

"Rebecca! Come see! Land! Look! We made it to land! Come check it out!"

She stuck her head out of the forward hatch, which she could open again now that he'd removed the rope that was holding it down. Ahead in the distance she saw a thin sliver of land that looked much like the little island they had left behind, only smaller. Most of the shoreline appeared white, and she knew that was sand reflecting in the sunlight. There were some larger rocks in the middle and stacked up near one end, but she saw no trees at all, and hardly any vegetation. There was nothing else there, no sign of human activity, no boats in sight—*nothing*.

"We made it!" Russell shouted again. "We've reached the Jumentos!"

Rebecca wondered how he could be so sure of where they are. She only saw one island, not a chain of them, like Larry described. But still, her curiosity led her to go back up to the cockpit and get a better look. When she got there, Russell was staring off to the south of the island through her grandfather's binoculars.

"There!" he said, handing the binoculars to her. "Look right down there, and you can see the next island. There will be more. It's a whole string of them and they lead the way south, like stepping stones to Cuba!"

With the binoculars, she could see the island he was pointing to. It looked a bit bigger than the one they were near, but with the sun so low it was mostly in silhouette and she couldn't make out any details.

"How do you even know which islands these are? Larry said there are hundreds of little islands in the Bahamas."

"There are, but I know these are the Jumentos because they're right where I expected to find them from plotting our course on the charts. What we need to do is sail to the other side of that closest one, and then we can find a place to anchor and get some sleep. Tomorrow, we can explore the chain and find the best place to hang out for a while."

Rebecca was glad they had found land, whether these islands were really the Jumentos or not. The longer they kept sailing, the harder it was going to be for her to find her way back to Green Cay. Russell may have been wired while they were moving, but she knew he had to be tired and that once they stopped, he would probably sleep for a long time. She didn't know if she would have her chance then or not, but the more she thought about it, she figured she would not. He wouldn't go to sleep without tying her up or at least locking her up in her cabin again. He might be stupid, but he couldn't be that stupid. That got her thinking that maybe she shouldn't wait. He was tired now but she had gotten some rest and even napped several times during the long day while she was in her bunk. As they neared the island, the wheels were turning in her mind. It might not happen, but if the right moment came along, this could be her chance because Russell was distracted by the sight of the land and focused on getting through the reefs and shoals to the other side before it got dark.

He had the chart book spread out on the coach roof in

front of the cockpit and asked her to take the helm while he studied it and stared at the shoreline of the little island.

"I'm pretty certain we're here," he said, holding up the chart and pointing. "There's plenty of water on the north side of this cay as long as we stay about a quarter mile off it. I'm going to stand up by the mast where I can see and I'll tell you if you need to make a course correction."

Rebecca was willing to do everything she could to help him avoid hitting any obstacles. It would do her no good if they ran the *Sarah J.* aground, so it was in her best interest to help Russell navigate while they were in dangerous waters with the sun setting soon. He pointed and yelled a half dozen times as he directed her to the areas of bluer-colored water that indicated sufficient depths. He had already retracted the centerboard, so as long as they had a bit more than four and a half feet of water they were good. But as they passed the north end of the island, Rebecca could see vast areas of green water with a white sand bottom, most of it far too shallow even for the *Casey Nicole*, never mind the *Sarah J.*

Once they made through the cut to the southeast side of the cay, Russell came back to the cockpit and took the helm, turning the boat to the southwest to aim for the larger cay they'd seen in the distance that was now visible without the binoculars. The engine had been running again to get them through the pass, but now Russell wanted to shut it down and sail.

"Keep us pointed directly at that other island," he said, giving her back the wheel. "I'm going to kill the engine and get the sails back up. We can sail down there and find a place to anchor. There's no shelter here at all if the wind picks up."

She was steering almost into the setting sun now, the light making it hard to see anything. Russell had the main and jib set and had returned to the cockpit, where he stood on the edge of the deck looking at the first little island sliding by a quarter of a mile to the north. The wind was still out of the southeast, so the boat was on the port tack and heeled over in the direction of the island, putting Russell on the low side of the boat, his back to her as she steered. Rebecca didn't know if it was the best chance she would get or not, but there might not be another before he forced her back to her cabin and locked her up. She didn't ever want that to happen again, even if he probably would let her out again in the morning unharmed. There was a metal winch handle in it's holder within easy reach, and Russell was too busy studying the island to notice when she leaned over to grab it with one hand. He had one hand on the bimini frame beside him, but his grip was relaxed and where he stood, the lifelines were touching his legs at about mid-thigh level. If she did this right, they wouldn't stop him from going overboard.

Rebecca switched the winch handle to her stronger right hand and stepped up onto the cockpit seat, directly behind Russell. She swung the makeshift club with all her might, hitting him in the back of the head before he was aware she'd left the helm. The result was not what she'd expected. Instead of going right over the side into the water,

Russell buckled a bit at the knees and reached up with his free hand to feel his head. As he did so, he turned to face her and she knew she had to act fast. She brought the winch handle back the other way in a backhand sweep that caught him in the side of the head this time, and before he could react she shoved him hard in the chest, sending him backwards over the lifelines.

The sails began flogging as the boat headed up into he wind with its helm unattended. Rebecca looked over the side first to make sure Russell wasn't hanging on, then grabbed the wheel and fought to bring the boat back under control. She looked over her shoulder as it slowly moved away, and saw Russell's head bobbing in the wake. The CO_2 inflator had activated upon immersion, just like it was supposed to, and the PFD was keeping his head clear of the water as he drifted. But he still appeared to be unconscious or maybe even dead. If not for the PFD, she knew he likely would drown if he wasn't dead, but with it, the wind and waves might eventually carry him to the shore of the little island.

Rebecca kept glancing back over her shoulder as she steered on the same course Russell had set to the other, larger island. She was shaking with adrenaline as she realized what she'd done. She was free of the man who had taken her captive, and she had her mom's boat back! But it was going to be dark soon and she knew she had to stop somewhere for the night before she turned to sail back to Green Cay. She could not imagine navigating all night out here by herself. She needed more sleep first and she needed daylight to see where she was going. The other island Russell had wanted to go to seemed like a reasonable option. If there was indeed a place to anchor, she would do so, and in the morning she could start back to the northeast and try to find Green Cay.

CHAPTER 25

"THIS IS GETTING RIDICULOUS!" Tara said, as she paced the deck with yet another cup of coffee, her eyes scanning the horizon to the north for any sign of Larry and Jessica.

"It's still three hours until sunset," Artie said. "I'll bet they'll show up any minute now. It probably took longer than Larry expected to check the whole island."

"He would have been back to get us by now if the boat was there. He hasn't found it. That's why he's still out there. He's looking in the wrong place and all this time that man is heading somewhere else, getting farther and farther away with my child! I knew I shouldn't have listened to him! Every time I have it's been a mistake!"

"I understand how you're feeling, Tara. I really do. Believe me. When all this first happened all I could think about was finding Casey. I know she's older than Rebecca, but she's my only child too. And I never would have found her without Larry's help. You've got to have faith in him. He knows what he's doing."

"I don't have to have faith in anything!" Tara said. "After all this, how could you expect me to? All I can say is they better get back soon. I'm not sitting here waiting and waiting while Rebecca is being taken God knows where by that lunatic!"

Artie hoped it didn't come to an argument with Tara over when they would leave, because he wasn't planning on going anywhere without Jessica and his brother. He didn't expect it to go that far though because he had plenty of faith in Larry whether Tara did or not. Larry would be back with Jessica soon. He knew it. And a shout from Casey confirmed it.

"There they are!"

"Well, we will know soon enough what they found then," he said to Tara, as they all turned to see the tiny sail in the distance, slowly coming into focus as it approached.

"What are they doing now?" Grant asked, as the boat suddenly veered more to the west, angling away from the coast of the island instead of coming directly at them.

"Maybe just adjusting their course to take advantage of the wind?" Casey speculated.

Artie watched the dinghy with the others as it continued on this new course. It was still too far away to see Larry and Jessica clearly, but he waved at them anyway. For some reason they continued on the new course, as if they intended to give the catamaran a wide berth rather than sail directly to it. As the dinghy continued on, it passed within a quarter mile of the *Casey Nicole*, and when the two figures seated in it were no longer in the shadow of the sail, they could see that they were not Larry and Jessica.

"Someone has taken the dinghy!" Casey said.

Artie wished he had the binoculars Larry had taken with him, but even without them, he could see well enough to tell that the two occupants of the dinghy were men—both of them black men and likely Bahamian islanders. *But why? Why were these two strangers sailing the dinghy instead of Larry and Jessica?* Artie felt knots of fear in his stomach as he realized why the dinghy had veered away. Obviously, the two men who had taken it were not expecting to see the catamaran anchored there, and had changed course to avoid passing near it. Artie knew Larry would never give up that dinghy without a fight. If these men had managed to take it, what had they done to Larry and Jessica and where were they? There was only one way to find out.

"We've got to catch them!" he said.

"I'll get the anchor up! Can you give me a hand, Casey?" Grant was already moving forward to the front trampoline.

"There's no time!" Artie shouted, as he reached into the galley for a knife. I'll just cut the rode. You and Casey get the main up! Tara, you take the helm! We can catch them if we get going now!"

Artie didn't hesitate to slice the nylon rode attached to the *Casey Nicole's* best anchor. It would have taken an extra 10 or 15 minutes to haul it in by hand and that was

10 or 15 minutes they didn't have. As soon as Grant and Casey had the main set, Artie set to work on the jib halyard. Tara brought the helm over to fill the main and the catamaran was moving. When Artie glanced out at the dinghy, he saw that the two men had reacted to the sight of the sails going up and had turned to the northwest, running before the wind away from them as fast as they could go.

"Let's get the foresail and staysail up too. We need to put on everything we've got!"

The catamaran was moving well and would pick up speed fast, but the dinghy had a good head start and it was out in better wind, far from the lee of the island where the *Casey Nicole* had been anchored. With that breeze, the little boat was still gaining on them, but Artie figured that would change once they got the catamaran a little farther out.

"They're heading straight for a line of shoals!" Grant yelled from where he was perched by the shrouds on the port side cabin top. "Check the charts! I'm not sure we can get over them! I can't tell if it's just sandbars or reefs!"

Artie scrambled for the chart book in a panic as he told Tara to just stay on course until he said otherwise. He had not paid close attention to what was in their immediate vicinity since Larry had prior knowledge of these waters and it had been his decision to anchor where they did. Thankfully, Larry didn't take the chart book with him, but it took Artie several minutes to find the right page and then pinpoint their approximate location.

"They're going on across! Maybe it's deep enough!" Grant shouted from the cabin top.

When he finally found the shoal area Grant had to be seeing, he saw that it was a large area of sandbars and shallow reefs, stretching almost all the way between Staniel Cay and several small low cays not far away to the west. Although much of the area showed three or four feet, there were hazards less than two feet deep in spots. Larry had said the dinghy drew even more than the catamaran with the centerboard down, but as the two men in it were running almost straight downwind, they didn't necessarily need the centerboard. If it was raised, the little boat could skim along in mere inches of water. Artie didn't know what else to do but take a chance. They needed to catch those guys to find out what happened to Larry and Jessica.

Tara was saying nothing, just steering with her focus on the dinghy. Artie didn't know how she felt now, but he figured it couldn't be good. He stood there beside her, a rifle in his hand for when they closed the gap to effective range.

"Shoals coming up!" Grant yelled. "Cut it to port a bit!"

Artie held his breath as they sliced into an area of clear white sand, the water over it so clear it was almost as if it wasn't there. The next thing he knew he was flying forward across the cockpit until he landed at the base of the foremast, a sharp pain in his upper right arm where it had struck something solid. The boat had plowed into the sand and come to a sudden stop. Only Tara had managed to keep her feet, hanging on to the wheel through it all. When

Artie scanned the decks around him he saw that Grant and Casey were still on board, but were sprawled on the forward deck of the port hull.

"Are you okay?" he asked, directing his question at both of them.

"I think so," Casey said.

"Damn! I didn't see that in time," Grant said.

"I didn't hear anything break. It must have been just sand."

"It is," Tara said. Artie saw her step up onto the cockpit seat, looking around the boat on boat sides. "It looks like we ran smack onto a big sandbar."

Grant and Casey were on their feet and Grant was standing up on the highest part of the cabin top again.

"They're getting away! It looks like they're headed to one of those little islands out there."

"We'll never catch them now," Artie said. "We're hard aground."

"We've got to get it off," Casey said. "We've got to go look for Larry and Jessica."

"Maybe I can get an anchor out off the stern and we can pull it back to deep water the way we came."

"Maybe. But now we're missing our best anchor too. I wish I hadn't cut the rode now."

"It doesn't matter," Grant said. "We've still got three more and plenty of line."

"The tide is about its lowest right now," Tara said. "Just our luck. We could have gotten over it at high tide, I'll bet."

"Well, since we didn't, we're in luck that it *is* low. At

least we know we've got more water coming in if we can't get off now."

"I don't know how you can call it lucky. There's nothing lucky about any of this. Now we still don't know if Rebecca and my boat is at Staniel Cay or not, and even if they were when Larry and Jessica got there, they may not be now."

"I didn't mean it like that. I just meant lucky with the state of the tide. Believe me, I don't think there's anything 'lucky' about this. My brother and Jessica could be dead, for all we know."

"Don't say that!" Casey said. "I don't want to think about losing Uncle Larry—or Jessica! Maybe they're okay. They're probably on Staniel Cay now, and needing a ride. As soon as we get the boat off, we can go find them."

"I know, Casey. I'm just worried, that's all. I can't imagine how anyone could have taken the boat from them. I wouldn't have expected Larry to go ashore. But then again, maybe he found that house Russell was talking about. Maybe that's how it got stolen."

Grant jumped over the side and asked them to pass him the large Danforth and its chain and nylon rode he'd pulled out of one of the anchor lockers. The water was nearly waist deep off the stern, but the bows were firmly buried in the sand where it was well under two feet deep.

"You need to get it well off the stern in deep water so we can pull it straight back," Artie said. "Larry told me about a trick to do that without a dinghy. Said he'd done it often."

Artie went to one of the storage lockers and fetched two of their empty 5-gallon water containers. They were the rigid plastic kind so he didn't see why they wouldn't work well for the purpose. He tied them together at the handles with a short piece of line and handed them to Grant.

"Put the anchor between them and use them to float it out there when it gets too deep to wade. That way you can swim it out all the way to the end of the rode.

Grant agreed that it was a great idea and soon he had the anchor as far from the boat as possible. Watching him swim back with the water jugs, Artie felt another wave of dread and horror sweep over him as he thought of his brother. What would they do if something terrible had happened to Larry and Jessica? Rebecca was already missing and that was devastating enough. Now they had no idea where Larry and Jessica were, and they were stuck. And when Grant was back aboard, he and Artie both cranked on the big winch for all they were worth, while Casey and Tara tried to help by pushing on the bows. But nothing worked. They were going nowhere until the tide returned.

CHAPTER 26

RUSSELL CAME to when he felt the painful sensation of his legs dragging across something sharp. He spat out a mouthful of seawater as a cresting wave broke over his head, smashing him against the jagged rocks beneath the surface. Realizing it was going to happen again if he didn't move fast, he turned all the way around to get his bearings and saw the sand of a beach less than a hundred yards away, on the other side of the breaking surf that was pounding him.

The inflated PFD was keeping his head above the surface but the water was too shallow to avoid the coral and rock hidden under the waves. He cried out in pain as another wave swept him over the reef, and then he was in the clear, floating in four or five feet of calm water on the inside. He could see blood in the water around his legs and feet, and he knew he had been badly cut and gouged on the rocks. His arms and hands were okay though, so he swam to the beach and crawled out onto the sand, thankful to get out of the water before the sharks found the source of the blood.

His legs and feet were sliced and scraped from the knees down, as well as a nasty scrape on the back of his right thigh. He'd been wearing only shorts and a T-shirt and the inflatable PFD. Russell also felt a throbbing pain from the side of his skull and when he reached up to touch it, discovered he was bleeding there too. It was from the winch handle. He remembered seeing it after feeling the first blow to the back of his head and turning in surprise to see the girl attacking him. He'd been so stunned and surprised by her first strike that he couldn't react fast enough when he realized what she had in her hand. Now he remembered seeing it coming, but he didn't remember the impact or how he got in the water, but obviously he had fallen overboard. The automatic PFD had inflated, saving him from drowning while he was unconscious, and the wind and waves had carried him to the island they were passing when it happened.

It hurt like hell, but Russell struggled to his feet to try and see. Where was the little bitch now? Had she already sailed over the horizon, out of sight forever? He was sure that she had, but oh, if he could only get his hands on her now! There would be no more Mr. Nice Guy trying to be her friend. He would straighten her out and he would do it quick. He looked out to sea due south where they had been sailing when it happened and saw nothing. Turning slowly, and almost falling in the process, he scanned the horizon to the southwest and then west, in the direction of the next island in the chain he remembered seeing from the boat. And there it was—*a sail!* It had to be her. He squinted and stared until he was certain it was. The triangle of sail was about right and after looking several minutes; he thought he could tell he was looking at the hull from astern. It was pretty far away, too far to see any details, and he was sure it would only get farther with those sails up and the wind still steady. It looked like she had kept the boat on the same course he'd been sailing, aiming for that next island, probably with the intention of anchoring for the night.

And night was coming soon. The sun had set and now the biting sand fleas called "no-see-ums" were out in force, attacking Russell's exposed skin and his wounds and swarming his face, ears and neck. He slapped them in the places where he wasn't cut or bruised, but without clothes or a way to make a smoky fire, he had little defense until they went away after full darkness arrived.

Taking stock of his surroundings, Russell didn't even have to move to ascertain that he was in a far worse predicament here than he was the entire month he was marooned on Green Cay. The little cay was *tiny!* And there was *nothing* on it—no trees—and barely any bushes and plants of any kind. He was certain that he would find no abandoned cistern here as he did on Green Cay; because it was highly improbable that this cay had ever been inhabited. There was little reason for anyone to even set foot on it, especially since it was not big enough to even create a lee in which a cruising boat could anchor. And to make matters worse, Russell already knew it was absolutely in the middle of nowhere—even farther off the beaten path than Green Cay. He was surely and truly fucked this time, stranded here with no water, nothing to eat, little clothing and no tools, not even a knife, much less a fishing spear. And to make matters worse, he was bleeding all over the sand and wracked with pain from his bruises and lacerations.

How could he have been so stupid? Why did he let the girl out of the cabin in the first place? He had been a fool to trust her so soon. He should have left her locked up until he reached a secure anchorage where he could deal with her while not occupied with navigating and sailing the boat. It was a stupid mistake on his part, one that had nearly cost him his life and might anyway if he didn't figure out a way off this miserable speck of sand and rock.

He made his way to the highest part of the island were there were some large, exposed limestone rocks several feet tall and found a place to sit down with his back supported. He had removed the PFD and deflated it. It might be useful for something, but he had no idea what. Nevertheless, it was now the only thing he owned other than his T-shirt and shorts. How quickly his fortunes had changed again! He'd had everything he could hope for considering the circumstances: a fine sailing yacht, a rifle and ammunition, and still weeks of food for him and the girl, not to mention a few bottles of cheap liquor. All of that in the palm of his hand, and now *nothing!* It wasn't fair! Life had never been fair to Russell. All his life, it seemed his dreams had been just out of reach. Every time he'd thought he was closing in on making one of them come true, something happened to derail him yet again. It was the story of his life. The story of a loser. Maybe he'd be better off dead anyway. At this point, did it even matter?

Russell was so exhausted from staying awake for the entire passage from Green Cay that he slept despite the pain of his wounds. None of the cuts and scrapes seemed deep enough to be life threatening, and though they bled a lot and hurt like hell, no major veins or arteries were cut. The no-see-ums disappeared after dark and only returned for the first hour of early morning light, before the sun was high enough to warm the rocks and sand of the little cay.

Russell's head was throbbing and the knot from the winch handle still hurt to touch, but worse than the pain was the thirst he felt upon waking. He hadn't swallowed any that he knew of, but seawater had gotten into his mouth and nose when he was in the water and the salt only aggravated his thirst. Looking hopefully at the sky for signs of rain, Russell was disappointed to see only clear blue overhead. If it didn't rain, he would die in another day or two.

Grabbing the rock behind him to assist, he managed to get to his feet and stand to look around. When he did, the first thing he saw was the triangle of sail he'd last seen before dark the evening before. Now the sun was behind him instead of behind the boat, and he could see the white of the hull as well as the sail. He had no doubt it was the *Sarah J.*, and it was heeled over with the sail full of wind in the exact spot he'd last seen it nearly 12 hours before. *What the heck? How could that be possible?* The boat should have long been out of sight or else if the girl anchored it, sitting upright with the mast bare. But there it was, apparently still under full sail and going nowhere. Russell wondered if he could be hallucinating, and figured that probably had to be it. He had been hit in the head, had nothing to drink since yesterday afternoon, and had lost a fair amount of blood. But when he deliberately looked away, rubbing his eyes and focusing on other objects both near and far, the boat was still there in the same exact spot when he turned back to look for it. He stared and mumbled to himself, and then it hit him all at once. The boat was aground! That had to be it. The stupid little girl had knocked him overboard, but then she'd run into a reef or a shoal before she reached the next island. If he had binoculars, he might be able to tell for sure, but he was quite certain that was what happened. There were shallow hazards all around this chain of islands from what he'd seen of the charts, and that was likely why they were still so pristine and seldom visited.

It almost made him want to laugh, thinking about Rebecca in her new predicament after what she'd done to him. It served her right, that was for sure, but the only thing that wasn't funny about it was that even though he could see the boat stuck out there, it was still completely out of reach. He figured it was probably two miles or so from his little cay, and even if he were uninjured and had food and water and a mask, snorkel and fins, it would be a long and hazardous swim. With his legs cut up the way they were, it was out of the question. It was painful to even stand there.

Even if he could make it, if she saw him approach it might be difficult to board the boat. He still had the padlock key in his pocket, so she couldn't get to the rifle, but she could throw things at him or hit him with something else as he tried to climb aboard in his weakened condition.

But he couldn't just sit here and die of thirst with the boat and all the stuff aboard it in plain sight. He had to figure out a way to stay alive long enough to get out there. There was one thing Russell could be pretty sure of. If that Tartan 37 was really hard aground, there was no way a skinny 14-year-old girl was going to get it off by herself. She would be there until she either ran out of food and water herself, or some other boat came to either help her or help themselves to everything aboard.

He knew it was a long shot getting there, but seeing that boat stuck out there like a carrot on the end of a stick gave him new motivation to live. It would truly suck to sit here and die with so much, so close. He limped around the perimeter of the little island as best he could, scanning the high tideline just as he'd done every day on Green Cay, looking for something—*anything*—that might help him survive. When he found nothing but a few discarded plastic bottles and fishing floats, he began scouring the rocks of the interior. It was there that he found another ray of hope that he might just hang on. In the middle of a particularly large slab of pockmarked limestone rock partially covered by the sand, there were several shallow potholes eroded away over time. Some of the holes contained a little dirty-looking water at the bottom, and when he first saw them, Russell wasn't sure whether the water was left by rain or a particularly large wave that had swept the rock. But when he knelt down and scooped a handful to his lips to taste, it was sweet and fresh. He would not die today.

CHAPTER 27

"I'M SORRY, Jessica. Please excuse my language, but I just had to vent." Larry had remained pretty calm as he stood there holding her hand until the two men were gone in the dinghy, then he had turned away, kicking at the sand and cussing the two thieves and his own stupidity for letting his guard down. He didn't mean to put on such a show of rage in front of Jessica, but he was really pissed.

"I understand, Larry. Don't apologize." She gave him a reassuring hug as his breathing began to return to normal. "I understand exactly how you feel. I can't believe we just got robbed liked that."

"Yeah and marooned at the same time. I don't know which is worse. But at least they didn't kill us. There's that. They could have just as easily shot us in the head and no one would ever know."

"I guess they really just wanted the dinghy."

"No doubt. And I can understand that. They were

probably fishermen before the collapse and probably wouldn't have considered the idea of stealing someone else's boat. But life has gotten hard. You do what you gotta do to survive and eat. And here in the islands, it's hard to do either without a boat."

"And now we don't have one."

"Yeah, that's what set me off."

"The one man said something about a little dinghy on the other side of the island. Do you think he was just lying to keep you from trying something?"

"I'm sure he was. But it won't hurt to look. What else have we got to do? I sure don't want to have to swim to Bitter Guana Cay. Do you?"

Larry was beating himself up inside even if he had outwardly calmed down and stopped his cussing. He wondered after all this time and all they had been through how he could have still done something so stupid. This could have been completely prevented by taking the simple precaution of carrying the shotgun with him when they stepped ashore. He doubted he would have had to shoot the two men, because they probably wouldn't have even shown themselves when they saw that he was armed. Instead, like a dumbass, he'd left the shotgun in the boat and lost everything as a result. And he knew they were truly lucky that these men were probably just honest fishermen driven to desperation. If they had even a streak of the bad in them that so many they'd encountered did, there's no telling what they would have done, especially to Jessica. But they had what they wanted and now they were gone, sailing off to the south in the same direction Larry and Jessica needed to go to return to the *Casey Nicole*.

On top of the inconvenience of losing their ride back to the catamaran, there was the real possibility that it wouldn't be there much longer if they didn't find a way to get back in a hurry. Larry had given Tara permission to take charge in his absence if he didn't get back in a reasonable time, and now, considering the predicament he and Jessica were in here, he didn't see how they could. The island they were on was closer to Staniel Cay than it was to Bitter Guana, It would be possible to swim to Staniel, but then what? Hope that someone in the anchorage would be kind enough to give them a ride? But when they made their way through the rocks and bushes to the west side of the little island, Larry saw they might not have to try that after all.

"There *is* a dinghy!" Jessica said.

There was something there that might pass as a dinghy, but it certainly wasn't in the league of Tara's father's hand-crafted wooden beauty. Larry picked his way down to where it was pulled up on the sand and turned upside down, glancing at the hull bottom before stooping to flip it upright again. It was an ancient and battered fiberglass hull, built of the cheapest construction using chopped fiberglass sprayed into a mold. It was heavy and poorly shaped and designed, barely over six feet long and nearly four feet wide. A big chunk of fiberglass had been broken off the starboard sheer near the bow, but there were two rusty oarlocks still in place and in the bushes nearby, Jessica found a pair of oars.

"What an utter piece of crap!" Larry spat. When he saw the oars, he just rolled his eyes. They were the clunky, plastic-coated aluminum kind with stubby, plastic blades more suited use with a pool toy than a real tender. And they were only six feet long. No wonder those two men wanted their dinghy bad enough to steal it at gunpoint. Being stuck with this sorry excuse for a boat was a punishment worthy of purgatory. But, Larry had to admit that it probably *did* beat swimming. Maybe.

"Do you think it will float?" Jessica asked.

"Oh I'm sure it will. That's about all it will do, but it will do that. The question is whether or not we can get anywhere in it. Especially with those pathetic toy oars."

"I'll leave it up to you to be the captain!" Jessica said.

"Thanks a lot!"

Larry had no time to waste complaining though. It was going to take some time to row this tub to Bitter Guana Cay, and if they were going to make it, they had to get started now. With Jessica's help, he dragged it to the water and held it steady while she got in. The tiny boat was barely big enough for two adults. It was the most minimalistic dinghy imaginable designed to ferry a crew of two smaller than average adults from their boat to shore in the calmest of harbors. Larry seldom saw dinghies like this anymore, but he knew they were more common back in the 60's and 70's when young, adventurous couples with little money were sailing to the islands in much smaller cruising boats than those typically seen today. This type of dinghy was the biggest size that would fit on the decks of boats like that. It would do the job for which it was intended, but it would do it so much better with a real pair of oars of the proper length. As it was, they would have to make do. And he was glad that Jessica was a young, slim and agile female. It certainly would not have worked with another man his size as crew.

As it was, they were scrunched into the short boat facing each other, the seat so close their knees were touching and Larry feeling as if he were invading her personal space each time he bent forward to set the oars for another stroke. Jessica didn't seem to mind though; she just smiled and tried to stay out of the way, impossible though that might be.

There were two more small cays between the island they'd been stranded on and Bitter Guana Cay. Larry aimed for the first one, to break up the crossing and minimize their exposure in the unseaworthy little boat. It seemed much more reasonable to make the short hops between each cay than to contemplate more than a mile of rowing the thing in choppy seas. Even the short hops were risky, and the boat took on a lot of water from bashing into the waves. They had no life jackets, or anything with which to bail, so when they reached the first stopover, Larry aimed for the beach and they pulled the dinghy up and dumped out the excess water.

"I told you it might be an adventure, didn't I? You're probably wishing you had stayed on the boat now, huh?"

"Not for a minute. I think I'm starting to like adventure and just sitting there waiting would be boring. You'd probably rather me not be in your way though. Not to mention having the extra weight slowing you down."

"It's not *you* slowing me down, believe me. This thing isn't exactly a racing shell. But hey, don't think I don't want you tagging along. I just meant I hate you're having to endure this. And that it could have gotten you killed back there."

"Maybe I'm the reason they didn't do anything to you. Seeing you have a woman to take care of and all. They probably thought I was your wife."

"Or daughter," Larry said.

"No way! You don't *even* look old enough to be my dad. You don't look a day over 30, beard or not."

"Thanks, but you know I am."

"Does it matter? It doesn't to me. Anyway... that's probably what they thought. I don't think they thought I was your daughter."

"Maybe not. It doesn't matter anyway. What counts is that we're still alive. We'd better get going though. Tara is going to be chomping at the bit to go look for the *Sarah J.* herself. She's convinced I'm totally incompetent, and when I come back with this piece of junk instead of her dad's fine sailing dinghy, she's going to have her proof. I hope you're prepared for the show."

"Don't worry about her. I've got your back. I know you want to impress her and all, but she's got to understand this isn't a game."

"I don't care about impressing her. Not after our trip

across the Gulf. I'm ready to find her boat so I can skipper the *Casey Nicole* again and let her have it."

Jessica expressed her doubts about this and Larry detected a hint of jealousy in her tone. He didn't quite know what to make of this. Was Jessica just insecure around other attractive women because she was used to getting all the attention, or was it something more? Was she really interested in him? Or was she just interested in using him to make Grant jealous? Larry didn't know, but he knew he didn't mind their close proximity in the dinghy, and their pleasant conversation. Tara was more than a handful and Rebecca was her priority. Jessica, on the other hand, was unattached. If Grant didn't take the opportunity he was given during all that time they were together on the passage from Cat Island, then he clearly was more interested in Casey. Maybe Jessica had come to that conclusion herself by now. Larry rowed on, the two of them having to work together to stay in sync so that he didn't push her backward over the stern with every stroke. By the time they got to the next cay, they were laughing about the absurdity of it. But the boat was getting them there. After another stop to empty it, they pressed on and soon stepped ashore on the north end of Bitter Guana Cay.

"I think it'll be easier to hike the rest of the way to the anchorage than to row. It'll be faster and we need to hurry before they decide to leave."

"Won't we need the dinghy later, since we don't have one?"

"Maybe. But I hate to even put this thing aboard the

Casey Nicole. One thing about the catamaran is that we can always beach it or anchor in waist-deep water if we need to get ashore. I'll decide after we get there. We can always sail around here and pick it up. But we need to go now."

Bitter Guana Cay was rugged and difficult to hike. Where it was not rocky, it was choked with dense bushes, many of them thorn-bearing. The going seemed easier along the rocky cliffs of the east side, where they were able to pick their way along the precipice overlooking the pounding surf below. It was slow going and it was already late afternoon, but Larry was pretty sure his brother could keep Tara calm at least until dark. But when they finally found a path to the crest of the island overlooking the spot where he'd anchored earlier, the *Casey Nicole* was gone! Larry couldn't believe it. Why in the hell was Tara that impatient? Anyone would know that a trip like the one he and Jessica undertook in a small boat could be slightly delayed. He could understand it if they had not gotten here until the next day—but this? It wasn't even fully dark yet! Even though he gave Tara permission to take the *Casey Nicole* if he didn't return, Artie and Casey and Grant should have been able to prevail upon her to wait just a little longer. They couldn't effectively search for anything in the dark anyway, doing so would only put them at risk. It made no sense at all, and Larry was utterly disgusted as he tried to figure it out.

"Wow, we're really stuck, huh Larry? Unless they come back."

"Why would they? They wouldn't have left in the first

place if they were planning to come back." Larry looked at her and wondered how yet again so much could go wrong so fast. He'd lost the dinghy, and now he'd lost his whole damned boat! He had nothing but the clothes on his back. Well that wasn't exactly all. He had the company of a gorgeous young woman who was quite content to be here with him, regardless of the circumstance. It might have been a dream to be stranded with her this way some other time but now, in addition to trying to save his own sorry ass, he was responsible for her as well, and she deserved better than this.

CHAPTER 28

REBECCA WAS nervous as she steered the *Sarah J.* into the setting sun. She could see the low silhouette of the other cay out there far ahead of her, but in the blinding light she could see little else. It was impossible to see the color of the water ahead of the boat, so she had no way to judge the depths. The chart did her little good other than to remind her by the numbers printed on it that dangerously shallow water was all around her. She was simply steering on faith, hoping to find a place close to the other island to anchor so she could sleep until morning.

For a long time, she had been able to see the bright red of Russell's PFD bobbing in the waves behind her. It had grown smaller in the wake until it finally disappeared from sight. It looked like he was drifting closer to the island they'd been passing when she hit him, but she couldn't be sure. She kind of hoped he would make it there, if he weren't already dead from the blow to the head. She didn't really want to kill him. She couldn't imagine taking a life, other than her own back when she still wanted to do that. But she had to get him off the boat, and once the decision was made and she saw her opportunity, doing it was easier than she'd expected. If he made it to the island alive, maybe someone would find him. But she couldn't worry about it any more. She had enough to worry about trying to skipper this 37-foot boat all by herself. Rebecca had never been all that interested in sailing, even though she'd enjoyed going out on the *Sarah J.* in the summer with her grandparents, sailing along the Gulf Coast. She'd picked up a few things about the boat through simple osmosis, and had learned much more from Captain Larry in recent days, but she was in no way qualified for what she had to do now. She worried about how she was going to get the sails down and then back up again after she stopped. She worried even more about hauling the anchor. She had worked the windlass a few times, but had never completely weighed anchor by herself, manually cranking in more than a hundred feet of heavy chain. Then there was the bigger issue of navigation. She had to find her way all the way back to Green Cay—a tiny island in the middle of nowhere. Even Artie and Grant and Jessica had screwed up on their navigation, nearly wrecking the *Casey Nicole,* and they all knew more about it than she did. How was she going to get it right her first time with far less experience and knowledge?

All this was on her mind as she watched the sun touch the water on the horizon in front of her bow. And it was at about that same moment that suddenly none of it mattered, because her voyage came to an end before it really began. At first she didn't realize what was happening. The boat suddenly slowed and felt heavy and sluggish. The feeling seemed to go away for a moment, as if whatever was holding it back had let go. But then she felt it again, a sudden deceleration as if someone had put on the brakes in a car. But sailboats have no brakes and the sudden slowing didn't make any sense. The boat seemed to inch along for a few more seconds, before coming to a complete stop. Rebecca was baffled. She turned the helm back and forth, but it made no difference. The wind was the same as before, and the sails bellied out and full. But the boat was no longer moving at all. Rebecca let go of the wheel and looked over the side. The light was fading fast, but she could clearly see the problem. The water around her looked shallow enough for wading. It was clear and green, and beneath it she could see an endless expanse of wave-rippled white sand. She knew then she had run the boat aground, apparently right onto a sandy bank. But there had been no sound of hitting anything solid, and no crunch of breaking fiberglass or other destruction. The boat was simply stuck and stopped dead.

She looked over the other side and it was the same there too. When she made her way to the bow, she saw that the water was shallower in front of the boat than beside it. In fact it looked like it was only inches deep farther ahead. She had run smack into a huge sandbar, and there was no way the *Sarah J.* could have floated over it or missed it on the course she was sailing. The only way Rebecca could see to get off was to go back the way she came, but how? The boat was already stuck, and it was not budging. It was still leaning way over just the same as it had been when under sail. She didn't know if the full sails would make it worse or not, but she was afraid to try and take them down with so much wind, because she knew you were supposed to head into the wind to do that, to make it easier. All she could think of to try that might help was to start the engine and see if the boat would go backwards under power.

She knew how to start the diesel. That was one of the things her grandpa had shown her that stuck over time. But she also knew that Captain Larry said it didn't need to be running until he fixed it. He said it would burn it up to use it, but Russell had done it anyway and nothing bad had happened so far. She decided it would be okay to try it and see if she could go backwards with it. If it worked, she would turn it off again and use the sails.

It cranked like it was supposed to when she turned the key and pushed the button. She went back up the cockpit to the engine controls beside the helm and moved the shifter lever to reverse, and then she revved it up slowly to see what would happen. She could feel a lot of vibration through the hull and she could see that the prop was turning strong by all the silt it stirred up in the clear water. But nothing else was happening. The boat wasn't moving. She moved the throttle lever to the wide-open position and even more turbulence was created around the hull, but the boat still wouldn't move. She tried turning the wheel back and forth as the engine pulled, hoping to make it break free of the sand, but the only thing that happened was that something got really hot. That was obvious by the smoke pouring out of the exhaust at the stern. She quickly pulled the throttle back down to slow it and shut the engine off. Backing up wasn't going to work.

If Captain Larry was on board, Rebecca knew that he would know if the state of the tide was high or low. He kept track of it in his head and seemed to always know when it was coming in and going out. But she had not been paying attention to it and neither had Russell, as far as she knew. Captain Larry would have been keeping notes in the logbook during the entire passage, but Russell seemed to care less about such things, if he even knew how to do them.

Thinking about Russell again suddenly sent a chill of fear down her spine. It looked far away, but she could still see the little island they had been sailing past when she knocked him overboard. And if she could see it from where she was stuck, then she was sure anyone on that island could see the *Sarah J.* as well. While she had kind of hoped he would wash up on the island rather than die, it now terrified her to think that he might actually have. What if he came to and survived and then saw the boat out there aground and helpless? Could he possibly swim that far? Rebecca didn't know, but he did have the PFD, so she thought he probably could, and he would be really moti-vated to do it. He would want to get her back for what she'd done, and the boat would be his only chance of getting off the island.

This new fear gave her a renewed sense of urgency; not to get the boat unstuck, which she knew she couldn't do, but to get at the rifle Russell had locked away in the cockpit locker. She knew he had the key that had been hanging on the bulkhead. It was probably in a pocket in his shorts when he went over the side. Whether it still was or not didn't matter. That one was gone for good, but she was sure her grandpa must have had a spare hidden away some-where and she had to find it. She had a feeling she would need the rifle, whether to fend off Russell or someone else who might arrive in another boat. Without it she was help-less and exposed, an easy target out there in the wide open. It would soon be dark though, so she felt that gave her extra time to find it. Even if Russell was alive and had made it to the island, maybe he wouldn't try to swim out there until morning.

It was weird going down below with the boat heeled over so far, yet not moving. She would have to live on it at that uncomfortable angle but she knew she would get used to it. At least she had a place to sleep and plenty of food and water. There was probably enough to last her for weeks, but she wondered if even that would be enough. She'd seen enough in the little sailing she'd done to know that when boats were hard aground like the *Sarah J.* was now, they generally required assistance from larger boats to get free again. She knew she might never get it off without help, unless she was lucky enough that the tide was at its lowest and enough water would come back in to float her free. Thinking of that, she decided that no matter how tired she was, she had to make herself wake up every couple hours or so to check. She did not want to sleep through the high tide cycle if one came during the night. It might be her best and only chance to get out of this mess before the wind or a storm made it worse, or Russell made his way out there to get his revenge.

Getting up to check the water level through the night only brought her more disappointment when she discovered that it had not been low tide when she hit the sandbar. She guessed it was somewhere in between, because although the water level rose a few inches between midnight and dawn, it was even lower than the evening before by the time the sun came up. She had tried the engine again in the dark when it seemed the highest but had no better luck than the first time.

While she was awake, however, she had discovered the spare key to the padlock Russell put on the cockpit locker. It was tucked away in a small box in the drawer of the Nav station, and when she tried it the lock opened immediately. The rifle was inside the locker, just as she'd thought. She lifted it out. It was heavy, but fairly short. Rebecca didn't know much about guns, but she knew that if it was loaded, and she was sure it was, all she had to do was flip the switch from "safe" to "fire" to make it shoot. If she saw Russell swimming her way, she intended to do just that.

When the sun was high enough the next morning to reflect off the white sand of the beach he might have swum to if he survived, Rebecca scanned the island with her grandpa's binoculars, but saw no movement. There were large rocks on parts of the little island, and she knew he might be behind one, if he was there at all, but since she didn't see him she studied the waves between her and the island instead, looking for anything that could be a swimmer coming her way. She was tired from staying up all night, and dozed off on the cockpit seat when she saw nothing out there. But when she woke up a half hour later and checked again there *was* something. But it wasn't what she was looking for, and it wasn't between her and the little island, or on it, but far beyond it, on the other side. *It was a sail!* And as she studied it through the binoculars for several more minutes, she was certain that it was coming her way.

CHAPTER 29

SCULLY WAS at the helm of *Intrepida*, steering east-southeast in the direction of a tiny cay they could see on the horizon in the midmorning sun. They had anchored near an equally small one some five miles to the northwest, and had set out at first light on this new course, which the chart showed would take them to the main islands in the Jumentos chain. The sight of this next little cay right where it was supposed to be confirmed the course was good. Scully asked Thomas to take the helm while he went forward to the base of the mast on the cabin top with the binoculars. He knew one could never be too careful in these reef-strewn waters, and he wanted to keep a good lookout as they passed near the cay. It would be easier to spot the shoals as the sun got higher, but aboard such a shallow draft vessel, Scully wasn't especially worried.

They were within a half-mile or so of the cay and he

was scanning the horizon beyond for the next one after it when he spotted something totally unexpected—*a sail!* It was far away and even with the binoculars he could not make out the hull beneath it, but from the angle it pointed at the sky he was sure that it was not a catamaran. Only a monohull sailboat would heel that far over. If it was an average sized-cruiser, he doubted they would catch it in the little seventeen-footer, and he was surprised he had not seen it sooner. At least he knew it was there though, and they would keep an eye out for it as they worked their way down the Jumentos chain. To be here sailing the course they were apparently sailing, the crew of this other boat had to be seeking out these islands, and would probably anchor somewhere along the way. Scully returned to the cockpit, telling Thomas to keep the same course he was steering.

"I hope they're friendly folks if we run into them some-where ahead," Thomas said.

"Only got to watch out an' see. Maybe we knowin' soon, mon."

Mindy was in the cockpit with them now, having made them all tea from the rapidly dwindling stores of such luxu-ries aboard *Intrepida*.

"The water here is even more beautiful than at Andros. I didn't think that could be possible," she said.

"We finally made it to the real Out Islands of the Bahamas," Thomas said. "It would be awesome if it were the pleasure cruise we'd dreamed of."

"We'll make the best of it anyway. At least we're safe here."

"I hope," Thomas said.

Scully checked the distant sailboat again and was surprised to see that they seemed to be getting a bit closer to it. He wasn't sure how the other boat could be sailing that slow on the same course they were, but he knew too that the distance could play tricks on the eye and that it might take another hour to really know if they were gaining on it or not. He passed the binoculars to Mindy when she asked for them, saying she wanted to look at the nearby island. They would pass within a half-mile of it, but from what Scully had already seen, there was nothing of interest there; only barren sand and a few big rocks.

"Hey! There's somebody on that island!" Mindy said. "Somebody is waving at us!"

Scully found this hard to believe, but when she gave him the binoculars and he looked for himself, he saw that it was true. A lone figure was standing on one of the highest rocks, waving something red back and forth over his head. He had to be a castaway, but how did he get here? As Scully watched the man continued his waving, while also running and hopping about with an apparent limp.

"He must be stranded," Mindy said. "Should we help him?"

"It might be a trap," Thomas said. "Maybe he's just trying to lure us in. Can you tell if he's armed or not, Scully?"

"Can't see nothing, mon. He got somet'ing I t'ink is only de life jacket."

Scully turned the glasses back to the distant boat, and saw that it was now closer to them than ever.

"I t'ink dat sailboat, she on de ground, mon. Mehbe dis fellow, he fallin' off an' he boat go on de reef."

"Can you tell if there's anyone on the boat?"

"Too far. All I see is de main and jib up. Should be sailin' fast wid de wind in de sail like dat, but de boat she don't move. Got to be on de bottom, mon."

"That's got to be it!" Mindy said. "If the guy on the island has a life jacket, he's bound to be a sailor. He must have fallen overboard. We can't just leave him. He'll die on that little island. There's nothing there. I'll bet he's already suffering from thirst."

"Lotta people dem dyin' dese days, you know. Can't help dem all. Too many."

"We would have died too, if not for you, Scully. You helped us. Now I want to help someone else. Maybe just for the good karma, I don't know. Besides, this man is clearly a sailor, just like us. Maybe we can take him to his boat."

"If de boat she hard aground, not gonna get it off wid only dis little boat an' no diesel to pull."

"Yeah, but even if we can't, he'll have a chance of survival on his boat. You know he won't last long on that little island," Thomas said.

Scully thought about what they were saying. His life just kept getting more complicated, but helping Thomas and Mindy had proven beneficial to him in the long run. He was here at least; in the island chain that he knew was Larry's eventual destination. And he would certainly not be here now if not for Thomas and Mindy. He shrugged his shoulders and handed the binoculars to her. It wouldn't hurt to at least sail closer and see what the situation was. The AK was close at hand if it were indeed some kind of a trap, but Scully didn't think it was. From everything he'd seen, it was pretty obvious what had happened here. He asked Mindy to keep an eye on the man with the binoculars while he steered closer to see if they could find a place to anchor near the island.

Shallow sandy flats extended a good two hundred yards out from the beach though, and between that area and deep water was a line of reefs with a light surf break. There would be no way to get any closer with *Intrepida*, so Scully headed up into the wind while Thomas dropped the sails. Scully then set the anchor just outside the surf zone. From this point they could hear the man on the island calling out to them to please help him.

"Okay, I goin' in de kayak an' see what he say. I can pick him up an' bring him back to de boat if everyt'ing okay. You both need watchin' what he doin' an' look for trouble. Don't t'ink it's gonna be a problem but you can't be too careful, you know."

Scully pulled the kayak alongside *Intrepida* and stepped in, putting the AK in the cockpit between his feet before Thomas passed him his paddle and he set off for the island. The surf between him and the beach was an obstacle, but he was able to read the waves to pick a route through a cut in the reef and soon reached the calm shallows inside. The stranded man had limped to the water's edge to greet him before he could step out of the kayak.

"Man! Am I ever glad to see you! I didn't expect another sailboat to come along way out here anytime soon, much less today."

"What happen, mon? How you end up on dis island wid no boat?"

"*That's* my boat out there! And my daughter is alone on board! We were sailing past this island late yesterday when the boat jibed and I got hit in the head with the boom." The man pointed to a large knot on the side of his head. "I'm lucky to be alive, I tell you that. If I hadn't been wearing this automatic PFD I'm sure I would have drowned. It was a nice bit of luck this island happened to be here too. My daughter was down below when it happened, and I guess she didn't even know at first. When I finally made it to the beach I saw that she had run aground way down there," the man pointed at the boat again. "She's only 14. There's no way she could get it off herself and no telling how bad it's stuck. We lost our dinghy too, a long time ago, so she has no way off the boat to come get me. Man, I was just thinking about trying to swim for it today until I saw your sail out there this morning. I doubt I would have made it between the currents and the sharks, but I know I wouldn't last long here on this rock either and I can't leave her out there alone."

Scully considered what the man was telling him. He

didn't really look old enough to have a 14-year-old daughter, but perhaps he married really young. No matter about that, his story seemed to add up. The boat was there all right, in plain sight, and here he was on the island with an inflatable PFD. Scully could see that his legs and feet were badly slashed and scraped from being swept across the reef, which was why he was limping and grimacing in pain. It would be a simple matter to take him back to his vessel and reunite him with his daughter, but Scully doubted they could do much for him when it came to freeing his boat. If it was truly hard aground then that's where it would stay, but at least the two of them would be together and would have food and water until whatever provisions they had aboard ran out.

"Okay mon, I take you back." Scully pointed to the front seat in the tandem kayak. "Push it out some, an' hop inside mon."

"Dude, I can't tell you how much I appreciate it! Today is my lucky day, even if yesterday was my unluckiest!"

Scully slipped the kayak back through the cut in the reef and aimed for *Intrepida*, where Thomas and Mindy were anxiously waiting in the cockpit.

"Whoa, that's a *little* boat, man! Three of you are sailing in that? Where did you come from man?"

"De boat little, but she a good one, mon. We sailin' from Florida."

Scully knew it would seem even smaller with a forth person on board, even for the short sail to the grounded boat. But he also thought this man should keep his mouth shut and be grateful for the ride, no matter how small the boat.

When they pulled alongside, Thomas and Mindy welcomed him aboard and Scully introduced them as the man climbed out, repeating the story he'd told Scully.

"Russell," he said. "My name's Russell. You guys are braver than I am, sailing all the way from Florida in a boat like this."

"It was better than the alternative," Thomas said. "Florida is not a place you want to be right now."

"Tell me about it. I was just trying to convince some friends of that recently. I wouldn't go there for anything! So what brings you guys all the way out here to the Jumentos Cays? This place sure isn't on the way to anywhere else. Are you just looking for a good refuge, or what?"

"Yes, and our friend Scully here is looking for his friends. They were all headed here to these islands on two different boats, but they got separated and delayed and now he's trying to find them. Have you seen any other boats here?"

"No, but my daughter and I just arrived the morning before this happened. What kind of boats are your friends sailing?" Russell asked, turning to Scully.

"One, she a 37-foot monohull. Built by de company dem call Tartan. De otha one she a Wharram catamaran—36 feet. My friend Larry an' I we build dat one on the de beach in Culebra."

Russell had a strange look on his face for a second as he took this in, but then he just looked back in the direction of his boat before replying. "I'd guess there must be plenty of monohulls that size around the islands, but Wharram catamarans are kind of rare. I know of them. I've seen a few over the years. Funky boats and not my style, but I haven't seen one since the collapse. Maybe you'll run across them somewhere out here, though."

CHAPTER 30

EVERYONE aboard the *Casey Nicole* was awake and ready when the tide peaked at around 3:00 a.m. This time Artie was at the big winch while Grant, Casey and Tara were all in the water at the bows, pushing as hard as they could while Artie cranked up tension on the rode. At first it seemed nothing was going to happen, but then it moved a little, and then a little more. There was just enough water to lift the knifelike keels out of the deep sand and once it started going, the catamaran slid backwards until she was completely afloat once again.

"ALL RIGHT!" Artie shouted. "Let's get that anchor up and get out of here!"

Tara climbed back on board first, and Artie saw Grant lift Casey up before coming aboard himself. Tara had been a nervous wreck all night, pacing back and forth and trying the windlass to no avail, too impatient to wait on the tide. Artie had been holding it together himself, though he was just as worried for Larry and Jessica as he was for Rebecca. Actually, he was more worried for them. Seeing the two Bahamian men in the dinghy did not bode well for his brother's well being. Artie knew Larry wouldn't give that boat up without a fight. Rebecca was in the hands of an idiot, but he didn't have any real reason to kill her and probably didn't want to, if he could avoid it. But Artie had to face the reality that his brother and poor Jessica may already be dead. If those men had wanted her, she would have been in the dinghy with them. Since she wasn't, she may have met the same fate as Larry.

"It's still nearly three hours until daylight," Grant said.

"I know. We can't really sail into the harbor at Staniel Cay in the dark. There'll be too many boats, if it's anything like Larry said it would be. No one is going to want to talk to us at this hour and they may see us as a threat if we go sailing in there at night."

"We can't just sit around doing nothing for three hours," Tara said.

"No. We can sail closer to the harbor. Maybe look around some of the outlying areas, but it's going to be hard to see anything in the dark anyway. It's not worth the risk to run aground again and next time it may not be soft sand we hit. You know as well as I do there are reefs everywhere around here. Believe me, I want answers just like you do. I want to find out as soon as possible if anyone around here saw Larry and Jessica and might know where they ran into those two guys."

"I hope they just went ashore and the boat got stolen

then," Casey said. "If so, maybe they are waiting on us to come pick them up. Like you said, maybe they found that house Russell was talking about and went to check it out."

"I hope you're right, Casey. And I hope we find the *Sarah J.* and Rebecca there as well."

It was just a short sail to Staniel Cay and they dropped the anchor again to wait on the daylight before entering. The wind was light when morning came and with full sails up they were barely ghosting along as they cruised into the crowded anchorage. Many of the occupants of the boats there were awake and on deck, watching them and unsure what to make of the strange catamaran arriving so early in the morning.

"We're looking for a Tartan 37 named the *Sarah J.,"* Artie shouted, as they slowly sailed past the first two boats that were rafted together near the entrance to the harbor. "And also a man and a woman who sailed this way yesterday afternoon in a wooden sailing dinghy. They were from our crew."

"Haven't seen the *Sarah J.,"* a heavily bearded man yelled back, "but we saw the two in the dinghy. They said they were looking for the *Sarah J.* too."

"Did you see which way they went?" Casey asked.

"Saw 'em sail right through the middle of the harbor, heading east, but I don't know after that. They didn't come back this way or I would have noticed. They could have taken the cut to the outside, but I wouldn't have in a little boat like that."

Several more passing conversations as they worked

through the anchorage verified what the first man said. Larry and Jessica had definitely sailed through here, but no one had seen them come back this way. And no one had seen a Tartan sailboat named the *Sarah J.* Hearing this, Tara was devastated. She had thought they were getting close to finding Rebecca, but now they had no more knowledge of her whereabouts than when they'd left Green Cay. Actually, they had less because at least then they thought they knew where to look. Now, it was anyone's guess as to which way Russell had really gone.

"What do we do now?" Casey wondered.

"I say we sail on through that cut that fellow told us about," Grant said. "If they went that way, maybe that's where they lost the dinghy. We can at least keep a sharp eye on the shoreline for any sign of them."

"I agree," Artie said. "No point in going back the way we came. We already know we won't find them there. We'll sail around Staniel hopefully along the path we saw those guys coming from."

Artie was as devastated as Tara, but he was trying to keep an air of confidence and hope despite the sinking feeling of doom that fell over him. If the *Sarah J.* had not been spotted here, then Larry and Jessica's loss of the dinghy was unrelated to Russell. That meant almost anything could have happened. The men they'd seen in the dinghy could have simply shot them as they sailed near the shore somewhere. If they were then dumped in the sea or had fallen overboard, Artie knew he might never learn what happened. And even if their bodies were ashore somewhere, they might or might not be visible from the water and it would be impossible to search the entire island and all the other little cays near it. All he knew to do was to sail on around Staniel Cay. The dinghy had come from that direction, from the northeast, so the encounter must have taken place not too far from where they were originally anchored at Bitter Guana Cay. Larry would try to get back there if he and Jessica were alive, and if they were, they had to know that he and the rest of the crew would be looking for them by now.

Casey and Grant were both perched on the starboard cabin top, the one nearest the island as Artie steered the catamaran as close to shore as he dared. Tara was slumped in the cockpit, fighting back her tears as she had been since they found out for sure they were not going to find her daughter here.

"We're going to find Rebecca, Tara, if we have to sail to every island, cay and rock in the Bahamas. I promise you we will never give up. But it will be so much easier with Larry's help. I've got to do what I can to find him and Jessica. But we will find Rebecca, no matter what."

"I'm scared that it's already too late," Tara said. "Anything could have happened. That guy may have been trying to come here and didn't make it. We have no idea if he knew anything about sailing or not. All he did was lie. Every word out of his mouth was a lie. And now Rebecca has to pay the price for our stupidity in trusting him."

"It's not stupidity, Tara. We were just all trying to be decent human beings. And I hope we'll always try. Too many people have lost their humanity in the aftermath of this mess. Is it even *worth* surviving if one has to live like that?"

"No, and it's not worth surviving if I have to live knowing I failed to protect my daughter. There's nothing left for me if I don't find her."

"I understand. But until you've exhausted every possibility of finding her, you've got to stay strong, or you will fail her. I'm here to help you, Tara. I know what it's like. I have my daughter after all the worry and fear when I didn't. I have nothing else to do but help you find yours. But I'm really worried for Jessica and my brother. I can't imagine facing this situation we're in without his help, and Jessica has been through enough herself. I just want us to all be together and find some refuge where we can somehow put all this behinds us and start over."

"We would all be better off if Rebecca and I had stayed at Cat Island. The boats would have never gotten separated and all of you would still be together. Rebecca and I would have probably been fine there after those killers were dead. You said yourself when Larry first suggested it that it was a mistake to separate the crew on two separate boats. You didn't want to do it, and neither did Jessica. You were right all along."

"That was just my first reaction because I was so surprised when Larry suggested it. I don't think it was a mistake at all, because I don't believe you and Rebecca would have been safe there. I know you can't imagine anything worse than what has happened, but I think she is okay and we are going to find her and get her back unharmed. That's better than what could have happened if you had stayed at that place. And whatever has happened to Larry and Jessica is not your fault. Larry would not have had it any other way. There's no way he was going to leave you two at the mercy of whoever might have come to that island next. And yes, he found you attractive and that might have been a factor in his motivation, but my brother is a good guy, and he would have done it whether he thought he had a chance of something more with you or not. And now I know he was right to do so."

"I hope he's okay. I really do. I do hope we can find him and Jessica, but do you really think we will?"

Artie didn't answer. He didn't want to say because he was afraid to contemplate the truth. And though he'd tried to assure Tara that they would find Rebecca as well, the truth was that he wondered how they ever would. Every hour and every day that went by expanded the possible distance between them and the *Sarah J.*, as well as the range of destinations the lunatic could be sailing with her to. The truth was that the more time they spent here searching for Larry and Jessica, the lesser the odds of finding Rebecca before it was too late—if they ever did.

"That's the south end of Staniel Cay dead ahead," Grant pointed. "It looks like there's two or three small cays between there and the one where we were anchored yesterday."

Artie glanced at the chart and saw that Grant was right. He stayed in the deeper water away from the rocky shores of the little cays, and along with Grant and Jessica, scanned the coast intently for any clue or anything out of the ordinary.

"This has to be the approximate route the dinghy was sailing when we saw them," he told Grant, as they sailed across the final stretch of water to Bitter Guana Cay.

"Yeah, and there's no sign of anything. What do we do now?"

"Hey, look at that!" Casey shouted. "Isn't that some kind of dinghy?"

Artie and Grant turned to look to the northwest, where she was pointing. Sure enough, a tiny little speck of a boat was making it's way up the east side of Staniel Cay, heading in the direction of the anchorage they'd checked before circling the island. It was much too far away to make out any details, but they could see the motion of oars propelling it, and it appeared there were two people sitting in it. Artie turned the helm to change course while Grant sheeted in the jib on the other tack. The dinghy was moving slowly and keeping close to the shore. The two in it could be from any of the boats anchored there, but since it was so far from the anchorage, it seemed like a good idea to check it out. And as they changed their course, apparently the occupants of the dinghy spotted them as well. Whoever was rowing spun the little boat around and started pulling in their direction.

CHAPTER 31

THE LITTLE MONTGOMERY 17 was not the kind of sailboat Russell was expecting to see calling at these remote cays. When he'd first noticed its sloop rig coming out of the northeast in the early morning light, he had assumed it was a much bigger boat and that it was farther away than it really was. But then it sailed quite close to the island and he saw that the kayak trailing astern was longer than the boat itself. When the crew of three dropped anchor and one of them headed his way in the kayak, Russell felt quite sure they were coming to help him. It would be obvious to anyone that he had nothing of value to steal, so there was little reason for them to stop otherwise.

When he saw his opportunity to get back to the boat from which he'd been so savagely evicted, he quickly formulated his story, as it would not at all do to tell the truth. He was quite pleased with his brilliant performance when the black Rastafarian fellow approached the little cay and asked how he'd wound up there. It was such a logical narrative—as it was not at all surprising that a man could get hit in the head by a sailboat boom and knocked overboard into the drink. And that his young daughter, all alone and frightened, would then end up on a shoal or reef while trying to handle a big cruising boat all alone in unfamiliar waters.

Of course it worked on the island man in the kayak. He bought the whole thing without question and within minutes, Russell was sitting in the bow seat of the two-man boat, being ferried out to the diminutive mother ship the newcomers had arrived on. It was hard to believe three adults had sailed on that thing all the way from Florida, but then again, a lot of things that were happening now were hard to believe. Four people on board it would really be a crowd, but they only had a short distance to sail to reach the *Sarah J*.

The young white couple who were the owners of the boat seemed pleasant enough, but when they answered his question regarding what brought them to these particular islands, Russell was taken aback. He did a passable job of concealing his surprise, but it was a real shocker to learn that the Rasta guy was the very same friend that Larry the catamaran dude was planning to sail back to Florida to look for. Russell remembered now that Larry said his name was Scully, and now Scully had arrived at their planned rendezvous area after all, having sailed here on this tiny boat.

Scully was looking for Larry's catamaran and the *Sarah*

J., but the grounded yacht in the distance was still too far away to identify. Once they started towards it, it would be just a matter of time before they were close enough to read the name painted clearly on the stern. Russell wished now he'd taken the time to sand it off. Anyone in their right mind who stole a yacht would do so right away, but that had been the least of his worries considering the situation at the time, and it was something he planned to get around to later, when he thought of a suitable new name with which to christen his ship.

Russell had to figure out something quick because he knew that as soon as this island man saw the name on the boat, the BS story he'd concocted on the fly would be busted. This was going to be a problem. It was bad enough that the dude was over six feet tall and nothing but sinewy muscle—obvious to all as he wore nothing but a ragged pair of cargo shorts. But when Scully followed him aboard the little sailboat from the kayak, Russell now saw that he'd been carrying an AK-47 hidden under his legs as he paddled. He tried to keep calm about it, making a comment to hide how nervous he was.

"Whoa, dude! I see you weren't taking any chances when you came to the beach to check me out!"

"Nevah know about de stranger dese days, mon."

"We've run across some unsavory types," Thomas said. "If not for Scully and his AK, Mindy and I wouldn't be here now."

"I hear you," Russell said. "No doubt there are a lot of desperadoes around now. So many people just seemed to lose it when all their easy living got taken away. It didn't affect me much. I've been outside the mainstream my whole life. I've never needed all that shit most of them think they can't live without."

"Have you and your daughter been living aboard your boat for a long time?" Mindy asked. "Where you already cruising the islands when the solar flare happened?"

"Oh yeah, of course. I literally raised her aboard the boat. It's been just me and her for years. Her mom decided she didn't want a kid any more, and she sure didn't want me, so the two of us just took off for the islands. We've been all over the Caribbean and up and down the East Coast. One summer we went north all the way to Newfoundland."

"That's really cool. What's your daughter's name?"

"Rhonda," Russell said without missing a beat. "She just turned 14 since the blackout."

"What a life she's lived for someone so young! I would be envious if not for the way things have turned out now. But I guess she's coping with it better than most because of how you raised her. Good for you, Russell. I'm glad we came along when we did. It must have been awful for you, being stranded on that island, unable to reach her."

"I can't even describe it. But today seems like my luckiest day ever, seeing you guys come along. What are the odds? I figured I would slowly starve to death there. At first, I thought I wouldn't last much more than a day or two from lack of water. But believe it or not, I found some rocks with pockets of rainwater in them. If not for that, I might have been too weak to even notice your boat go by."

"And we wouldn't have seen you if you weren't standing there waving that red PFD."

"I wouldn't have been there if I hadn't been wearing it. Just goes to show you never know what's going to happen when you're sailing. You won't catch me on a boat again without it." Even as he said this, Russell made a show of putting the now-deflated PFD back on. Scully had tied off the kayak to the stern of the boat, and Thomas was going forward to retrieve the anchor. "Hey, I'd give you a hand with that man, but my legs are pretty torn up."

"Don't worry about it," Thomas said. "Everything's easy on a little boat like this. I've got it."

"I'll get you some anti-biotic ointment," Mindy said. "You don't want those cuts to get infected."

By the time she returned the tube of ointment, Scully and Thomas had the boat underway again, and Russell was getting nervous. Trying not to make it obvious, he kept an eye on the AK that Scully had placed in on the cockpit seat next to him as he steered. The rifle was his only real chance of overpowering this man. Thomas he could probably take without it. And Mindy would be easy enough to shove over the side. But Scully looked hard and serious, despite his smiling demeanor and easy-going attitude. Russell could read people well and he could just tell from looking at him that Scully was bad news. He would have to take him out first and he would have to be ruthless and quick. It was a shame really, because they only wanted to help him, but once this man found out he had taken the *Sarah J.* from his friend Larry, there was no telling what he would do. And if they just sailed up to the grounded boat, Rebecca would surely tell them the whole story and that would be game over.

Russell felt the knots tighten in his stomach as he sat there, rubbing the ointment onto his cuts and scrapes. The only way he was going to get that rifle was if Scully left the helm for some reason and didn't take it with him. He only needed to leave it for a few seconds, but whether he would or not remained to be seen.

The little boat was moving faster than Russell would have liked, giving him little time to make a plan. He hoped that Rebecca was down below, asleep or something so that they wouldn't see her until the last minute. Scully would recognize her when he saw her, even if he didn't recognize the boat first. But his time ran out when Thomas asked Mindy to pass him the binoculars. Scully was still steering, but Thomas wanted to get a better look at the boat as they sailed towards it. Standing at the base of the mast, leaning against it to steady himself, he raised the glasses as Russell cursed under his breath.

"The *Sarah J.*," he said. "The *Sarah J., Biloxi, Mississippi*. I thought you said you were based in the Bahamas?" he turned to Russell.

Before he could answer with another hastily concocted story, Thomas raised the binoculars again, saying he'd seen someone on the deck. Scully also stood up from where he'd been seated at the helm, asking Thomas what he'd just said. Things started happening fast at that point.

"Turn the boat, Scully! She's got a gun and she's aiming it at us!"

Just as he said it, a hole appeared in the mainsail two feet above Thomas' head and they all heard the report of a rifle shot ring out across the water. Scully put the helm down hard, swinging the boat around off the wind so fast that Thomas nearly lost his balance and fell. A second shot followed the first and Russell saw Scully waving both hands over his head, trying to make himself visible to Rebecca even as he steered the boat with one foot on the tiller. Thomas and Mindy were still clearly confused even if Scully had figured out what was going on, and Russell knew if he was going to act, now was the time to do it. He grabbed the AK off the cockpit seat right from under Scully's feet, and was racking the slide to make sure a round was chambered when the island man kicked him in the face. The blow sent him back against the cabin bulkhead, but Russell held on to the rifle, inadvertently pulling the trigger and firing a round over the rail as he stumbled. Dazed from the blow to the face, he struggled to bring the muzzle of the rifle in line with his foe, getting off one more shot before he felt a weight crash on top of him and take him to the sole of the cockpit. Russell was vaguely aware of Scully collapsing at the helm before he realized that Thomas was on top of him, trying to choke him from behind. He twisted and lunged, breaking the smaller man's hold on his neck as he threw him hard to the rear of the cockpit where Scully was clutching his leg in a pool of blood. Russell had dropped the rifle and now he bent to pick it up, his full focus on finishing the job he'd started. Thomas had hit his head on something when he fell and his weight on top of Scully was keeping him pinned down as well. Russell smiled as he raised the AK to aim at Scully's head, his troubles with the islander about to be eliminated with a pull of the trigger.

It was his single-minded focus on what he perceived to be the only threat that proved to be Russell's undoing. Before he could steady the sights of the rifle on the moving boat, an excruciating pain ripped through his side at his lower rib and his ears rung with the sharp bark of another gun fired from just two feet away. Russell turned to see what had happened as his arms felt weak and the AK fell from his hands. Mindy was standing in the open companionway below him with a pistol pointed at his chest. She fired it again and Russell felt more burning needles of pain before his knees buckled and he collapsed onto the seat behind him. Soon after, he was vaguely aware of hands on him as he struggled to breathe, and then there was the cool sensation of water surrounding his body. As he opened his eyes he saw aquamarine blue that stretched to infinity, the color contrasting sharply with the cloud of red spreading into it from around his torso. The beauty of the mixing colors faded within seconds however, supplanted by total blackness as the crushing pain in his chest took away his last conscious thought.

CHAPTER 32

LARRY AND JESSICA walked the beach in front of which the *Casey Nicole* had been anchored just hours ago, wondering how Tara managed to talk Artie into leaving so soon. He couldn't believe that Artie, or any of them really, could be foolish enough to leave already. Hell, it had only been a few hours. Anything could delay a boat as small as that sailing dinghy on a trip of several miles like that. What were they thinking? Larry couldn't believe they would simply leave the whole area to go off searching for the *Sarah J.* the same day. Surely they would wait until at least tomorrow? He knew Tara could be persistent, but with Casey and Grant backing him up Artie wouldn't give in that soon. Would he?

"What can we do now?" Jessica asked.

"I don't know Jessica. I'm fresh out of ideas, how about you? We're stuck on an uninhabited island with no water, no food, no weapons and no boat."

"That's not entirely true. We do have a boat. Well sort of."

"If you can call it that. I hate to use the word 'boat' for that piece of crap."

"It *did* get us here though."

"Yeah, but it's not going to really get us anywhere else. Especially not now. It's going to be dark soon. We may as well figure out where we're going to camp and settle in for the night. Maybe we'll dream up a better plan in our sleep."

"I don't think they would have just left us like this for no reason. I think they must have seen something. Maybe they saw the *Sarah J.* go by in the distance or something. After we left."

Larry considered this idea. It had not really crossed his mind until Jessica mentioned it, but the more he thought about it, the more that seemed like a real possibility. That could easily explain why Artie would leave. Maybe Russell *had* stopped somewhere out on the banks before he got here and they had unknowingly passed him during the night. They had gotten here first and after he and Jessica left on the dinghy, Russell showed up later. He might have seen the anchored catamaran and turned away to run for it. It would have taken Artie and the crew some time to get the anchor up and set the sails to give chase, so even if they caught up, which he was sure they would, it could be miles from here. The question was where though, and in which direction. Maybe the best thing they could do after all was just sit tight and wait. They would come back to look for him and Jessica regardless of where they went, maybe even before morning.

"Let's find a place somewhere up at the top of the cliffs. That'll give us a better chance of spotting them and hopefully we can signal them somehow."

"We could build a fire," Jessica said.

"Yeah, except that we can't. I don't have anything to start one with. Rubbing sticks together never worked for me and since it's been so long since the last time I burned a joint with Scully, I don't even have a Bic in my pocket."

"Grant knows how to start fires without any of that stuff. He showed me when we were looking for Casey on that river. It didn't look easy though. It was like a wooden drill and he had to make all the parts."

"Yeah, I've seen it done. Never tried it though. Anyway, we don't need a fire for any other reason than if we see them, and jumping up and down will probably work just as well. We sure don't want a fire up there on the high part of the island at night. No telling who it might attract."

"More men like those two who took our dinghy, probably."

"Or worse. Those guys just wanted a boat."

"Well I hope it sinks. That would serve them right."

"It won't. It's a damn good little dinghy. It will probably serve them well. Like I said before, they probably have hungry families to feed. It sucks that they took the boat, but we probably would have missed our ride regardless. If they did see Russell near here, it could have been right after we left. And we would have been gone a few hours even if nothing happened."

"I know, you're right. But it does suck that we're stranded here now. At least if we still had the dinghy we could sail around and look for them."

"It would probably still be best to stay put. Anyway, I'll bet we'll only be here one night. They'll be back to get us. Sorry you're stuck here with me instead of Grant, though. He could build a nice fire, too.

Jessica laughed. "Yeah and it would be so cold he would need to. I was stuck on the *Casey Nicole* with him for nearly a week and he acted like I was toxic or something. But I know what's up now. I *was* interested in Grant, but not anymore. He's exactly where he needs to be—with Casey. I hope it works out for them, I really do. It just took me a little time to realize he's not my type after all and I'm totally okay with that now."

"I'm glad you're okay with it then. I was afraid this was going to happen. I could see how he and Casey were around each other. I'm her uncle and I want her to be happy of course, but if it had been *me* in Grant's shoes..."

"Yeah?"

"I'm just saying *if*. Grant is a lucky young man, to have such a choice."

"I'll bet you've had more pretty girls fighting over you than he has... seeing how you're such a ruggedly handsome sailor and all."

"Yeah, right. Ask Tara about that."

"That was just a misunderstanding. She's over it now anyway."

"Nah. Too much drama there for me with the kid and all. Maybe she and my brother will hit it off. He's used to dealing with a daughter anyway, and likes it just fine. He'd be a much better match."

"So where does that leave you and me, Larry? We're just the odd ones out. And now we're stuck here on a deserted island while everybody else is having all the fun."

"It leaves us with no choice but to make the best of a tough situation, Jessica." Larry took her hand to lead her up to the top of the island. "But we're survivors, right? I think we'll do okay."

"I think so," she smiled. "Even without a fire."

As Rebecca watched the sail that appeared on the distant horizon that morning, her heart sank as she saw it change course to approach the little island she was afraid Russell might have swam to. When she turned the binoculars back to the island, her fears were confirmed. Now that the morning sun was higher, she could just make out a human figure standing on the highest rock of the little cay, waving something overhead to signal the boat. So Russell *had* survived! And now he had been spotted by the crew of the new boat that she thought might come to help her. Her hopes of that happening were dashed now. Russell would either lie to them or steal their boat to get back to the *Sarah*

J. She had no doubt he would do anything to reach her after what she'd done yesterday.

She went back into the cabin and grabbed the rifle off the bunk where she'd left it. She was determined to keep Russell from ever stepping foot aboard the *Sarah J.* again, because she knew that if he did, she was as good as dead. She didn't know who these other people on the other boat were, and she didn't want to hurt anyone unless she knew they were tying to hurt her, but if they tried to bring Russell back to the boat, then she was going to stop them if she could.

With the rifle close at hand now, she stood there leaning against the stern pulpit, studying the scene on the little cay with the binoculars. She saw the sailboat drop anchor near the island and then she saw that it was towing something behind it. When someone from the boat got in the object astern and began paddling, Rebecca saw that it was a kayak, and that it was headed for the beach where Russell was now standing to meet it. She could tell that he got in it and she saw it going back to the sailboat. So they *were* helping him and she had no doubt they were bringing him back to the *Sarah J!*

Rebecca watched as the boat got underway again and started coming her way. She picked up the heavy rifle and rested the barrel across the stern rail to steady it. She had never shot a real gun like this, but she had used toy guns in arcades and knew enough to understand that the front sight had to be lined up in the notch of the rear sight. She wanted to shoot high, over the heads of the people on the boat in hopes of scaring them away, so she aimed at the middle of the mainsail, which even at a distance seemed a big enough target to hit. She couldn't see the people on the boat from this angle, because it was coming straight towards her and she knew they would be in the cockpit, sitting lower than the cabin top. It was unlikely that a bullet would hit any of them, but she had to take a chance because she didn't want them to get close enough for Russell to get aboard the *Sarah J.*, no matter what.

When she squeezed the trigger, the sound the rifle made was much louder than she was expecting and because she was holding it loosely, it punched her shoulder with a painful kick. The boat turned off to one side, making a bigger target so she pulled the trigger one more time to make sure it had turned because of her shooting. Then she set the rifle down hoping she wouldn't need to use it again, and grabbed the binoculars to take another look. That was when she realized how tiny the sailboat really was. It was way smaller than the *Sarah J.,* that was obvious by how big the people in it looked now that it was turned beam to her where she could see them.

She could see a man standing on top of the cabin holding onto the mast, and a woman in the cockpit with Russell. But it was the sight of the man in the back, the one who was steering, that surprised her the most. He was a tall and lean black man, with dreadlocks down to his waist, and he looked exactly like Scully, Captain Larry's best friend who had been left behind in Florida. When she pointed the binoculars at the kayak again, she *knew* this man was

Scully. There was no doubt that it was the same two-person yellow kayak that had been aboard the *Casey Nicole*, and Rebecca knew that Scully had been in it when he was last seen.

She saw Russell grab something and then there was a lot of quick back and forth movement before she heard two gunshots and realized that Russell had a gun. Scully had fallen where he was steering and the man who had been on the cabin top by the mast jumped on top of Russell and knocked him down too. Rebecca saw that they were fighting and then she heard more gunshots. Her hands were shaking as she watched through the binoculars, fearing that Russell would kill everyone on the little boat and then come for her, but instead, she saw the other man get back up and then he and the woman bending down as they worked together to roll Russell's limp body over the side of the boat and into the water. She kept the binoculars focused on the area around the boat, but she didn't see him come back up. She couldn't see Scully either, but she could see that the man and woman were bent down again, doing something in the bottom of the cockpit. *Was Scully dead?* She was quite sure he had been shot when the struggle started.

She wished she had a way to go to the other boat and find out, but all she could do was wait and see what the man and woman would do next. She stood at the stern rail and watched with the binoculars, and when the man looked her way she waved her empty hands overhead to let them know she wouldn't shoot at them again. The boat had been drifting with sails flogging since Scully had fallen, but now she saw the man turn the boat off the wind so that they filled again and then it started moving. It circled around to get back on course and then once again it was sailing straight at her.

CHAPTER 33

WHEN THOMAS READ the name *Sarah J.* on the stern of the grounded yacht, he knew immediately that something was wrong with this Russell guy's story. Scully had talked about the two boats he was looking for at length during their voyage together from Florida, and Thomas knew that the *Sarah J.* was one of them, especially when he saw that the hailing port lettering under the yacht's name read "Biloxi." It could be no mere coincidence, but he didn't fully realize the extent of Russell's ruse until he read the name out loud, so that everyone on board, including Scully and Russell could hear.

Russell's move for Scully's AK was unexpected and sudden. Scully's reactive kick was just as quick, but not decisive enough to prevent him from pulling the trigger. When Thomas saw him bring the muzzle back in line to fire again, he knew he had no choice but to act immediately. Even so, he feared he was too late as the gun went off and he saw Scully fall. He landed on the stranger's back from where he leapt from the cabin top, knowing that if he didn't subdue the man he and Mindy would be next. He thought he'd succeeded when Russell collapsed under his weight and dropped the rifle, but Thomas had little experience as a fighter. He knew nothing of the tactics of maintaining the upper hand once he had it and he had no idea how resilient a determined foe could be. And so it was with great surprise that he found himself practically upside down on top of Scully. Russell had somehow managed to get up enough to flip him violently off his back. And upon landing, Thomas hit his head on the side of the cockpit seat; causing him to see stars and momentarily lose all motivation to continue the fight. Time seemed to stand still as he was vaguely aware of Russell getting to his feet and standing over him, the AK-47 in his hands again. Like that night when he knelt helplessly on a lonely beach in the Florida Keys waiting for the inevitable, Thomas fully expected to receive the bullet that would punch his clock for good.

He heard the sound of a gunshot and winced and closed his eyes as he did, but there was no pain that he could perceive. There was blood on the cockpit sole beneath him, but it had been there when he fell and he knew it was Scully's. He heard another shot and opened his eyes in time to see Russell fall onto the starboard seat, and then he realized it was Mindy who'd done the shooting when he saw her emerge from the companionway with the pistol in her hand. When she was sure Russell was out of action, she put the gun down and knelt beside him.

"Are you okay?"

"I think so. Scully is hurt though. He got shot!"

Thomas pulled himself off of the wounded man. The blood was everywhere now, and now he saw that Scully was holding his leg just above the knee with both hands, trying to slow the flow of the blood pouring from the wound just below his knee.

"Hang on, Scully. We'll get it stopped."

"We've got to make a tourniquet. Use the end of the mainsheet. Anything! If we don't he'll bleed to death."

Thomas knew she was right as he grabbed for the end of the Dacron line that was tangled on the seat nearby. Scully looked weak and grimaced in pain when Thomas told him what he was doing.

"Just let me get a loop around your leg. You can let go with your hands as soon as I pull it tight. It should work better than trying to hold it."

Scully nodded and the Thomas tightened the tourniquet, wrapping it several turns around his leg. His hands were slick with Scully's blood by the time he was done, but the bleeding slowed to barely a trickle. The bullet from the rifle hitting his leg at such close range had done tremendous damage. It was impossible to tell just how much, but Thomas had no doubt that bones were shattered in addition to the torn veins or arteries that had caused him to lose so much blood.

"Help me for a second," Mindy asked, and Thomas saw

that she was struggling to push Russell over the side. More blood now covered the cockpit seat from the two wounds in Russell's torso, and it was obvious he was dead or dying, but his eyes were still open and Thomas couldn't be sure if he was already gone or not. Together the two of them lifted him up to the edge of the cockpit coaming and then rolled him off the edge of the narrow side deck. He hit the water with a big splash and slowly sank into the clear depths.

Thomas looked back at Scully, still slumped in the cockpit sole and then at the boat they had been sailing towards. He saw the girl standing at the stern rail waving her hands, and when he checked with the binoculars, he saw that she wasn't holding the rifle any more. Reaching for a rigging knife he kept just inside the companionway, Thomas cut off the excess end of the mainsheet so that sailing the boat wouldn't interfere with Scully's tourniquet, then he turned *Intrepida* off the wind to fill the sails. As he got back on course towards the *Sarah J.*, Mindy began dipping up bucketfuls of seawater to wash the blood off the decks and out of the cockpit scuppers.

"How many you see on de boat?" Scully asked Thomas, looking up from where he still lay slumped in the cockpit sole.

"I didn't see anybody but the one girl. I think it's the teenaged daughter you told us about."

"Rebecca."

"And that guy just completely lied to us, saying she was his daughter and her name was Rhonda," Mindy said. "I wonder what happened here. How did he ever get on the boat in the first place, and did he really fall off like he said he did?"

"Maybe we'll get the answers soon," Thomas said. "I'm going to ease up to the stern end and hope we have enough water there to tie alongside without getting stuck on whatever she's on."

When Thomas and Mindy saw how firmly the keel of the *Sarah J.* was buried in the sandbar Rebecca had sailed into, they knew it was beyond their means to get the yacht afloat again. But fortunately, the water at the stern of the bigger boat was just deep enough for the little Montgomery 17 to raft alongside, and once they had their boat secured and exchanged their stories, the next question was what they were going to do for Scully.

"That would be great if we can find him," Mindy said, when Rebecca told her that Captain Larry's brother, Artie was a doctor. "He absolutely needs a doctor. That leg is awful and I'm afraid he's going to lose it."

Scully was weak from the blood loss and had been in and out of consciousness since he was shot. They had to get him out of the hot sun and keep him well hydrated and immobile. Then, they had to get him some help. He might not survive if they didn't and Thomas knew he and Mindy owed him their lives, so he was determined to do everything in his power to save Scully's.

"We need to get him aboard your boat, Rebecca. *Intrep-*

ida's cabin is so small there's no way to make him comfortable in there and he wouldn't be able to get any rest while we're underway."

"We can get him on board with the Lifesling," Rebecca said, pointing to the rescue device mounted on the stern rail. "We've used it before and it works great. All you have to do is crank the halyard winch to hoist him up. We can get him down into the cabin and he can sleep on the starboard bunk. The way the boat's leaning over, he'll be on the low side and he can't roll off."

All this was easier said than done, but with the three of them working together they accomplished the task and Scully was safely aboard the larger yacht an hour later. There was a decent first aid kit on the *Sarah J.*, and with it Mindy did her best to bandage Scully's shattered leg. There was nothing she could do about the damage to the bones, but when she was finished wrapping it the bleeding slowed enough to make it safe to remove the tourniquet. Maybe the leg could be saved or maybe not, but there was nothing else she knew to do for him other than try and find the doctor who was the brother of Scully's best friend. When she was finished Rebecca showed her and Thomas where Green Cay was on the chart.

"Captain Larry had been talking about going to the Jumentos Cays in front of Russell, and I guess that's where he got the idea to come here. But before that, he wouldn't shut up about some friend's house he wanted to go to on Staniel Cay. He tried to talk Captain Larry into taking him there, but that was out of the question with Scully missing in Florida. Russell refused to go there with Captain Larry to look for him, so that's why he took our boat and me along with it. The catamaran was on the beach and the mast was down, so it was easy for him to get away. I think as soon as they got it ready to sail again, my mom and Captain Larry would go to that Staniel Cay place to look for me before they would come here. They would never think Russell would come here because he wanted to go there."

"Wow, that's a long way from here," Mindy said, tracing her finger over the chart. "They could be almost anywhere in the Exumas."

"Yeah, especially if they went to Staniel Cay and didn't see the boat. There's no telling what they would do then," Thomas said.

"They would keep looking, that's what. Captain Larry would never give up trying to help my mom find me and her boat. And after that, he could do what he planned to do and sail his boat to Florida to look for Scully. But now Scully is here and he has no way of knowing that."

Thomas had never been to the Exumas, but in all their dreaming of sailing to the Bahamas before the collapse, he and Mindy had read and heard a lot about those islands, as they were so popular with cruising sailors. He had thought he would never get to see them, but now sailing there to look for Larry's brother was the only hope of finding a doctor who would be willing to come here and help Scully. Rebecca's mother and all the rest of the crew on the catamaran would be immensely relieved to know that Rebecca and the *Sarah J.* had been found and that she was safe.

With the catamaran and all her crew, they might even have a chance of getting the *Sarah J.* off the ground. There was really no other choice they could make. An hour later, Thomas and Mindy were sailing north, bound for the southern Exumas. They would work their way along the chain, checking every anchorage between their landfall and Staniel Cay, and hopefully intercept the *Casey Nicole* in her search for the *Sarah J.*

Tied to the stern of *Intrepida* was the two-seater kayak, just as it had been since Scully first joined them in Florida. They were bringing it for good reason. As they were discussing their plans in the cabin of the *Sarah J.* with Rebecca and Scully, Mindy had voiced her concern that Larry and the others on the catamaran would have no interest in a little 17-foot sailboat like *Intrepida*. What if they saw them somewhere in the Exumas and tried to flag them down? They could not possibly catch up to the much faster catamaran, and Larry and the crew would be wary of strangers and too busy looking for the *Sarah J.* to be inclined to stop for a smaller boat. Hearing this, Scully said the solution was to take the kayak in tow. He said Larry would recognize it anywhere because it was not a make and type that was commonly seen in the islands. If he saw it behind their boat, they wouldn't have to try and flag down the *Casey Nicole*, because Larry would run them down to find out why they had it when Scully was last seen in it off the coast of Florida.

Thomas hated to leave Scully and Rebecca stranded on a grounded boat with no way off, but Scully insisted they take it, so they did. He said they would be fine. There was food and water and Rebecca had already proven she could use the SKS if Scully was unable to get to the deck in the event of an attack of some kind. But he wasn't worried about that in such a remote place and he also insisted that Thomas take the AK and leave the old hunting rifle with him. This was a suggestion Thomas had no hesitation about. Sailing to the Exumas would put them in contact with a lot of other boaters, all of them on larger, faster vessels, and he felt much better having the firepower of the semi-automatic. He also had a newfound respect and admiration for Mindy, who had saved them all with her willingness to use the handgun despite her inexperience with firearms. There were eight rounds remaining for the pistol, so with it and the AK, he felt they were as prepared as they could be given the circumstances.

CHAPTER 34

"IT LOOKS like you got the bad end of the deal in your dinghy trade," Artie said, as the *Casey Nicole* drifted alongside Larry and Jessica so they could catch hold and climb aboard. Artie was so happy to see him he couldn't resist this little attempt at humor with his brother, but he made sure to keep his voice low enough that Tara didn't overhear. He was absolutely thrilled to find Larry and Jessica alive and unhurt. Truthfully, it was not what he'd expected after seeing those two men sail away in the dinghy. But here they were, bobbing along in a tiny fiberglass boat that had certainly seen better days but was never much to begin with.

"We thought we were going to have to build another catamaran with driftwood on the beach after we got back to Bitter Guana Cay and found you guys already gone. What's the deal? Did you see Russell go by in the *Sarah J.* or something?"

Artie told him they had not, but instead had seen the men who stole the dinghy and tried to catch them.

"I'm not surprised the bastards got away. We'll never get it back, but hey, it could have been a lot worse. They got the drop on me and they didn't have to leave us alive, but they did."

"I take it you haven't seen any sign of my boat or my daughter," Tara said, as Larry climbed aboard the *Casey Nicole* behind Jessica.

"Unfortunately, no. And none of the folks we talked to in the anchorage have either. So either he hasn't made it here yet because he stopped somewhere along the way, or he decided to go elsewhere."

Tara sank back onto a seat in the cockpit, her face buried in her hands. "That's just what I was afraid of. And just what I tried to tell all of you!"

"Well you didn't have a better idea of where to look, did you? I don't recall you telling us if you did, but I'm all ears if you do now. Look, I'm sorry, and I know this is rough on you. We're going to do all that we can and my boat is at your disposal. So you tell me. Where do you want to look, because that's where we'll go."

"I don't know! I've never been to these islands before. I just have to find my daughter. I still can't believe this has happened."

The tears were streaming down Tara's face now, and Artie sat down beside her and put his arm around her shoulders as Larry stood there not really knowing what else to say, other than to assure her that they would leave immediately to continue their search. Larry asked Grant to help him and the two of them pulled the junky little dinghy up onto the forward deck.

"I hate to put this thing on my boat, but unfortunately, it's all we have now."

As they were lashing it down, Artie heard Larry ask Grant where his primary anchor was, and why it was missing from the bow roller where it was always stored when the boat was underway. When Grant told him they had cut the rode in order to try and catch the men in the dinghy, Larry said they had to go back to Bitter Guana Cay and find it.

"That Rocna is worth its weight in gold, especially now. I don't know where I'd ever get another one, and we're sure to get in a situation where nothing else will do. I don't suppose you put a float on the rode?"

"No," Artie said with a bit of embarrassment for the oversight. "I didn't even think about it, to tell you the truth. We were in such a hurry to try and catch those guys and I was so worried about you and Jessica. I wasn't expecting to ever have to go back and look for it, really."

"That's all right. I'll find it. I know about where I dropped it and the water is clear."

Larry did find the anchor after just a few minutes of searching with mask and snorkel after they returned to Bitter Guana Cay. He brought up the severed end of the nylon rode and Grant hauled it aboard. When he was back in the cockpit, Larry spread out the chart for the Exumas and pointed out the likely spots he thought Russell might have gone since he did come to Staniel Cay. All of them were to the south.

"I just think it's highly unlikely that he's north of here. To go farther north from where he started, he would just about have to come here first to miss the banks that stretch out to Green Cay. He would have passed close enough to Staniel that someone on one of those boats would have seen him. I think the folks we spoke to would have told us if they had. They had no reason not to, because it was a strange boat passing through that none of them could have known anything about. He may have been trying to come here and failed to make landfall where he planned. I have no idea how much he knew about navigation, but since I know he was full of shit about most things, I doubt it was much.

"The wind would have likely been too much on the nose for him to go straight down to Georgetown, on Great Exuma, but he may have ended up at one of the other cays between here and there. There are lots of anchorages that way, as you can see," Larry pointed out at least a dozen on the chart.

"The best thing we can do is hit all of them one-by-one and hope we get lucky. If we don't find him between here and Georgetown, I'll think of another plan then."

Their systematic search of Exumas anchorages had taken them to Darby Island by late the next afternoon. Larry was disappointed and a bit surprised they did not find the *Sarah J.* among any of those islands. He didn't let Tara know it, but he felt the odds of finding it farther down the chain on the other side of Great Exuma were slim. Sure, George-town was a popular anchorage, but did Russell really have the ability to sail there without the use of the engine? Larry figured he might have used it anyway, without the water pump, but he would have had to motor quite a bit to work his way in there. It would have been so much easier for him to sail to one of these anchorages on the west side of the middle Exumas and Larry had really expected to find him there. But if he had come here he was gone now, and if they didn't find him in Georgetown tomorrow, Larry wasn't quite sure where to look next. He had more questions than answers but then everything changed and the answers all came in the most unexpected way possible. Artie spotted a sail coming in from the horizon to the southwest shortly after they dropped anchor to spend the night and wait for daylight to head to Georgetown.

The boat was apparently arriving at the Exumas from the open sea, and Larry was curious because of the direction from which it sailed. There was nothing to the south but the Jumentos Cays and Ragged Islands, where he'd been planning to go all along. If this boat was coming from there to the Exumas, he wondered if things might not be better there after all. It would be interesting to ask them, but he doubted he would get the chance. As it got closer to landfall, the boat began angling off a bit to the northwest. On that course it would pass fairly close by Darby Island and probably stop at one of the anchorages they had already searched. Larry had already dismissed it from his mind when Artie called out to him again:

"That's weird. They're towing something that looks longer than their boat."

Larry had little interest really, but if he still had his binoculars, he might take a look out of curiosity. But like the shotgun, his expensive Steiners had been in the dinghy when it was stolen. He was ready to forget about the other boat as long as it kept enough distance from them, but that was not to be. When he looked out at it again, he saw the sails luff as the crew apparently spotted them anchored there, and then it tacked and turned directly towards them.

"Crap!" Larry was tired and aggravated and the last thing he needed now was another confrontation. He went below to get a rifle, getting mad all over again at being reminded he'd lost the binoculars and the shotgun along with the dinghy. And that was the second lost shotgun. Scully had already lost his personal Mossberg back in the Pearl River swamps of Mississippi.

As he stood there on the deck of the *Casey Nicole* with the rest of his crew and watched the boat approach, Larry soon realized that it was a *really* small vessel—a tiny pocket cruiser just a fraction of the size of a typical cruising boat. The crew must have seen that he was armed, because whoever was steering put the helm hard over to turn away when they were within a couple hundred yards. Larry saw a woman step up the cabin top, waving her arms back and forth and shouting something he could not quite make out, and that's when he also saw and recognized what the little boat was towing.

Larry had his kayak back aboard the *Casey Nicole* and the anchor up and sails set within a half hour of meeting Thomas and Mindy at Darby Island. It would be dark within an hour but he wasn't going to wait, even though a night passage would put them at the cays where the *Sarah J.* was grounded well before daylight. It was a clear night and Larry expected there would be enough moonlight at the time of their landfall to find it. If not, they would stop and wait for dawn, but he sure wasn't going to wait here with Scully in need of Artie's care. And learning that Rebecca was safe and Russell was gone, Tara wasn't about to wait either.

He felt bad about leaving Thomas and Mindy behind after the risks they'd taken to come here and find them. But they were exhausted from all the sailing they'd done and their little boat couldn't possibly keep up with the *Casey Nicole* anyway. They would stay in the anchorage at Darby Island and set out for the return trip to the Jumentos in the morning. Larry told Thomas to keep the AK until they got there and he gave him a couple more full magazines for it when he learned that they only had one. Casey and Jessica put together a small package of food from the galley stores to share with them as well.

Rebecca was awakened from a sound sleep in her sharply tilted bunk by what sounded like shouting from outside the boat. She was sure it was a dream, because that would be impossible for the voices to be real unless for some reason Thomas and Mindy had already returned aboard *Intrepida*. But the shouting was persistent and when she climbed out of the bunk she saw that Scully was awake too.

"Do you hear that? I thought I was dreaming?"

"I t'ink it's a dream too. Sound like Larry, calling my name, an' de woman, callin' for you."

Rebecca climbed the companionway and slid the hatch open. Right off the stern of the *Sarah J.* illuminated in the moonlight, was the most incredible sight she could have imagined. The *Casey Nicole's* twin bows were pulled up around the stern of the *Sarah J.* so close that the front beam of the catamaran was almost touching her rail. Her mom was standing there on the beam and as soon as she saw Rebecca emerge from the cabin she leapt aboard into the cockpit and crushed her close in a frantic hug. As her mom held her, Rebecca was vaguely aware of Artie and Larry rushing past her and down into the cabin where Scully was still sitting up in his bunk.

Casey and the rest of the crew all joined them in the cockpit, but everyone stayed out of the way until Artie was finished with whatever he was doing for Scully. Daylight was breaking by then and when Artie finally came back on deck, everyone wanted to know about Scully's leg.

"The good news is that I don't think he'll lose it. The bullet went all the way through, but it did a lot of damage on the way. Thomas and Mindy did the right thing to use the tourniquet and also to remove it when they did. I'm going to have to keep a close watch on it for infection, and he'll probably always walk with a limp, but he'll get through it. Scully's a pretty tough hombre."

Rebecca had been telling her mom over and over how sorry she was that she made such a mistake and ran the *Sarah J.* aground. And she had replied that they did the same exact thing in the catamaran, even though it draws even less water.

"I still feel stupid. I don't know how we'll ever get it off. Scully said it would be really hard."

But when Captain Larry heard all this talk he had a different perspective. "Hey Rebecca, people have been running aground all over the Bahamas since the first ships ever sailed here. Cruising folk did it all the time before the blackout, and it was a lot easier to navigate then with the help of GPS and depth sounders and all that other fancy stuff. You did a great job keeping the *Sarah J.* safe. The main thing is that you got Russell off the boat before he hurt you or completely wrecked it in his stupidity. And, we're right where we wanted to be, in the Jumentos Cays. Scully is here now, so everyone is accounted for and we have both boats. Now I don't have to sail to Florida to look for him, so I have nothing better to do than figure out how to get the *Sarah J.* floating again. So don't worry about it. I've got some ideas and I've seen far worse. We've got plenty of anchors between us and when Thomas and Mindy get back we'll have even more help. I know a great little cay with a good anchorage not far from here where we can take all three boats once we're sailing again. It will be the perfect place to hang out while we make a plan and figure out what we're gonna do next."

BOOKS IN THIS SERIES

ABOUT THE AUTHOR

Scott B. Williams has been writing about his travels and adventures for more than thirty years. His published work includes hundreds of print and online magazine articles and more than two dozen books. His interest in trekking, sea kayaking and sailing small boats to remote places led him to pursue the wilderness survival skills that he has written about extensively in both his fiction and nonfiction works.

A solo sea kayaking odyssey of nearly two years, undertaken at age 25, set Scott on his path to becoming a storyteller when he authored the account of that adventure in his 2005 travel narrative: *On Island Time: Kayaking the Caribbean*. That journey and countless others that took him far off the grid for extended periods gave him the inspiration to delve into his passion for fiction and to write action and adventure tales like the ones that shaped his own desire to travel and explore.

With the release of his first novel, *The Pulse,* in 2012, and the subsequent sequels to it that became a popular post-apocalyptic series, Scott moved into writing fiction full time. Later and ongoing projects include the *Darkness*

After series and the *Feral Nation* series, with more new works currently in development. To learn more about his upcoming books or to contact Scott, visit his website at: www.scottbwilliams.com

Made in United States
Troutdale, OR
10/11/2023

13624667R00190